THE LITTLE BRUDDERS OF MISÉRICORDE

The
Little Brudders
of
Miséricorde

A novel

DAVID M. WALLACE

TIDEWATER
PRESS

Published by Tidewater Press
New Westminster, BC, Canada
tidewaterpress.ca

978-1-990160-08-0 (print)
978-1-990160-09-7 (e-book)

LIBRARY AND ARCHIVES CANADA CATALOGUING IN PUBLICATION

Title: The little brudders of Miséricorde : a novel / David M. Wallace.
Names: Wallace, David M. (David Michael), author.
Identifiers: Canadiana (print) 20220141339 | Canadiana (ebook) 2022014141X | ISBN 9781990160080 (softcover) | ISBN 9781990160097 (HTML)
Classification: LCC PS8645.A467365 L58 2022 | DDC C813/.6—dc23

Front Cover Illustration: Emma Francis
emmafrancis.bigcartel.com,
instagram.com/emmafrancisartist

Printed in Canada

For my daughter, Emma Francis.

"Faith is to believe what you do not see; the reward of this faith is to see what you believe."

AUGUSTINE OF HIPPO

"I got you to look after me, and you got me to look after you, and that's why."

Of Mice and Men, JOHN STEINBECK

Ash Wednesday

I have a visitor.

He sits framed in my bedroom doorway. A little grey mouse. *Une petite souris grise.* He sits upright on his rear legs. With those in front, he gives his whiskers a thorough grooming. The lamp on my nightstand is positioned in such a way that the light catches him at a low angle. His form throws a stark shadow behind him as though he is sporting a long, black cape. All the while, he keeps his gaze steadily on me.

This confirms what I have suspected. For several evenings in a row, I have sat up reading in bed. *Le Petit Prince, en français.* It is part of my strategy for achieving my bilingual bona fides since arriving in Montréal last July. On previous evenings, I'd caught just a blur out of the corner of my eye. *Ce soir, c'est différent.*

Ordinarily, house mice are timid creatures. They keep a low profile. In the winter they are like refugees, finding warmth, maybe, but not welcome. Feeding on crumbs. But this is no wee, sleekat, cowran, tim'rous beastie. This guy is cocksure.

"If you're staying, you're paying rent, pal." He swivels an ear in my direction.

I repeat myself in stilted French: "*Si tu veux rester, tu dois payer le loyer, mon chum.*"

He nods solemnly. Or maybe that is my imagination. Lowering himself onto all fours, he saunters toward the living room, pausing for just a moment to give me one final glance.

"*Bonne nuit.*"

I make a mental note to set traps tomorrow.

Thursday, Second Day of Lent

In the morning, before my French class, I manage a perfunctory sweep of my apartment. I anticipate that the broom will capture some mice droppings. *Rien. Souris imaginaire? Souris constipée?* I haven't time to play detective; French class begins at 8:30, and in this weather it will take me a full hour to cycle to the school.

I check *la météo* on my phone. *Moins douze degrés.* Geared up, I step onto the balcony to get a sense of what minus twelve is going to feel like today. It is nice that I can cycle in daylight now, though this Sunday the clocks will change, and for some weeks I will be riding, again, in the uncertain light of dawn. Spring forward, fall back. I say this to myself to make sure I've got it right—the sun will rise an hour later.

Spring forward, fall back could also describe my progress in French class. I seem to lose as much as I learn daily; my memory is not what it once was. There was a time, while I was still doing theatre, when I would remember all my lines letter-perfect and even the lines of all the other characters in my scenes. At university, by the end of an eight-week summer theatre run, I had memorized nearly all the dialogue in *The Importance of Being Earnest*. And that was during my drinking days. Even twenty years later, when I directed my own students in a production of *Earnest*, I could prompt them from memory. Those days are gone. Now I can't even keep *sont, ont, vont et font* clear in my mind.

My thoughts are interrupted by a whirring mechanical sound. Below my balcony is the entrance to the underground parking garage. When I first moved in, I worried that the sound of the door opening and closing would disturb me. But scarcely anyone in the building seems to own a car. A few times, especially last September when I moved in, I'd seen the landlord, *le propriétaire*, Nick, coming or going in his white Subaru.

Speak of the devil. Nick emerges from the parking garage, *sans voiture*, and stands in the entrance speaking rapid French into his cell phone. I can't understand a word. He steps out onto the sidewalk and looks north up the street. After a moment, I see a jet-black Plymouth Valiant turn into the entrance driveway below me.

I recognize the distinctive flares over the front and rear wheels, the molded chrome bumpers and the boxy grill. Vintage 1960s. The driver rolls down the window. Nick says something. He looks up as he gets into the passenger seat. Perhaps he senses my presence? Our eyes meet briefly but he offers no greeting and I look away. The car disappears and I hear the garage door closing.

Nice vehicle. I remember Phil Cucovich in high school. He was the only guy in school with a full beard and he was the owner of a copper-coloured '66 Valiant. By then the Valiant was less flashy: the flares over the wheels had evolved into a single sleek line and the cat-eye taillights were no more. But it still had that indestructible slant-six engine. He and my brother, Ian, had worked on it together in Auto Shop. Back then I envied the manly goings-on of the older boys gathered under the chassis of cars up on the hoists. I was actually pretty decent at identifying makes and models—all those Meccano Dinky Toys and Mattel Hot Wheels in my childhood collection. I would sometimes annoy Ian by correcting him: "No, it's a '63. That's when the divided grill came in and the dual headlamps." But once I became involved in all those school plays, I was banished from the company of the Grease Monkeys, the regulars in Auto Shop. My brother and I never talked much anyway, and by then we almost didn't talk at all.

Now, though, I'm curious why Nick needed to usher in the car and driver. None of my business. Yet strange how that car just floated into view like a ship out of the fog, towing a bit of my youth in its wake.

I observe the trees across the street in the park, swaying in the wind. Moderate breeze. Not enough to make me consider taking *le métro* instead of cycling. My hands are cold. Back inside I grab the broom I had been using to search for mouse droppings. It is leaning against the table next to the stereo. Still on the table is the little ceramic Nativity scene I have set up each Advent since my daughter, Clara, was born. My fingers are a little stiff from the cold and I lose my grip on the broom for a moment. The handle taps the table on the way down and topples Joseph and one of the little sheep. I rescue them before they hit the floor. Juggling the figurines, I feel a little rush of adrenaline in my chest. Second day into Lent and I still haven't put away all the Christmas paraphernalia. I take a deep breath and set Joseph and the sheep back in position.

As usual, I am first to class and set my damp gear on the radiator under the windows. Étienne is five minutes late, also as usual, and comes in with a coffee, a broad smile and forced enthusiasm. Half the class will show up at *la pause*—more than an hour late. Part of me wants to tell him to start each class with something that is both important and fun. Something that the students need to do, want to do and must all be together for, in order for the class to be successful.

Marie, who taught my *niveau quatre* class was all business. Well organized. High expectations. *Ses élèves sont arrivés à l'heure.* We felt like a team. *Une équipe.* I had adapted several of my drama games for practising verb conjugations and for vocabulary acquisition, and she had readily incorporated them. Several times I even led the class. But *niveau cinq*, with Étienne, is a bit of a slog and he has done little to put his students at ease with one another.

After French class, I leave my bicycle thawing on the mat just inside the entrance to my apartment. Spreading out my notes on the far side of the bed, I settle in under the warmth of the comforter for an afternoon of studying. Exams are scheduled for next week. I feel confident I can pass *compréhension écrite* and *production écrite*. With the aid of a dictionary, I can read simple French prose and fashion childlike sentences. I am more concerned about *compréhension orale* and *production orale*.

"*T'inquiète pas.*"

I look up. I must have dozed off. My bedroom window is dark. *La nuit est tombée.* The same mouse from last night is sitting in the same position in my bedroom doorway, the same elongated, black shadow flung out behind him as though he has been blasted into that position from some other dimension.

"*T'inquiète pas,*" *dit-il.*

And then he is gone.

CLARA

Spence sat in Café Orange, waiting for Clara and her fiancé, Gabriel. He had taken *le métro* to and from class today and left at *la pause*—the 10:00 am break—to ensure he had plenty of time to get there by 11:30, as arranged. The entrance to the restaurant was just below his balcony, but his building was not old enough to sport one of the ornate spiral stairs/fire escapes so common in the city. That would have allowed him to simply descend from his balcony and arrive on *la terrasse* of the café. However, his place in NDG—Notre-Dame-de-Grâce—was not entirely charmless and the price was right.

Spence felt his phone vibrate: "5 mins. Sorry. Running late." Just like Clara. To the point, no excuses offered. *Tête-à-tête*, Clara was a lively conversationalist. Otherwise, when she had something to say, she painted or wrote poetry.

Spence had already finished one cup of coffee. It was shortly before noon, and the place was still not full. On a Saturday, the waitress who was coming by with the coffee pot would have given him a look that said, "*Commandez ou partez, monsieur,*" looking pointedly at the queue outside the door. Today she was all smiles in her orange apron that matched the upholstery of the booth and the décor. He declined a second cup but reassured her, "*Ma fille va arriver dans cinq minutes, madame.*" Then he switched to English and told her the coffee was excellent.

Spence had discovered that Montréal was the most difficult place in the world for an anglophone to learn French. About half the city was bilingual and anyone in a service position was generally fluent in both English and French. If you began a conversation in French, you were likely to be met with a barrage of fast *français*, often sounding nothing like the recordings you so diligently studied. Spence had developed a habit of starting his conversations in French, for practice, but also to be courteous. Then he would switch to English to signal that it was the language at which he was more adept.

6

Spence's table was by the window and through the glass he saw Clara and Gabriel approaching from the direction of Station Villa-Maria. They must have taken *le métro* for the length of one stop, from Vendôme, to avoid walking up the hill. Her arm was through Gabriel's and she leaned her head on his shoulder as they walked.

Gabriel was wearing the same knee-length leather coat with fleece trim that he had sported all winter, a dark-haired version of Ryan Gosling in the remake of *Blade Runner*. He *is* handsome, Spence had to acknowledge. The two of them walked right past without noticing him waving through the restaurant window.

Spence slid out of the booth and stood in the little glass-enclosed entranceway. Gabriel was consulting his phone, probably double checking the address. The lobby and entrance to Spence's building was at the rear, so likely neither had noted Café Orange during their visit at Christmas. He watched Clara raise her arms in mock dismay and turn in circles as if to say, "Hopelessly lost!" Gabriel playfully grabbed one end of her long Gryffindor scarf and used it to spin her around. She feigned dizziness and contrived to fall into his arms. The waitress came and stood at Spence's vacant table, perplexed. He waved to her and pointed outside to where Clara and Gabriel stood kissing in the middle of the sidewalk. The waitress, a woman about Spence's age, grinned and raised her eyebrows when he mouthed, "*Oh là là.*"

Spence opened the exterior door and called to them, "Break it up, you two." Clara rushed to him as if she'd not seen him for ages, though he'd been at her place just last week, receiving instructions concerning care of the houseplants. He was surprised and pleased as she threw her arms around him and kissed him on both cheeks, greeting him in exaggerated French fashion.

"We're going to Paris! We're going to Paris!" Clara was thirty yet still occasionally had to produce her ID when she bought wine. When she was happy, she could display a girlishness that charmed Spence's heart. When she was happy, she abandoned herself to that emotion, just as her mother used to do. When she was sad, she withdrew to some faraway land. The trip to Paris was to meet her future *belle-mère*. Gabriel's parents were divorced and his mother had remarried a well-to-do Frenchman and moved overseas. They were leaving Montréal the next day for a quick visit to Mont-Laurier to visit his father, whom Spence had yet to meet.

"Sorry we're late. It's Gabriel's fault."

"Me?" her fiancé threw up his hands as he approached.

"Moi?" she teased him. She let go of Spence and gave Gabriel a quick kiss.

Inside, Spence and Gabriel performed an awkward little waltz as they simultaneously offered to help Clara with her coat, until Gabriel smiled and raised his hands in a kind of mock surrender. Spence was not sure if he was pleased that his future *beau-fils* was so solicitous toward Clara or if he was a tad jealous that she was happier than he could remember. Maybe both.

Though Spence had known him for about half a year now, they saw each other infrequently. Clara and Gabriel still kept separate apartments; Gabriel lived in Le Plateau, needing his own space to work on his thesis—something to do with Environmental Biology. Clara had turned her bedroom into a painting studio and converted half the living room into a sleeping space. Their plan was to get a bigger place together when they returned from France in three months' time.

The bells from St. Augustine's across the street began to sound, as they do every day at noon. The waitress came by with the coffee pot. Spence noticed she appeared to have applied some fresh lipstick. She offered coffee all around and Spence accepted a second cup. Over the sound of the bells, she described the lunch specials.

"I want pancakes," Clara said. "It is Pancake Tuesday. We are all having pancakes." She ordered for the three of them, snatched up the menus and handed them to the waitress. It would be pancakes with fruit and whipped cream and real maple syrup.

The church bells across the street had been ringing for a full three minutes. Spence was accustomed to the way the knells grew softer and further apart. Seated beside each other on the orange bench of the booth, Clara and Gabriel gazed into one another's eyes, their lips moving, miming the sound of the last few chimes, as if the suspense before the final silence was the most wonderful thing in the world.

Young love.

Spence thought of his late wife, Serenity. Her vivacity. Her impulsiveness. The sheer recklessness of her emotions. The current of relentless melancholy that flowed just below the surface until she finally drowned in her own sorrow. *That is not going to happen to Clara.*

"Daddy. What's new?" Clara asked abruptly.

"Not much. Class in the morning. Studying in the afternoon. Reading in the evening."

Lacking any other news, he mentioned that he thought he'd seen a mouse in the apartment, though he wasn't entirely sure. Clara, who loved all creatures, excitedly began to describe the menagerie of animals that surreptitiously shared the neighbourhood: skunks, groundhogs, wild turkeys, raccoons, feral cats. Gabriel added his expert commentary on habitat and adaptability and, somehow, they concluded that they were going to adopt a dog when they got back from Paris.

When breakfast arrived, Clara let out a girlish squeal. Spence drizzled maple syrup over a stack of pancakes and strawberries. He hesitated with the whipped cream. In English, the day was Shrove Tuesday: to shrive, to make confession and receive absolution. In French it was *Mardi Gras*—Fat Tuesday. It referred to all the rich, fatty foods that one consumed in a final hurrah before Lent. He heaped on several spoonfuls. When in Rome.

"Remember when we used to have breakfast at . . . what was it called?"

"Banners," Spence said. "Banners Family Restaurant."

She turned to Gabriel. "My dad used to entertain me while we waited for the food to be served. He would turn the cutlery into little puppet characters and act out stories."

Spence was glad it was a happy memory for Clara. He remembered Banners for being a restaurant near the house where Serenity had rented a basement suite after they had separated. Spence would pick Clara up Friday mornings and then drop her at her daycare on Monday. It was the apartment where Serenity died, shortly after they reconciled.

"Are you going to Mass, tomorrow, Dad? For Ash Wednesday?"

"Uh huh," Spence's mouth was full. "I thought I might actually go to L'Oratoire Saint-Joseph. I haven't been since I went with you two."

When Spence had first arrived in Montréal, Clara and Gabriel had shown him around a little. They'd climbed Mont-Royal to the viewpoint that looked over the city, the best vantage from which to admire the giant mural of Leonard Cohen. Visited Le Musée des beaux-arts. Had a picnic in Parc La Fontaine.

"He really wants you to like him, Dad," Clara had confided. "He's very nervous around you."

"I do like him," Spence told her. "If you are happy, I am happy."

And it was true. Over the course of the previous year, since she and Gabriel had been together, Spence had received no panicked phone calls from Clara, his daughter hyperventilating at the other end. Gabriel had arranged an appointment for her with a young doctor of his acquaintance at McGill. She began taking medication for her anxiety and she'd joined a support group. Both were helping tremendously. In just a few months, Gabriel seemingly accomplished what Spence could not, despite providing years of expensive therapists. Love. Had it really been that simple all along?

"Gabriel climbed the steps to the Oratory on his knees when he was a boy," Clara said, and took a bite out of a huge strawberry, as if that somehow proved the veracity of the claim.

"Really?" Spence looked at him. "That's a hundred wooden steps, I believe."

Gabriel looked up from his pancakes, a little startled to be put on the spot. Clara took her paper napkin, dabbed the corner of his mouth, and kissed him on the cheek as if he'd performed the feat just for her and maybe saved her from a dragon while he was at it.

"Ninety-nine," he said. "I was a kid," he added, as if he was apologizing for performing the devotion. "A lot of people used to climb the stairs, especially on Good Friday."

Spence wondered what it was about a strict Catholic upbringing that turned children like Gabriel into confirmed atheists in adulthood. Spence had converted to Catholicism at twenty-seven and had attended weeks of courses in preparation for his baptism and confirmation. Serenity had agreed to allow Clara to be baptized on condition that their daughter would not be catechized in the Faith. It was a promise he honoured even after Serenity died.

"So, what would you think if Gabriel and I got married in France?"

Spence set his knife and fork on his plate. He thought of making a joking remark but tears brimmed in his eyes. He gulped a few breaths, trying to swallow the sobs that rose unbidden and for no reason that he could understand. The waitress arrived to clear their plates. Spence looked out the window. He did not like being surprised by his own emotions.

"Not quite finished," Clara said. She slipped onto the bench next to Spence and put her head on his shoulder. The flood was released and Spence sobbed quietly for a couple of minutes before he could compose himself. The sobs came in little shuddering waves. Part of him wanted to go lie in the snow and cry for a week. Another part was ashamed that it was his daughter comforting *him*. Surely it should be the other way round. He should be *her* strength and *her* comfort. And then it passed. He kissed her on the forehead.

"It's okay. I'm okay. I guess I was just taken by surprise."

He managed a wan smile. Excusing himself, Spence made his way to the washroom, glancing down as he passed the waitress who was readjusting the strings on her orange apron. The washroom had one of those old-fashioned porcelain sinks on a pedestal. It could have doubled as a birdbath. He filled the basin with cold water and plunged his face in several times until the puffiness around his eyes subsided. He blew his nose and patted his face dry with a paper towel. He didn't dare look into the mirror.

The waitress was standing just outside the washroom door when he emerged. She smiled. A little speck of red lipstick had smudged one of her front teeth.

"May we have the check, please?"

"All taken care of. You okay?"

Spence nodded. Sympathy did not help. It only threatened to send him into another bout of tears.

"Thanks," he said. "*Bonne journée.*"

Clara and Gabriel already had their coats on. Spence donned his. They walked across the street without talking until they stood on the sidewalk in front of St. Augustine's.

They all smiled, trying to figure out how to say goodbye.

"Thanks for lunch," Spence said. He took a deep breath to calm himself. "You two get married whenever and wherever works for you. Elope if you like."

"It was just something we talked about, Dad. Nothing's decided."

They stood silent for another few moments. A robin flew close to Gabriel's head and he ducked. They all laughed.

"But if we did decide to get married in France, you'd be there, right? I can't get married without you. You're supposed to give me away and all that."

"I'll be there wherever, whenever you need me," he said. "Promise."

"I know you will." Clara threw her arms around him. "You are always there for me."

Spence knew that wasn't true. But it was encouraging to hear her say it. Gabriel held out his hand, but to both their surprise, Spence gave him a quick hug.

"Say a prayer for us tomorrow." Gabriel smiled. "Isn't Saint Joseph the patron saint of travellers?"

"Refugees, I think," Spence said. "And I'm not going up those stairs on my knees."

They laughed again. And then Clara began crying. Spence held her for a moment before passing her to Gabriel.

"*Adieu.*"

He smiled and watched them depart, arms around each other's waist and leaning together as they walked away.

Friday, Third Day of Lent

I wake with a start when my phone alarm sounds. Still fully clothed, my notes slide off my chest and onto the floor when I sit up. It takes me a moment to realize my phone is in the front pocket of my trousers. I silence the alarm and look around me, *déconcerté*.

When I was a child, I could vividly remember my dreams. In fact, for a time, I had lucid dreams. That is to say, I frequently knew when I was inside a dream. Some people have the impression that lucid dreamers can control their dreams. That was not the way it worked for me. I have heard people describe their experiences on LSD and I would say lucid dreaming is more like that. You know it isn't real, but it feels real. I stopped lucid dreaming at about the age of eleven. I don't know why. At some point, I stopped remembering my dreams all together. Certainly, I still dream. But the dreams dissipate almost as soon as my eyes open in the morning.

T'inquiète pas. Don't worry.

That bit of my dream I do remember. Evidently, I am now receiving advice from a francophone mouse. There is something on the floor near the door to my bedroom where I'd imagined I'd heard the mouse speaking. I stoop and pick it up. It is a well-worn dime, a young Queen Elizabeth II, her simple coronet still faintly visible. Above her, in Latin, *Dei Gratia Regina.* Queen by the Grace of God. On the reverse, the familiar schooner, *Bluenose,* and the date: 1957.

The year of my birth.

Back then, dimes were made of mostly silver. When I was a boy such a dime could buy an entire Oh Henry! chocolate bar. Perhaps it is my imagination but, nestled in my palm, this dime feels more substantial than the more recently minted steel sort.

"*T'inquiète pas,*" I say to myself.

Maybe it's my lucky day.

Jean-François

"You've lost some weight," JF said.

"Nearly forty pounds so far."

"You look good, Spence."

When Spence's friend and mentor had called him and said they should get together for a chat, Spence had suggested Granville Island. They could grab a coffee at the market. Maybe go for a walk. It was a warm afternoon. They sat with their coffee on the long row of steps overlooking False Creek. A half dozen seagulls waddled toward them, looking for a handout. From the middle of the channel a yacht gave a blast of its horn for no discernible reason and the gulls took flight. They circled and settled a little farther along the steps.

Jean-François Sauvé had been the principal of Queen of All Saints until his retirement two years ago after his seventy-fifth birthday. He might have even carried on, but the Diocese applied the same rule to him that governed priests: at seventy-five, it was compulsory to submit one's resignation. There had been a faction in the school who had ardonically referred to the principal as "The Saviour."

JF had never given up on a student. In all the time Spence knew him, JF had never suspended a student, much less appealed to the Discipline Committee for an expulsion. The year before Spence started, nearly half the staff had walked out because JF would not initiate proceedings against a boy who had pulled a knife on a teacher.

JF had just returned from Rome where he and his wife, Sylvia, had spent several weeks and had managed to attend the Easter Mass in the Basilica.

"How's his Holiness doing?"

"We didn't get a chance to chat."

"So . . . the Vatican. Nice?"

"A bit over the top for my taste. Sylvia sent away for tickets ages ago. For the Easter Mass. After Trump was elected." JF took a sip of coffee and added, "Brave new world."

"Uh huh. Some kid spray-painted a fucking swastika on the roof of the school as a graduation prank. Part of me is glad I'm not teaching this year."

"Listen, Spence, I would have reached out sooner but, you know, Sylvia's sister was very ill. We stayed at her place in Toronto for a while. Until she passed."

"So sorry," Spence said.

JF nodded thanks. "When we got back, Sylvia had her cataract surgery. Then the three months in Europe, which we'd been putting off since forever."

"No worries, JF. I'm fine."

"They said you had a heart attack?"

"Let them think that," Spence laughed. "It was probably a panic attack. Clara used to get them, until very recently. The only reason they did all those tests on my heart was because it was racing. Probably just the stress. And letting myself get so fat. My heart is fine. I mean, it apparently has a few quirks, but still going strong."

"You got enough sick leave?"

"Hell, yeah. I had over two hundred accumulated days. When did I ever take a sick day? Maybe I'll go on extended leave and then collect the other one hundred next year. Fuck them."

"That doesn't sound like you, Spence." JF looked at him, amused.

"Actually, I am officially retired as of April Fool's Day. Which fell on Easter morning this year. Now you know where you were on the big day."

"Congratulations."

"Thanks."

They sat in silence for a few moments. Then JF nodded toward the Arts Club Theatre a stone's throw to his right. "You ever do a show there?"

"Nope. Their roster of actors was pretty cozy, back in my day. Got a couple call backs, that's it. Clara got an autograph from what's-her-name? Woman from *Deadwood*?"

"Molly Parker?"

"Right. We saw her in some melodrama about Dracula same year I started teaching. Clara has this thing about vampires."

Another long silence. The gulls began edging toward them again. They watched a woman and her three children walking along the wharf. She was carrying her youngest. A girl of maybe five clung to her skirts. Her son, a toddler, ran ahead, his feet trying to keep up with the rest of him. Spence was forty feet away but his hand instinctively reached out as the boy stepped too close to the edge of the wharf.

"So why *did* they cut all the drama programs? Truth. Is that on me?"

"No." JF shrugged. "Maybe a little. Look Spence, I asked around. They actually did have to cut something to make budget. They considered Music , but it has too much support among parents. They looked at a lot of things. It probably didn't help that some of your plays were . . . "

"What?"

"You created controversy, Spence. But that's who you are. And the kids learned a ton. And they loved you for it. Trust me on that. It was worth it, Spence."

"You always made me take in all your little misfits." Spence laughed. "'Give the kid to Spence. Let him run around in Drama. Maybe he'll learn some social skills.' Used to drive me crazy."

"Drama is a very social environment, Spence. You made it a safe one for them."

"Yes. But I wanted to take risks. I had things I wanted to accomplish. And I wanted students who worked hard to produce superior results."

"And I told you your job wasn't to produce superior results, Spence. Remember?"

"Oh yeah. I remember. It wasn't easy to hear. You also told me I only really loved the talented kids. The ones who worked hard. In fact, you told me my job wasn't to teach drama but to use drama as a way to love the kids."

He looked at JF and then looked out over the water.

"Thanks, JF."

JF stood up and stretched. His knees cracked. A seagull wandered toward him and then reversed course and took flight.

"Your knees sound like mine," Spence said.

"So, what are you going to do in retirement?"

"Clara is in Montréal. I've decided to move there."

"She's staying there, then?"

"Yeah. The art scene there is better. Anyway, I can't afford to live in Vancouver. Not on my pension. And she certainly can't afford the rents here."

"She got a sweetheart?"

"She was seeing a woman for a while. Now she's with this fellow, Gabriel."

"The Lord's herald," JF said.

"He's been good for her, I think." He was silent for a moment. "They are getting married."

"How do you feel about that?"

"I'm not sure, JF. I mean, I guess I knew this day would come. The upside is she calls me more often now. And she really hates telephones."

"Kids all text these days."

"Not Clara," Spence said. "Part of me is worried I'll move to Montréal and those two will pack up and move to—I don't know—someplace. Am I going to follow her around for the rest of my life? Does she really need me, or am I . . . "

Spence didn't finish. He stood, as well, and the men walked to the trash can and dropped in their cups.

"Clara adores you," JF said.

"Really?"

"Why do you think she became an artist?"

"Well, her mother dabbled, a little."

JF laughed.

"What?" asked Spence. "You mean me?"

"For a smart guy, you are pretty dense, sometimes."

"I always felt she was, I don't know, a bit angry at me?"

JF laughed again.

"What? Tell me." Spence said.

"If I tell you, how are you going to learn, Spence? Some things you have to discover. You taught me that one. Isn't that your teaching philosophy? Experience and discovery?"

"You're a real pain in the ass, sometimes."

"You need a lift?" JF said.

"Got my bike."

"Right."

"I'm heading up to UBC."

"Up that hill?"

"I've already climbed Prospect Point this morning. I'll do sixty kilometers today. Almost every day." Spence patted his belly.

"Wow."

"Truthfully, the doctor said I needed antidepressants. I said I'd prefer endorphins. I think I've got a sort of Forrest Gump thing going on with this bicycle."

The two men stood smiling at each other.

"Thanks, JF. Thanks for . . . everything."

"You're a fine teacher, Spence. A master teacher. We were lucky to find you."

They shook hands and promised to stay in touch.

JF died of a massive stroke just two weeks before Spence moved to Montréal. It was standing room only in Holy Rosary Cathedral for his funeral. Spence was not the only one there who felt he had lost a father.

SATURDAY, FOURTH DAY OF LENT

I am sitting, picking at the remains of my omelette and wondering if I should have another cup of coffee and risk the heartburn. The mild guilt I feel at the extravagance—breakfast out at Café Orange—is taking some of the pleasure out of this solitary excursion.

I can't really afford this for much longer. Late tonight, Clara and Gabriel will get back from Mont-Laurier and will spend the night at Gabriel's place.. Early tomorrow, they will be flying to Paris to visit her future *belle-mère*.

With them gone from Montréal, I am alone in the city I have adopted. Apart from my classmates, I know no one in this city. Stilted conversations in French with the other students—*Comment s'est passé ton weekend? Bien, et le tien?*—have not provided the groundwork for any meaningful acquaintances. I nod to the handful of faces I recognize among my fellow parishioners at St. Monica's where I attend Mass. Polite greetings with Carl at the entrance, whom I find a little too effusive. A perfunctory "Peace be with you" to the two elderly ladies who generally sit behind me and who prefer not to shake hands at the signal to exchange the Sign of Peace. Only Clara and Gabriel have visited my apartment, and that was more than three months ago, when I cooked Christmas dinner. Now they will be in France until June, maybe longer. I will observe the traditional Lenten fast by being starved for company.

I promised Clara I would water her plants every Saturday during her absence and decide to walk rather than ride my bike. I make my way down to Station Vendôme, following the route Clara and I walked when I first arrived in Montréal. My new life. Retracing my steps might give me some perspective.

The heat in her apartment has been off since Tuesday. It is not as cold as I had feared and the plants seem to be doing fine. Last summer, when I arrived in Montréal, I lived with Clara while I looked for a place to rent. The plan had been to stay a month. But I suppose I had been feeling so isolated for those many weeks I'd been on sick leave, I contrived to stay a second month. Sick leave might be a bit misleading. There was nothing really physically wrong with me. I suppose I was just sick of everything. Especially the circumstances of my final days at Queen of All Saints Secondary. Over the preceding three years I'd only seen Clara once, the first summer after her move to Montréal to study Fine Arts at Concordia. She had flown home to visit for a few weeks, during which I realized how much I'd missed our conversations. It was even a pleasure to have my opinions gently critiqued as she educated me on the more nuanced aspects of fourth-wave feminism and intersectionality. Maybe old dogs *can* learn new tricks. And if not, they can still wag their tails and feel loved.

For those two months, I tried to make myself useful so as not to wear out my welcome. I removed all the double-paned windows and washed them. I replaced the flush valve gasket in her toilet tank. The bathroom window had been painted shut, and I spent an afternoon releasing it, only to discover that the pipes outside provided an excellent route for rats. So, I fastened a mesh covering around the frame. I got her kitchen sink draining properly and replaced the charred pans under the stove elements. Maybe I was compensating for those times, when she was young, that my nurturing had fallen short. Especially the year following her mother's death. Small comfort that I am now becoming the father I wish I could have been, especially now that I seem to be passing on the role of protector to Gabriel.

I step out onto the balcony to make certain she's left nothing that might be carried away by the wind. The noon bells at St. Raymond's across the street begin to sound. One bell, really. And it more clanks than resounds. I shiver. My first Mass in Montréal had been at St. Raymond's, a dismal affair. Granted, it was the Canada Day long weekend and, possibly, a lot of people were out of town. There were six of us, not counting the priest. And I was the youngest. I noted all of the weekday morning Masses were in Italian. Maybe the 9:30 Italian Sunday Mass had been full. But truthfully? The place was a little unsettling: the tiny frosted windows delivering some feeble illumination and positioned so high the place felt like a dungeon; the garishly painted statues and the Stations of the Cross, grotesquely carved in what looked like cherry wood. Several medieval-looking wooden chandeliers, fitted with electric candles, hung from the rafters. They were as charmless as carcasses dangling from hooks in an abattoir.

I lock up Clara's place and trudge back home. My new friend did not make an appearance last night. No more vintage coins have mysteriously appeared and I am almost inclined to believe I've been dreaming the whole thing. Nevertheless, I am still considering laying some traps.

Je me dis: t'inquiète pas. Don't worry, I tell myself.

I take a nap. When I wake, it is already dark. I snap on my bedside lamp, and he is there. The little grey mouse. Sitting on the top rail of the footboard. His ears swivel like tiny radar dishes, as though he is trying to divine my thoughts.

"*Qu'est-ce que tu fucking fais?*"

Absurdly, I am shouting in French. Face first, he climbs down the vertical rail to the floor and out my bedroom door. A moment later he returns with something in his mouth and drops it at the threshold. I wait a few minutes until I am certain he is gone before climbing out of bed. It is an elaborate, gold-coloured sewing thimble. The tip is mottled with tiny dimples; the base has delicately carved foliage and flowers inlaid with turquoise beads. Victorian, perhaps.

An offering?

The Drama Queens

"It's out of my hands, Lyle."

The new principal, Audrey Morton, was the only one at Queen of All Saints who called Lyle Spencer by his given name. Everyone else called him Spence. It was a nickname he had acquired—readily adopted, really—shortly after he'd left home at seventeen. Even most of his students called him Spence. Only the very youngest called him Mr. Spencer.

"They're cutting the drama program but they are keeping Latin? They're cutting a healthy, popular program but still keeping a dead language on life support? Unbelievable."

"I know, Lyle, I know. I'm so sorry. I'm told it was a very difficult decision. All the secondary drama programs have been cut."

"All except St. Francis," Spence said.

"They only do musicals, Lyle. Their program is integrated with the music program."

Audrey was seated in one of those plush ergonomic chairs. When she'd assumed her new duties, she'd had the entire office refurbished. Her new desk had sleek curved lines that swept around her as invitingly as a castle's moat. So different from JF's old oak desk that used to be standard in every classroom, decades ago.

"We both know what this is about."

"That is not true."

"The Drama Queens. This is about the Drama Queens."

The Drama Queens was the informal name that a group of Spence's students, among others, had given themselves. While many provincial school districts encouraged GSA clubs—Gay Straight Alliances—Queen of All Saints was an independent Catholic school, governed by the Diocese, ruled by what Spence referred to as the Conservative Cartel. GSA clubs were forbidden and so the Improv Club, which met twice weekly at lunch in Spence's studio-classroom, transformed themselves into the Drama

Queens. They still practised improvisation, but the meetings were really informal gatherings where LGBTQ students and others could find a convivial place to socialize and support one another.

"You're not hearing me, Lyle. All the secondary drama programs have been cut, not just yours. Everyone knows how hard you work and how much you have done for this school. Everyone is extremely grateful."

Spence stood and looked out the window at the dilapidated statue of the Virgin Mary that had been slowly disintegrating in the courtyard since he began teaching more than twenty years ago. Her benevolent gaze still tilted to heaven but her nose had crumbled away. Her hands, folded in prayer, lacked several fingers. Lichen was overtaking the surviving streaks of blue paint on her cloak.

"JF would not have allowed this." JF had been Spence's constant advocate. Together they had weaved the drama program into the fabric of the school. JF had encouraged Spence to produce work that supported curriculum in English and Social Studies. His students performed for the local elementary schools, and Spence's office was decorated with children's drawings that depicted scenes from stories he had adapted from Robert Munsch.

"JF isn't here anymore, Lyle. And I doubt even he could have prevented this."

"My program is integrated, too. Every student in this school passes through my studio. In many cases, several times a year."

"I agree all of our students have benefited from your program, Lyle. But not all of them are enrolled in your courses. Our funding is based on enrolment."

It was true that enrolment had been declining for years but Spence had always had a full roster of students.

"I don't cost any more than an English teacher. Less, probably, since I don't need texts. I built that studio. JF and I built that studio. And all of the productions are financed by me. What the Diocese contributes doesn't even cover royalties for the number of plays I produce in a year. I finance those productions out of pocket and have to make the money back from ticket sales. I'm practically running a business here."

"Lyle. You are a wonderful teacher. There are likely other positions coming open in the Diocese. In any case, your seniority guarantees—"

"What am I supposed to tell my students? How am I supposed to motivate them for the rest of June? They have nothing to work toward now."

"I am sorry that this is so last minute. I'm told it was decided at an emergency meeting of the Archdiocese. There was a funding crisis that needed to be addressed."

"Funding crisis. They don't lack funding. They lack integrity."

"Lyle, I'm asking you to take the rest of the day off. I've already arranged for Tom to take your classes this afternoon. You don't have to be the one to give the news to your students—let our vice-principal do it. Take a few days off. You have every right to be feeling upset. We are scheduled to meet with all the students enrolled in Drama today. We are taking them out of their classes by grade this afternoon. They will be choosing new elective preferences for next year and—"

Spence didn't wait to hear the rest. He walked abruptly out of Audrey Morton's office.

"Queen of hypocrites and homophobes," he muttered.

Spence knew he was too angry to trust himself behind the wheel of his car. He walked to the little park a few blocks down the street from the school. His heart was racing. Really galloping. Spence checked his pulse to get a sense of his heart rate. His alarm grew. He took out his cell phone and searched heart palpitations: "Breathe deeply. Splash cold water on your face. Stress and anxiety will make the palpitations worse."

He spotted a drinking fountain next to a bench. It produced a weak little stream and Spence had to wait until it began to run cold.

He took a few sips and splashed a little on his face. The veins in his temples were throbbing. He sat on the bench, in the shade of a sprawling oak tree, his eyes closed, breathing deeply. He sat so still that a starling flew down from a branch and lighted on his knee.

After an hour, Spence felt calmer and his heart had settled back to normal. He walked around the park several times, ruing that he had allowed himself to get so fat over the past decade. Buying a car had put paid to his old habit of cycling to school. At half past three, when he felt the coast was clear, he returned to the school. He was halfway resolved to cleaning out his desk and just quitting.

The door to his studio was open. Sitting on the floor, in a near perfect circle, were the thirty or so members of the Drama Queens. They were all holding hands. Arranged around the studio, sitting silently, were another twenty or more of Spence's students. Tom, the vice-principal, was standing glumly by the door.

"Spence. Do you think you could . . . "

"Get out."

Wordlessly, the students sitting on the floor shifted a little, expanding the circle to allow him a place to sit. He walked to the centre of the circle and stood for a moment, surveying the upturned faces of his students.

It was here he had begun his first class, surrounded by a similar circle of students. He had asked them to stand shoulder to shoulder in a circle, instructed them to widen their stances, and to keep their hands at the ready in order to protect themselves. "Don't push me. Simply stop me. I will choose a new direction," he'd instructed. Then he closed his eyes, crossed his arms over his chest, and walked without hesitation to the edge of the circle. Halted. New direction. Halted. New direction. After a couple of minutes, he began to run, still with his eyes firmly closed. Each time the students absorbed his momentum. Sometimes with squeals of fear and nervousness. But always with care for his safety.

For more than twenty years, the studio had been a sanctuary for a generation of kids. But it had been his sanctuary as well. It was here Spence had learned to surrender his power. And that became the source of his authority.

Spence walked to the edge of the circle and bestowed a weary smile on Derek and Anthony. They were among the youngest in the room. Fast friends. Rarely apart. They had first arrived in the studio to escape the bullying they endured. They were both autistic but, with them, autism could only be called a disorder if utter sincerity and mutual devotion were, somehow, an affliction. He reached out his hands and the boys helped him to a sitting position. The room had been silent until this moment. Then his knees produced a loud crack. Brief laughter and then, once more, a sea of solemn faces.

Across from Spence was Sam, the captain of the Improv Team. He was the one who had first dubbed this group the Drama Queens.

"We've decided to stage a sit-in, Spence. We aren't leaving until the Diocese changes their decision."

There was a murmur of assent around the room. Spence had known Sam for five years. Since the boy was in Grade 8. Since he had been Samantha. He had watched the boy slowly and confidently transform himself from Samantha into Sam until, now, he could not remember ever thinking of him as a girl. His shoulder-length hair, by stages, gave way to a crewcut. He'd defiantly worn high-top sneakers instead of the black pumps de rigueur with the girls' uniform. It was Sam's activism that convinced JF to amend the school's dress code, making skirts optional. Once in trousers, he soon swapped out his sweater for a boy's blazer and, finally, seemed utterly at ease with himself.

Many of the teenagers in the room had some similar story of transformation. Big or small. Not from the very beginning—and not all at once—Spence's studio had begun to gather in the misfits. The broken kids. The boys without fathers. The girls with stories they had been forbidden to tell. Sam's transformation had also changed perspectives, including Spence's.

Patrick sat next to Sam. In Grade 12, he was one of a handful of openly gay or lesbian students. His courage to be himself, Spence knew, drew boys like Derek and Anthony, who were still not sure what to make of their intensely close friendship. Spence smiled at Melody who was seated halfway up a ladder that leaned against the wall. Last year, she had written and performed a powerful monologue about dealing with her mental illness. Her honesty disabused the notion that self-harm was some new fad. No one mocked Amy's stutter here. Or told Craig to remove his mascara and eyeliner. It was not as though the studio was utterly spared pettiness and conflict. But it was a place where unity was valued. Where mistakes were made and were forgiven.

"I appreciate what you are doing," Spence began.

"We're not doing it just for you," Sam said. "We're doing it for all of us."

The room suddenly erupted. Everyone talking at once.

Spence sat silent for several minutes. Then he spoke, softly. "We have all lost something important," he said. "And when we experience a loss, it is natural to grieve. The first stage of grief is denial."

Spence removed his tie and loosened the top buttons of his shirt.

"No!" A girl named Sophia threw her water bottle at the wall. It bounced and rolled back toward her. Melody lowered herself from her perch on the ladder, picked up the bottle and sat next to Sophia.

"The second is anger." Spence smiled. He pressed the palms of his hands against his temples. He could feel a headache coming on.

"Bargaining, depression, acceptance." Lydia spoke. Lydia had been Spence's stage manager all that year. She was leaning out the window of the lighting booth. Spence turned and looked up at her. Her sister had died of a fentanyl overdose last year.

"Mr. Spencer?" Derek tugged at the sleeve of Spence's shirt. "Mr. Spencer, you are sweating quite a bit. Are you okay?"

Spence took a few deep breaths. His heart was racing again. His skin felt suddenly cold. There was a sharp pain behind his eyes as if he'd been struck in the face. His field of vision was slowly collapsing, like a scene change in an old silent movie.

"Derek, please go to the office and get Mrs. Morton," he said calmly. "Sam, would you kindly call an ambulance?"

I'm a little groggy. After being startled awake last night by *la petite souris* I had trouble getting back to sleep. I suppose, technically, he had roused me from a late afternoon nap. But had I slept through the night, I might not now be feeling so out of sorts, having lost an hour's sleep to the absurdity of Daylight Saving Time.

I check my phone. No text from Clara. I should know better than to expect one before she boards the plane to Paris. She has never been the sort of person who sends a lot of texts. When she was twelve, even before teenagers were all routinely carrying cell phones, I had bought a pair of them so that we could stay in closer touch. They were the flip sort, like the communicators on *Star Trek*. I thought that might intrigue her since she was a fan of the TV franchise. When she was younger and her mother was still alive, she would insist I play imaginary *Next Generation* episodes, since I could manage pretty decent Commander Data and Captain Picard impressions. As Lieutenant Worf I would growl: "That is not honourable!" And then we might engage in some elaborate wrestling. But she greeted this gift with near indifference and to this day is frustratingly slow to respond to texts. It might be nice, though, to get just a little note before she is 30,000 feet above the Atlantic.

I am sitting at the table with a coffee, the little ornate thimble, a half-dozen wooden mousetraps and a pencil. There is a part of me that wishes that the next time the little fellow appears he demand, "*Dessine-moi un mouton.*" I think I might happily draw him a sheep and call him *mon petit bonhomme,* as in *Le Petit Prince,* just to have someone around for company. But little princes, in our world, are few and far between and never seem to arrive when you really need them. When you are feeling stranded.

I load the spring on one of the wooden traps and test it with a pencil. It snaps the pencil in two. With luck, it will be quick. Merciful. No suffering. Yet aren't I being ungrateful? I don't know much about antiques, but I know that Victorian sewing thimbles are collectible. I fit the thimble onto my ring finger and tap the bowl of my coffee cup. Soon my child will be soaring above the clouds and here, below, I am plotting an execution like some evil baron in a nineteenth-century melodrama.

I am not really squeamish about such things. A little later in the morning, at St. Monica's, I reflect on this as I kneel before the altar. Nearby are the Stations of the Cross that are, in essence, a torture gauntlet. Given my regular Sunday milieu, why would I have delicate feelings about ridding myself of a mouse who evidently possesses the instincts of a magpie?

St. Monica's is the second church I attended in Montréal. Clara had taken several Religious Studies courses at Concordia and one of the instructors was the pastor of St. Monica's. Clara said she thought he was a good guy. St. Monica's is the only church I have ever attended where children outnumber the adults. It is on rue De Terrebonne, good earth, which I took as a positive sign. And nearly forty years earlier, I had performed a supporting role in a play called *Righteousness*. Among other characters, I assayed the role of Augustine's son, Adeodatus, which means gift from God. St. Monica is Augustine's mother. Whatever my ambivalent feelings toward Augustine the theologian, I liked his mother. Or maybe I liked the memory of the woman who had played his mother. We had been close, for a time, despite our age difference. In any event, I felt a connection.

When I introduced myself to the priest, he said, "Call me Larry." And I do. Larry is a no-nonsense Jesuit with a passion for films and is a genuine scholar. But what I mostly like about him is the way he invites all the kids up to the altar for the Lord's Prayer. They sit around the altar as if it were just some ordinary kitchen table and it seems to me more sanctified than usual surrounded by their guilelessness.

I am tired today and in a rotten mood. But for some reason the words of the responsorial psalm strike me: "Be with me, Lord, when

I am in trouble. You who dwell in the shelter of the Most High, who abide in the shadow of the Almighty, say to the Lord, 'My refuge and fortress, my God in whom I trust.'"

But I am thinking of *la petite souris*, not myself. I suppose, in a way, my apartment is his refuge, at least until spring arrives. I am his shelter and he is abiding in my shadow. The idea deserves some contemplation.

Monday, Fifth Day of Lent

"I can offer you $200."

"Really? The turquoise alone must be worth that," I say. I blow into my hands to warm them. Somehow, I managed to lose my gloves today, somewhere between locking up my bike at school and the walk up three flights of stairs. Expensive ski gloves.

"Turquoise *is* enjoying a renewed popularity right now. But stones of this quality and size, I'm sorry, won't fetch $200. You are correct, the thimble is Victorian. There is a market. I know a collector who might be interested. Maybe."

It was a shorter than usual French class this morning, just a two-hour exam. I am in an antique shop on Victoria just south of Sherbrooke. The proprietor gives me a steady look.

"You can set a price and I could sell it on commission, if you prefer," he says.

I take the $200. I am tempted to ask him about the 1957 dime but I change my mind. Maybe it will bring me luck. As I am fussing with the lock for my bike, I get a text from Clara.

"*Nous sommes arrivés à Paris! Je t'aime!*" I note that she has conjugated *arriver* correctly in *passé composé* and remembered the plural. *Très bien, ma puce.* My hands are too frozen to immediately reply.

Gloveless in Montréal in March.

Back home I consider the four mousetraps I have placed on the kitchen counter. They are not yet baited and loaded. It seems churlish, now, to trap a mouse who has, essentially, paid nearly a week's rent. I put the traps back in the box.

I deliberately stay up later than usual, waiting for him to show up, perhaps to offer some other collectable tidbit. I keep nodding off. Just before daybreak I am startled awake by the sound of squeaking. Then nothing. My little friend does not make an appearance.

My alarm sounds. Off to class.

TUESDAY, SIXTH DAY OF LENT

Fresh snow has fallen. There is construction in progress along de Maisonneuve and, returning home from class, I am obliged to dismount and push my bike on the sidewalk for a couple of blocks. Everyone agreed that this morning's *examen de compréhension orale* was much easier than expected. Nevertheless, I am feeling a little out of sorts. A young woman is walking toward me. I smile. I recognize her. She was a student of mine from Queen of All Saints who played the part of Viola in *Twelfth Night*.

Gisele.

I am just about to greet her when I realize. Her familiar face dissolves and becomes the face of a stranger. This happens more frequently than one might expect. Since arriving in Montréal, I often seem to see the faces I had been accustomed to seeing in Vancouver. Colleagues from school. Students. People from the old neighbourhood. It is as though my mind begins to idle and the half-seen faces *des inconnus* default to *visages familiers*.

Trying to think in French is surprisingly tiring. At home, I am tempted to take a nap. But I resolve to do a little housework instead. Exam week. I need to stick to a proper sleep schedule. I still have a collection of some hundreds of vinyl albums. Most of them belonged to Serenity, actually. I need something upbeat for housework so I put Ry Cooder's *Bop Till You Drop* on the turntable and survey the living room. Certainly some dusting is in order.

I resolve to pack away *la crèche*, the Nativity figurines on the table next to the stereo. I've had it too long to risk clumsily breaking a piece while dusting.

Odd. Joseph is missing. I spend a frustrating half hour searching. It occurs to me that, *peut-être, mon ami le rongeur—amicus meus rodent*—maybe my little rodent friend has absconded and taken St. Joseph with him.

"How is Baby Jesus going to manage without a father?" I say aloud. "Coins and antique thimbles are one thing. St. Joseph is a theft of a different order. Sentimental value, pal! Some might consider this sacrilege."

I am so tired and annoyed that I am shouting over the music.

"*Tabarnac!*"

He appears from under the sofa.

"Some people is tryin' to sleep. 'av some *ostie de* respect, *câlisse.*"

LATER . . .

His name is Thierry.

After my initial shock, I feel surprisingly calm. Almost relieved. It is as though I have been absolved of some guilty secret. Or as though I have always held some unspoken suspicion that has now been justified. I understand that no one is going to believe me. I know that. But perfectly sane people believe crazier things than this. Moses talked to a burning bush, after all. The history of half the world is shaped by that unlikely conversation.

"What you do wid dat timble, man?" Thierry's mouth is full and he sprays bits of cheddar cheese as he speaks. He rotates the little chunk I have given him like a sculptor expertly executing his craft.

"I sold it."

"*Vraiment?* 'ow much you get?"

"$200."

"Dat much?" He sputters and more bits of cheese go flying.

"It's a Victorian antique," I say. "Where did you get it, by the way."

"Dat ol' lady in de apartment above you."

"You stole from a little old lady?"

I don't know her so I can't pretend to be outraged. I have never heard a sound from the apartment upstairs.

"She is dead."

"You stole from a dead woman?"

"She not gonna miss it. By de way. You bedder call de cops or somebody. She gonna start smellin' preddy soon. Nobody ever visit 'er. *Pas mal triste.* It preddy sad."

I fire off a text to my landlord, Nick, expressing my concerns for my neighbour. He replies almost immediately: "Thanks! I'll look into it tomorrow morning."

"She not goin' nowhere," Thierry says, wiping bits of cheese from his whiskers. "You got any beer?"

"No."

"Too bad."

I learn that Thierry has been secretly living with me since New Year's Day. He had been sharing the apartment next door to me with a buddy of his, he says. Apparently, they had some sort of argument and Thierry decided to make alternative arrangements.

"We is still chums," he says. "We jes need some space, dats all. Anyway, de guy next door is a prick. Jean-Guy an' me both 'ate 'im."

"You what! You ate him?"

"*Non, tabarnac.* We 'ate 'im. *On l'haït.* Clean yer ears, *ostie.*"

I don't mind Thierry's bluntness. In fact, part of me admires it. Truth be told, I can be a little . . . reticent. Emotionally, I mean. I rarely say what I am feeling. Sometimes I'm not even sure what I am feeling. I ask Thierry why he has waited so long before reaching out.

"Most mice dun trust people an' people dun like mice. Except mebbe de white one wid de pink eye. Creepy." He shudders. "Also.

You 'ear de story. About experiment an' shit. Dat preddy barbaric."
He suddenly sneezes.

"*S'cuse-moé.*"

"*À tes souhaits,*" I say.

He looks at me, amused.

"*Pis,* you is learnin' French. 'ow come?"

"You know. When in Rome . . ."

He stares at me blankly.

"St. Ambrose's advice to St. Monica? *À Rome, fais comme les Romains?*"

Silence.

"What you do for a livin'?"

"I'm retired. I was a teacher."

"Uh huh."

"So . . ."

"You wanna know de truth? Okay. Nobody ever visit you, man. So, I tink, what de 'ell, why not take a chance. Mebbe dis guy could use de company."

Another silence. Night has fallen.

"Look, Thierry . . ."

"*Thierry.*" He corrects my pronunciation.

"*Thierry.*"

"Bedder."

"I'm going to have to sleep on it. I mean, if we are going to be roommates, *les colocataires,* we'll have to come to some sort of . . . arrangement."

"*Pas de problème.* What yer name, by de way?"

"Just call me Spence, okay? I'll see you in the morning?"

"I'll be asleep in de mornin'," he says. "*On se verra ce soir.*"

CHRISTINE

As he matured as a teacher, Spence developed a handful of strategies for bringing his drama classes to order. Even with a decade of experience, he still felt some anxiety before each class.

This afternoon, with his older students, he stood at one end of the studio facing the entrance. He closed his eyes. After a moment, two of his students came to either side of him and, wordlessly, linked their arms through his. Within a minute, all of his students were standing silently in a circle, arms linked. Many closed their eyes.

"Let's sit," he said. The class sat on the floor. He sat with them, cross-legged, surveying the faces around him.

"Where's Christine?"

"She'll be here in a minute," a girl named Emma said. She was chewing gum. She popped a bubble.

"Oops. I forgot." Emma ran to the wastebasket and spat out her gum.

"All right," he said. "Let's breathe together."

Spence had unconsciously borrowed certain features of the Mass, the various rituals that are performed in unison by the congregants. Even if one did not consciously reflect on the significance of each gesture and each reflexive response, the security of unity was present and the sheer repetition had an effect, like waves smoothing stones on the shore.

Early in his teaching training, Spence had been advised that he would need to develop eyes in the back of his head. He found that, in most instances, the opposite was true. If he closed his eyes, his students responded with almost a reverence. Not to him, of course, but to what Spence called the dramatic relationship that had been established. His authority came from his vulnerability. If he used no power, he encountered no resistance. That was one of the lessons of the Cross, Spence had come to believe. He wished he'd learned that at a younger age. But there's no substitute for experience.

They were rehearsing their next production, *Romeo and Juliet*. Clara, who had recently enrolled in a potpourri of courses at Langara College—Philosophy, Women's Studies, Introduction to Design—was going to help on costume and set design.

The studio was sometimes noisy and chaotic. Sometimes silent and focused. Occasionally filled with music. Spence had learned to assign responsibilities to his students, often allowing them to teach portions of the class. Students, he felt, needed a sense of belonging. A sense that they had some independence. A degree of competence. And they needed to know they had something to share.

He was occasionally discouraged to observe that certain inspirational quotes would gain popularity and appear on classroom doors at Queen of All Saints. "Nothing Works Unless You Do." Clearly school and learning were considered a job for children. "Failure is Not an Option." Great, Spence thought, let's make children fear failure. "Your Attitude Determines Your Direction"—this one from Mr. Owens, a sailing enthusiast. But what did that mean? Good attitude? Bad attitude? Wasn't it just a way of shifting blame onto the student who might be struggling?

So much seemed geared toward achievement and Spence had come to believe that the emphasis on striving was not always productive. "If you are not making mistakes, you are not learning," he would tell his students. It was a sentiment that all of the teachers at Queen of All Saints would approve. Still, many used marks as a tactic to ensure compliance—a reward. Dutifully adding up scores as if it were all a competition. As if secondary school were the farm team for the big leagues, the universities. We prepare them to excel, Spence thought, we don't prepare them for life. Even in this independent Catholic school, there was no class called, "Love Your Neighbour as Yourself."

"Christine is outside in the hallway, Spence." Unnoticed, Emma had slipped out and back into the studio while Spence's eyes were still closed in meditation.

"What is she doing there?"

"Crying." Emma shrugged, as if to say, "I already did everything I could."

"Austin? Your turn to lead the warm-up?"

Austin flipped his hair off his face and nodded.

"Okay. Something for energy. Something for listening and responding. Something for concentration."

Spence stood just as Clara opened the door to the studio a crack. She made an exaggerated sad face and mimed rubbing her eyes. Holding up five fingers, she mouthed "five minutes" and then gave Spence a thumbs up. Truthfully, he was a little relieved that Clara had the situation in hand. He sometimes found Christine difficult to deal with. Her moods could shift suddenly. One moment she would be fine and then something would set her off and she would flee the studio in tears. By the time the warm-up had concluded, Clara led Christine in and both were all smiles.

Stage violence—punches, kicks, slaps, hair-pulling—was the focus of the rehearsal. Not everyone in the cast needed to be able to handle a sword but Spence taught them all the rudiments anyway. He wanted the opening scene to be a real brawl.

By 5:30 everyone had dispersed. Spence groaned a little as he picked up a water bottle from the floor. He'd pulled a muscle in his lower back.

"Mr. Spencer. Do you think Shakespeare was Catholic?"

"Christine. You're still here? You know who this belongs to?" he asked, holding up the bottle.

The girl shook her head.

"Into lost-and-found with the rest of the orphans," Spence said.

"So, what do you think? Was he Catholic or not?"

She dropped her pack onto the floor and sat on it. It had started to snow outside and she brushed a few flakes off her sleeve.

"You came back to ask that? It couldn't wait until Monday?" Spence was teasing a little.

"Whatever," she said and stood up.

"No, no. Wait. We can talk about it," Spence said. She sat again and listened pensively as he explained that he thought Shakespeare was unlikely to risk his social ambitions by adhering to a forbidden faith.

"In general, best not to conflate the artist with their art," he added. "The plays are genius but Shakespeare himself might have been perfectly ordinary."

"Why did you cast me as Friar Lawrence?" Christine asked suddenly.

"I needed a strong actor in the role. That's all. And I needed to find a credible way to use girls in roles written for guys. Casting is a bit of a balancing act when we are doing Shakespeare. All the characters having been played by men and boys originally, as you know. If it weren't for the PAC, I'd probably make Romeo and Juliet lesbians just so I could use more girls in good roles."

Some of the parents on the Parent Advisory Council had not been keen on the idea of staging *Romeo and Juliet*. They didn't want the students seeing a play about children disobeying their parents. Or children committing suicide. "The play is about loving your enemy," Spence had argued. "The children are sacrifices, not suicides."

Christine sat silently.

"What? You're not happy in that role?"

"No. It's not that." She tugged at one of the straps of her backpack.

"What then?"

"I'm just not happy."

Spence nodded.

"Also . . . I don't believe in God so how am I supposed to be a friar?"

"I see."

"There's something wrong with me. What's wrong with me?"

"There's nothing wrong with you, Christine. You're intelligent. You have many wonderful gifts. You work hard."

Christine began soundlessly crying. Her face betrayed no emotions as tears poured from her. After a minute there was a little puddle on the floor near her feet. Spence walked to his office, got a box of tissues and sat on the floor next to her. She blew her nose repeatedly. Each time dropping the crumpled tissue at her feet. They accumulated there like a little bouquet of white roses. After a few minutes she spoke again.

"You're Catholic aren't you, Mr. Spencer?"

Spence nodded. Christine was among the few older students who called him "Mister." She wasn't making a point of offering respect. She was creating distance.

"You believe in God?"

He nodded again.

"I don't get it. You're an intelligent person. How can you believe in God?"

"Everyone believes in something, Christine. Everyone has, I don't know—ideals, values—something they cherish but can't prove are true. Universal. It is difficult to explain. It's not a matter of intelligence, Christine. In some ways it's not even a matter of belief."

"I don't believe in anything," she said. "What's the point?"

Spence was tired. His back hurt. He wasn't the counsellor. He wasn't the school's spiritual director. He was just a drama teacher. In the hierarchy of school subjects, he was at or near the bottom.

He glanced at the crucifix that hung above the door. There was one in each room of the school.

"We don't suffer alone, Christine." And then he added, "It gets better."

"When?"

"I don't know. It just does. Please trust that."

"Have you ever, you know . . . felt everything was hopeless?" she asked.

"Yes."

"What did you do."

"I suppose I prayed," Spence said.

"I don't know how to pray."

"Just say . . . " Spence hesitated. To be honest, he really did not pray all that much himself. "Say help."

She handed him back the box of tissues. She had no more tears.

"Yeah. Good luck with that," she said.

Christine slung her backpack around one shoulder and walked past Spence and out the door.

"See you on Monday," he said.

As ordered by the Diocese, *Romeo and Juliet* was cancelled. Even JF said it was the right decision under the circumstances. He told Spence that there was no way he could have known and that it was not his fault. Spence took seven days sick leave. He returned after Christine's funeral.

She had hanged herself in her bedroom closet. Her mother found her Sunday morning. She left no note.

Spence thought of Serenity. Her whole life she was crying, "Help." Had he really heard her? Or had he only tried to redeem himself by saving her? And now this child. A girl of sixteen, crying help, and he had given her a thumbnail sketch on Shakespeare's religious conformity. *Help.* And like some medieval monk, he'd suggested she pray. He had done everything he could.

Except hear her.

Before retiring last night, I went upstairs and knocked on the door of the apartment above me. Thierry's not a doctor, after all. How can he be certain she is dead? I knocked several times. No response. On my way to class, I meet Nick in the lobby. I can see an ambulance through the window and Nick thanks me for my text and explains that she seems to have died of natural causes, probably in the wee hours of Sunday morning. It occurs to me that Thierry might have accidently frightened her to death, but I set that thought aside. As it happens, I did know her slightly. I suppose the whole neighbourhood knew her slightly. She never went more than a block or two from the building. She walked at a snail's pace and impatiently refused assistance if anyone offered to carry her shopping bag or hold the door open for her. She died at age ninety-one, cantankerous and independent. I wonder, if I live another thirty years, will I become her?

This morning, my *examen de production orale* goes smoothly. In fact, Étienne does not even test me on any of the discussion topics the class had prepared. I chat with him, informally, in halting French for fifteen minutes. Then, he smiles and says: "*Veuillez demander au prochain étudiant d'entrer.*"

There is no scheduled class this morning, only individual appointments, so I am finished early. Cycling a leisurely route home, I find myself near L'Oratoire Saint-Joseph. I decide to stop in for a moment at Frère André's little chapel. Saint-Jean-Baptiste has been the official patron saint of Québec Catholics for more than a hundred years, but André Bessette, St. André of Montréal, is the unofficial patron of the city.

JF kept a photo of Frère André on his desk and I learned a little about him nearly ten years ago when Sister Jacqueline, of the Sisters of the Holy Cross, visited Queen of All Saints just prior to his official canonization. She gave a little presentation in the gym. Reflecting on Frère André's humble origins, his lack of formal education, his humility, and his almost simple-minded devotion to St. Joseph's power to effect healings, I suppose I developed a soft spot for a man who exemplified everything I am not. I don't necessarily believe Frère André actually performed miraculous healings. I think people sometimes blame themselves or get invested in their own helplessness, and it takes someone like Frère André to give them permission to forgive themselves or, maybe, throw away the crutches and get a bit of gentle exercise.

Nevertheless, I kneel at the old-fashioned communion rail in the modest chapel and say a prayer to St. Joseph. Not a prayer, really. At best, I have a contemplative moment. Then I head home.

LATER . . .

"*Salut.*"

Around eight o'clock, Thierry appears at my doorway. I am reading *Le Petit Prince.*

"*Bonsoir, mon petit bonhomme,*" I say.

"*Quoi?*"

"*Rien. Une petite blague.*"

I hold up the book to indicate I am quoting a familiar phrase, as a little joke. He stares blankly.

"*Alors?*"

"*Bienvenue, mon chum.* Make yourself at home. I have to study for one more exam in the morning. Tomorrow night we can discuss a few ground rules. Okay?"

Thierry nods, his tail gives a little flick, and he disappears into the kitchen.

Thursday, Eighth Day of Lent

Thierry and I have come to an understanding. I hope. His grasp of English is . . . imperfect. Although if I could speak French half as well as he manages English, I would be a happy man. Thierry, by his own admission, is *un voleur*—a thief. He has offered to steal money or jewellery or other valuables from the neighbours in order to pay a portion of the rent. I am not entirely comfortable with that arrangement.

"*Écoute.* I only gonna steal a lil something from a lotta different people. Most o' de time, nobody even gonna miss what I took."

I tentatively agree to those terms. Though, truthfully, I must confess to feeling a bit of a thrill at the prospect of participating in an illicit activity, even if it is only petty theft.

"I do need *some* privacy. I hope it is agreeable to you that I retain exclusive use of the bedroom and bathroom."

"*Quoi?*"

"I'd like you to stay out of my bedroom and the bathroom, if you don't mind."

"*Pas de problème.* But I get to eat anything dat fall on de floor in de kitchen. *D'accord?*"

"*D'accord.*"

A pause.

"I don't want to be indelicate. But there is the question of . . . um . . . offspring. Would it be too much to ask that you refrain from . . . um . . . mating?"

"You is kiddin', right?"

"No."

"Tell you what, man. I will eat any kid dat gets born."

"What the hell, Thierry!"

"*Une blague. Crisse.* A joke. I take de precaution. Okay? *Pas de problème.* I get it. Overpopulation. *Je catch.*"

I nod. Fair enough.

"Dats it?"

"*C'est tout.*"

"Okay den. *J'ai une surprise.*"

He scrambles to the far side of the sofa and briefly disappears, re-emerging with a bag of weed and some rolling papers. He deftly rolls a joint while I put a John Prine album on the turntable. We sit together listening to the opening track, "Illegal Smile."

"*Totalement légal maintenant.*" Thierry grins and stretches out on the sofa. He blows an impressive stream of smoke through his long, yellow incisors. I haven't smoked marijuana for more than thirty years. I take a drag.

J'ai un ami, I say to myself.

FRIDAY, NINTH DAY OF LENT

"Is not me. Is Jean-Guy. We is *chums* but 'e is kind o' a worry fart."

"You mean worry wart?"

"Dat too."

Thierry is up and about earlier than I expected. It is not quite dark.

"De guy next door. *Il a mis des pièges.* 'ow you say dat in English?"

"Traps? He's set some traps?"

"Dats right. Now me an' Jean-Guy, we been round de clock a few time . . ."

"Around the block?"

"Whatever. *Les deux.* Anyway, we is not likely to fall for *des pièges,* de trap, but you know it gonna be spring soon. More kid mice is gonna be born. Not mine for sure. I dun got no kid. But Jean-Guy, 'e got a soft spot *pour les enfants . . .*"

"How can I help?"

Jean-Guy has asked Thierry to check out the parking garage. Apparently, there are some old bait stations for mice down there. Jean-Guy wants to make sure they are *neutralisés.*

The parking garage is a bit of a mystery to me. I only go down there to dispose of my garbage and recycling and Nick is the only person I have ever seen entering or exiting the garage. As far as I can tell, none of the tenants use it. Oh yes—that black vintage

Valiant that Nick guided in the other day. All of the cars are covered with grey tarpaulins. If the Valiant is here, there is no way for me to know except to peek under the tarps.

The lighting is very poor. Several of the fluorescents are burnt out. Others flicker weakly. The pipes in the ceiling leak perpetually. The building, in general, is a little shabby. Repairs are routinely neglected. If the power fails during a storm, the hallways and stairwells are pitch black because the emergency lights do not function.

I have brought gloves, my camping trowel and a plastic bag.

"Pssst."

Thierry is by the wall near the utility meters. There are three rows of them, the old-fashioned sort with their mysterious dials. I think they are still analogue; my apartment is equipped with a fuse box rather than breakers. Frankly, the whole building is a bit of a fire trap.

"How did you get down here so fast?"

"*Un magicien ne révèle jamais ses secrets.*"

We follow along the walls and find several filthy bait stations. Most are empty. A few have a smattering of poison pellets. But obviously they have been largely neglected, maybe for years. We are greeted with a grim sight in the final one—the desiccated body of a mouse, as delicate as a dried flower crushed in a book.

"I'm sorry."

"Not yer fault, *mon chum*. Lots o' thing kill mice. Bird. Snake. Cat. Even de squirrel. Everything gotta eat."

"Nobody ate this fellow." I brush the remains into the plastic bag with the handful of pellets we've collected.

"We not gonna mention dat mouse to Jean-Guy. It just gonna make 'im sad. I'm gonna tell 'im de ghost is clear down 'ere."

"The coast."

Thierry looks at me.

"The *coast* is clear. It's idiomatic. Probably nautical in origin," I say.

"You is speakin' English, right?"

"Yes."

"Gimme dat." He takes the plastic bag in his teeth.

"*Attention, Thierry, c'est du poison.*"

He's gone.

SATURDAY, TENTH DAY OF LENT

I am in the shower when it happens for the first time. The second time, I am on the balcony enjoying a rare moment of sunshine when I see a little girl kneel and extend her hand, palm up, to offer a squirrel some morsel. The third time, I have Phoebe Snow on the turntable. She sings about a man who is reincarnated and comes back as himself. For some reason I find that unbearably sad. Sobbing over the song "It Must Be Sunday." And it is still Saturday.

They are brief episodes, but they take me by surprise. I rarely cry. And when I do, it is generally occasioned by the sort of things that make everyone cry. Ending a relationship. Someone dies. *Ce genre de choses.* Some years before my father died, he had been taking a medication to slow the growth of his prostate cancer. It drained him of testosterone. He once unexpectedly burst into tears. I didn't know how to respond—I had never seen him cry when I was a child.

I tell myself it is the stress of my French exams. The various unexpected expenses that keep thwarting my budget. Clara's absence. Maybe it's just me getting used to retirement. Please don't let it be my testosterone melting away.

Like most people, I suppose, I thought retirement would be a perpetual holiday. But truthfully? It takes some adjusting. An aspect of one's identity is snatched away. Who am I when I am not working? What is it I am supposed to be doing? It is like waking up with a stranger every morning. But the stranger is yourself. And now Clara is away and soon to be married. You never stop being a mother or a father but, I suppose, as children grow older, it is natural to fade into the background of their lives.

My usefulness has not been entirely extinguished. There are plants to be watered in Clara's apartment, as promised. Outside her building, someone has parked a truck in front of the fire escape where I usually lock my bike and I look around for an alternative. The sound of country music emerges from St. Raymond's just across the street. I notice someone has locked their bike to the railing on the wheelchair access ramp. I walk over and secure my bike beside the other. It is then I realize the music is live. A band is rehearsing in the basement of the church. I enter the vestibule and quietly descend the adjacent stairs to catch a glimpse. A woman about Clara's age is singing "All of Me." Another woman is on bass and a young man, in a battered cowboy hat, plays acoustic guitar. From where I'm standing, I can't see the drummer. I sit on the stairs and listen for a few minutes. Then, unnoticed, I climb back up .

In the vestibule, there is a bronze plaque commemorating St. Raymond of Pennafort with text in French, Italian, and English. An engraving depicts him floating across a narrow strait, kneeling on his own cloak, which is fastened to his walking stick to form a sail. Apparently he is making a miraculous escape. Photographs of former pastors line the walls, all of them smiling and projecting a reassuring benevolence. I survey them idly. Then I see him— Mallory Parent OSM 1968–69.

Just an unremarkable looking middle-aged man in an ill-fitting suit and a clerical collar. At that precise moment, I am aware of a peculiar smell. Like pine or mothballs. Camphor? I open the heavy doors to the church and peer down the nave. Perhaps someone is burning incense. Nothing. I wonder, for a moment, if I am experiencing—what is it called? When the senses become confused? Synesthesia? Curious. The sound of voices drifts up from the basement. The band must be taking a break. I pull my phone from my pocket and snap a photo.

Mallory Parent OSM 1968–69

I don't bother taking my shoes off in Clara's apartment. Bending down is still a little hard on my knees. I can give the place a sweep before she gets back. On my cell phone, I have the notes Clara gave me for the care of her plants. I do the rounds of the living room and the kitchen. In the studio I realize, I forgot the creeping fig last week. Who named it that? Some Renaissance prude surreptitiously fastening fig leaves to statuary to cover the naughty bits? Clara has given it a home inside a tall bamboo bird cage and its leaves spill up and out from between the bars.

Her paintings are neatly stacked against the walls. I suppose, in some ways, they are snapshots of her life. The ambiguous depictions of motherhood in her Madonna and Child series. The paintings of children with frightening adults looming in the background. The girls' faces hiding in layers of lovingly rendered fabric. In one, there is the mutilated body of a naked woman, both compellingly beautiful and repugnant. I know some of the pieces are visual dialogues of feminist theory, but I can't help but feel she is also processing emotions from her turbulent childhood.

After watering Clara's plants, I lie down on her sofa and nap for an hour with my shoes still on. Some days it feels like I am making up for years of lost sleep. But come evening, back home, I am wide awake. I sit up in bed reading *Le Petit Prince*. I have begun to memorize certain passages:

La preuve que le petit prince a existé c'est qu'il était ravissant, qu'il riait, et qu'il voulait un mouton. The proof that the little prince existed is that he was delightful, that he laughed, and that he wanted a sheep.

"'ey dere, brudder. It Saturday night, *saint-ciboire!* You dun gotta date?"

He appears in the bedroom doorway, takes a step into my room, then hesitates.

"*Puis-je?*"

I am pretty sure that *puis-je* is a very polite form—sort of the equivalent of "if I may." I assume he is being ironic. I nod my assent. A little company might do me good.

"Jean-Guy say tanks, by de way. For makin' de garage safe.'"

He manages to climb to the top shelf of my bookcase by pushing books into positions that make it possible for him to scramble up the shelves. His ingenuity is impressive.

"So, you read all des book?" he asks.

"Most," I say.

"You got a TV?"

"No. Sometimes I watch something on Netflix." I gesture to my laptop on the floor next to my bed.

"You mind?"

"Be my guest," I say.

He descends the bookcase at an alarming speed and exits my bedroom. A moment later he returns dragging a small mesh bag of marbles.

"Where did that come from?"

"*Le magicien . . .*" He winks. "You dun wanna ask too many question."

I watch, fascinated, as he frenetically manipulates the marbles in order to ferry my laptop out the door and into the living room. It is the sort of achievement that strips the shroud of mystery off the construction of Stonehenge.

"What yer password, *mon chum?*" he shouts from the living room. I shout back.

"You gonna have to write dat down."

He returns with a pen and a scrap of paper. I write my password and hand them back. He scrutinizes the paper intently for several moments.

"*Merci.*"

After a few minutes, "*Viarge!*" Then, "*Varlope!*" Another minute.,"*Vas chier!*" Still later, "*Vas te crosser avec une poignée de clous rouillés!*" At last, "*Voilà!*"

My cell phone gives off a little ping. It is Clara: "I love you, Daddy!" It must be the wee hours of the morning in France. The crying that I thought was behind me this morning starts again. I get up and close the bedroom door so that it is just an inch ajar and fall asleep to my own supressed sobs and to the muffled sound of *Incredibles 2*.

En français, bien sûr.

JF

"Mr. Sauvé," Spence extended his hand toward the principal.

"Call me JF," the older man smiled warmly. He examined Spence's face for a little longer than might be considered polite. As if he were searching for someplace on a map.

"Sit, sit," JF gestured to a battered armchair across from his solid oak desk that was piled high with books and papers and photographs. He shuffled through a little stack he had secured under the corner of his typewriter, an archaic looking Remington that might have been at home on the set of some old film noir starring Humphrey Bogart. JF must have noticed Spence's interest.

"It was my father's," he said. "We'll be getting computers, soon. I anticipate every classroom will have computers by the end of the year. Next year at the latest."

"Your father?" Spence gestured to a faded black and white photo in a silver frame. A tall young man in a dark suit and fedora towered over an elderly little priest in an old-fashioned black cassock.

"That's my dad in, I think, 1935 or '36 in Montréal. Before he was married. The little guy is Frère André."

Spence had never been to Montréal and had never heard of Frère André. His knowledge of Montréal didn't really go beyond a few novels by Mordecai Richler and maybe some poetry by Irving Layton. At university he'd become acquainted with the plays of Michel Tremblay in translation and, later, the work of Robert Lepage. For a moment, he considered making some small talk about French Canada. Sauvé must be a French name.

"So, Desmond tells me you had a 'mystical' experience," JF said. He looked up from Spence's résumé and smiled.

Spence shifted in his chair. Father Desmond, whom Spence had first met at Holy Rosary Cathedral, had been instrumental in getting Spence this interview but he hadn't expected such a question.

"Well, mystical experience might be a bit of an overstatement,"

Spence said. He worried he might come off as a bit flaky if he acknowledged this. "Who knows? Maybe I had one of those ministrokes."

"I hear you. My grandfather claimed Frère André cured the damage caused by the polio my dad had as a boy." He nodded to the photo on his desk. "Then again, maybe it was just all those daily leg massages my grandmother and his older sisters provided."

"Mysterious ways." Spence said. He glanced at the little priest in the photo again and then turned his gaze out the window for a moment. There was one of those old-fashioned statues of Mary in the courtyard. It reminded him of Our Lady of the Sea, near where he lived as a boy. That church had had something very similar.

"You're a widower," JF said.

So far, he'd not mentioned anything from Spence's résumé.

"And your daughter is how old?"

"Clara is eight."

"Clara. Bright. Clear."

Spence was briefly confused until he realized JF was providing the Latin origin of his daughter's name. JF sat on his desk so that he was positioned a little above Spence who leaned back in the armchair.

"Mr. Spencer," JF seemed to say this a little ironically, as though he were a student addressing a teacher. He glanced down at Spence's résumé. "So far you have been an actor, a bartender, a part-time manager at a bar, and you are a poet?"

"A dabbler," Spence said.

JF continued to smile down at him.

"I just thought it rounded out the résumé," Spence said. "That I've been published."

"A bartender who no longer drinks, a poet who dabbles, an actor who has done a fair number of performances for children and teens."

It was certainly the strangest job interview Spence had ever experienced. Had it really been necessary for Father Desmond to reveal his problems with alcohol?

"Your career plans now? Are you an actor or are you a teacher?"

JF looked at him steadily.

"A teacher," Spence said. "I want to teach. I mean, I want to learn to teach."

JF slapped his desk with his hand.

"All right, then. I will see you at orientation, this Friday morning. You start on Tuesday. The Diocese should have a contract ready for you tomorrow or the next day. They'll call."

"Friday," Spence said. At this point he was feeling a little dazed. He stood and added, "Thank you."

I am more composed today. No more unexpected crying jags. Whatever brought them on, I feel certain I have left all that behind—Spence is himself again. I have the apartment to myself during daylight hours. Thierry's presence in the evenings doesn't feel intrusive. I like the little guy. I haven't mentioned him to anyone, but then, why would I? I've been studying French at Centre Saint-Jérôme for nearly six months and in the course of the past few days I have spoken more with Thierry than I have with any of my classmates.

I don't blame them. Classes focus more on grammar and vocabulary than on conversation. Besides, I am not very forthcoming socially. I am older than all of my fellow students and, I feel sure, all of the teachers as well. The majority of my classmates are learning French in order to find employment. Many are receiving meager benefits from Emploi-Québec. Being older and retired, I suppose it must seem to them that I am pursuing a hobby. Their motives are more urgent and more consequential.

Thierry has become my only real friend.

This morning I discover that, in the night, he has quietly returned my laptop to my bedside, though he neglected to plug it in. I later learn that he is wary of electricity having once given himself a frightening shock while chewing through some wiring.

"*Mieux vaut prévenir que guérir,*" Thierry says.

"An ounce of prevention is worth a pound of cure. That's what we say in English."

"*La même chose. Plus ou moins.*"

Next to my laptop he has placed a paperback copy of Albert Camus' *L'Étranger*. His offering.

"A guy on de fourt' floor got a lot o' books just for show. I never seen 'im read nutin'. So, I tawt, you know, 'cause you like readin'," Thierry explains later.

Years ago, as an undergrad, I'd read *The Stranger* in translation. During the seventies the theme of alienation was enjoying something of a vogue. In the ensuing years, alienation gradually lost its literary sheen. I suppose, instead, it became our milieu.

MONDAY, ELEVENTH DAY OF LENT

I wake this morning and am gratified to find, slipped under my bedroom door, an only slightly chewed $20 bill and one teardrop pearl earring with what appears to be a speck of blood. *Je ne pose pas de questions.* Thierry is nowhere to be seen. *C'est bien.*

He'd explained, "*Je suis nocturne.*"

I appreciate his contribution to the rent, but I am a little annoyed to find this unwelcome addition: a trail of dark, rice-sized pellets along the base of the apartment walls. This is something new. I google mouse droppings. Apparently, they poop as they move—fifty or more droppings a day.

Brut!

I post a sign on the bathroom door: "*Thierry—La salle de bains n'est plus interdite. Utilises les toilettes, s'il te plaît.*" I'm capable of compromise. Maybe the living room is littered with droppings but my bare feet affirm that the kitchen floor has started the day spotless. As I prepare my breakfast, I am more than usually cavalier about the toast crumbs. All things considered—*jusqu'ici tout va bien.* So far, so good. I receive an alert on my cell phone. Clara has sent me a heart from Paris. I heart her back. It must be early afternoon in Paris. I don my cycling gear and step out onto the balcony with what is left of my morning coffee.

This is odd. Very odd.

A cream-coloured 1963 Pontiac Parisienne swings into the driveway leading to the parking garage. This is beyond coincidence. Clara just texted from Paris. A Parisienne appears. I am certain it is a '63 because I owned this exact make and model back in 1975. I had, drunkenly, driven it into a ditch on the night of my high school graduation. Mine was a beater, to be sure, and the one below my balcony has either been restored or lovingly preserved by someone. But I can't be mistaken. Parisiennes are an absolute boat of a car. I recognize the stacked headlights below the stylish curve of what seem like hooded eyelids. The side molding had been torn off mine, but this car still had that chrome streak etched with the name "Parisienne."

I hear the clank and whirr of the garage door opening. The auto glides down the ramp and out of sight. The door clunks shut.

Am I dreaming?

SOLEMNITY: FEAST OF ST. JOSEPH

Thierry's contribution this morning is a half-dozen blue laundry tokens. Disconcertingly, however, he has left them on my night-stand. I have not seen Thierry for the past two nights. Just because I relented on the bathroom prohibition doesn't mean I have granted unfettered access to my bedroom. Thierry and I are going to have a little parley *pour parler de certaines choses*. I go down to the *salle de lavage* and start a load of laundry. The tokens work just fine despite the pronounced tooth marks. Back upstairs, I take a moment to check my email on my laptop and discover the battery is almost completely drained.

Bizarre. Unless . . .

Je suis ben open but I confess I am taken aback to find my internet history littered with mouse porn. Some very happy childhood memories of Tom and Jerry have been ruined for me. Likewise, Mickey and Minnie.

Pas d'allure, Thierry. Pas cool.

On my way to toss the laundry into the dryer I lug a bag of

garbage down to the parking garage. Next to the elevator is one of those old-fashioned garbage chutes with an ornate cast iron door. It is labelled INCINERATOR and is welded shut. The carpet in the corridors looks like it might have been fashionable back in the seventies. Around the incinerator chute, it is worn and soiled by the approach of countless feet. Those days of burning one's garbage are long gone.

La salle poubelle is in the parking garage. A room about the size of my kitchen with a dozen large green plastic trash bins arranged along the walls. Everything is wrapped in plastic trash bags, but you cannot escape the odour of decay. Consumed quickly in the flames of an incinerator or slowly in some landfill. *Time is the fire in which we burn.* Where did that thought come from?

I stand for a moment surveying the dozen or so autos shrouded in grey tarpaulins. The parking garage is like a scene in an old horror film where a motley group of jaded English aristocrats, a brash American couple and an ex-Nazi with a monocle must spend the night in the spooky mansion in order to receive their portion of the inheritance from the will of some eccentric, distant relative. All the furnishings under ghostly dust covers as though it has been snowing ashes for years.

In the farthest corner I can just make out the silhouette of what must be the Pontiac Parisienne I saw yesterday morning. Who owns all these cars?

WEDNESDAY, THIRTEENTH DAY OF LENT

It has been two weeks since Thierry made his appearance, sitting in my bedroom doorway. Tonight, I am in bed reading later than usual, waiting for him. Among other things, we need to have a chat about poop and porn. I must have nodded off because near midnight I am startled awake by music blaring from the stereo. Groggy from sleep, I shamble into the living room where Thierry is reclining—and revolving—on the centre of my favourite Josh White LP. He is gripping a wooden matchstick in one hand like a microphone and mouthing the lyrics to "St. James Infirmary Blues."

"*Que-ce que tu fucking fais, Thierry?*"

"*Excuse.* I tawt you was asleep."

"Are you drunk?"

"*Non . . . ouais . . . . peut-être . . . . un peu.*"

"Where did you get those matches?"

"De guy next door 'as a lot. Fuckin' *connard.* I tawt mebbe dey will come in 'andy."

He keeps swivelling his head, shouting to me over the music while the vinyl LP goes around and round. He lurches as he tries to stand and uses the matchstick to steady himself. He slips and the match ignites.

"*Sacrament!*"

He runs squealing and staggering like a demented sprinter carrying the Olympic torch, going nowhere because he is running against the direction of the turntable. I blow out the match and switch off the stereo. He crumples into a dishevelled heap.

"*Je suis désolé,*" he murmurs. His tail performs a few languid flops. Then he pukes.

"I'm going back to bed. Try not to burn the place down."

"*Bonne nuit . . .*"

"*Maudit idiot.*"

Thursday, Fourteenth Day of Lent

For the first time since we began our arrangement, Thierry makes an afternoon appearance. Hunched, listless, tail drooping, he is more than usually unkempt. His whiskers are singed. Two have totally curled up from the flame.

"You still stink of booze." I am reading *Le Petit Prince*. I hardly glance up. I'm not kidding. He reeks.

"*Pardon.*" He lets out a sob. "*Mon chum, Jean-Guy, a été tué avant-hier.*"

I look up from my book. *Il est une petite image de dévastation.*

"Murdered? Oh, man, I'm so sorry." I set my book aside and put out my hand to help him onto the sofa.

"Tanks."

To my surprise he clambers onto my lap and leans his head against my belt, grasping a loop to steady himself. He's still a little drunk.

"I tol' you de bastard next door set *des pièges* . . . *des* trap." He takes a deep breath. "Is my fault. Me an' Jean-Guy was havin' a couple o' drinks. Jean-Guy gotta take a piss. I know 'ow 'e get when 'e 'as a few. I should 'ave gone wid 'im." He wails. After a few moments, he composes himself.

"Jean-Guy get caught in one o' dem trap." Thierry is breathing hard. "I never gonna forget dat sound. I go runnin' an' at first I'm glad cause 'e not dead. But den I see dat . . . 'is fuckin' back is broken. Jean-Guy is tryin' not to make no noise an' I is 'olding on to 'im. It is 'urting 'im so bad dat 'e bite me."

He shows me the teeth marks on his shoulder.

" 'e dun mean to. He just suffer so much. Den dat bastard finally wake up. 'e look at me an' Jean-Guy so I got no choice. *Je me suis enfui.*" Another moan escapes him.

"It's not your fault, Thierry. I would have hidden, too, in those circumstances."

"You know what dat bastard do? He make a fuckin' cup o' coffee and drink it." His little fists pound on my belt.

"Den 'e pick up Jean-Guy an' de trap wid some fuckin' tong." His chest is heaving. Trying to hold back his grief.

" 'e drown Jean-Guy in de toilet. *Mon Dieu* . . . de toilet."

He can hold it in no longer. He cries for a good ten minutes.

61

"*Quand même* . . . I got good an' drunk. *S'cuse.*"

I untuck my shirt a little. He blows his nose on the loosened folds and cries some more. As I pick up *Le Petit Prince* to mark my page, my eyes fall on this sentence: *C'est tellement mystérieux, le pays des larmes.*

It is so mysterious, the land of tears.

FRIDAY, FIFTEENTH DAY OF LENT

No sign of Thierry all day. No little offering under my bedroom door this morning. Nothing added to the trail of droppings drying against the base boards. *Juste un vendredi après-midi tranquille à Notre-Dame-de-Grâce.* Late afternoon and some feeble rays of sunshine pierce the narrow arches of the bell tower of St. Augustine across the street.

Then the wail of a distant siren. It grows steadily closer. And closer. Until it is blasting right below my third-floor window. It releases one final squawk and falls silent. From the balcony I see the red *camion d'incendie et les pompiers* in their familiar beige and yellow gear. They climb the steps into my building. For an instant I think of Thierry and the matches he'd filched. But there is no sign of smoke.

Shortly, a second siren. An ambulance. I go inside. The sound of boots in the corridor.

"*Monsieur! Monsieur! Ouvrez la porte!*" They are shouting to the guy next door.

Thierry?

A resounding crack as the door is forced open. For half an hour I hear muffled voices through the wall in fast, indecipherable French. I open my door a crack to see the paramedics wheeling out the guy next door on a gurney. He has an oxygen mask over his face. I click my door shut. Turn. There is Thierry sitting on the floor of the entranceway. He is holding an empty plastic bag. I recognize it as the bag we used to clean the bait stations in the parking garage.

"*Qu'est-ce que tu as fait?*" I whisper.

"Pfft. 'e will live."

He saunters into the kitchen and picks up a raisin that has fallen from the counter.

"It must 'ave been something 'e ate."

"Delighted to have a student teacher who is a fellow professional. So many dilettantes, if you take my meaning. 'Exploration of Self and Others?' Nonsense. Drama is one of the fine arts, not a form of therapy. Don't you agree?"

Mr. Fernsby. Spence's sponsor teacher for his first teaching practicum. He referred to his students, only half-jokingly, as "the enemy."

He was an English expatriate who wielded his genteel accent like one of those fancy fish knives at a formal dinner—ready to pluck away recent changes in the curriculum like errant fishbones. He was fond of name-dropping but even if he had attended RADA, as he frequently reminded Spence, his social circle could not possibly have included the entire roster of luminaries he claimed as acquaintances.

"You must see *Four Weddings and a Funeral*. Simon Callow was a dear friend, once upon a time. We still exchange Christmas greetings."

A man of, perhaps, fifty years. It was difficult to tell. His thinning black hair clung to his scalp like sparse strands of wet seaweed at low tide. He was the sort of man who seemed always a little moist from perspiration, as though every routine task he fulfilled was some tremendous labour. Spence had the impression that Mr. Fernsby was motivated more by the desire to lighten his own workload than by any intent to serve as a mentor.

"I'll be in the staffroom, darling, if you need me. Trial by fire, as they say. You will learn more if I am not constantly hovering over you like a stage mother."

Spence soldiered on. Despite the daily grind, he was feeling optimistic. He and Serenity had reunited after a long separation. That past summer, Serenity had completed ninety days in the Pacifica Treatment Centre for her heroin addiction. Before meeting his wife, Spence had thought all junkies staggered through disreputable back alleys, wild-eyed, shivering and scratching at unsightly sores. He had learned that the truth was that most drug addicts were no more or less capable of carrying on some semblance of normal life than are many others who soothed their fears with all manner of more socially acceptable balms. Certainly, Serenity's addiction was different from Fernsby's. Yet, Spence knew the little man was consumed by his sense of failure, feeding his fragile ego from a phantom bottle of comforting fabrications. Bitter pills.

Though Spence had been sober for a decade, he was still keenly aware of the lies he had been obliged to tell himself in order to justify his daily intake of alcohol. Had his life during that period differed so much from the lives of the Fernsbys of the world?

It was not the challenges of his coursework—the deadlines for papers, the long, unreadable list of official "expectations" compiled in the opaque prose of Edu-Speak—none of these could cause Spence to falter. It was Serenity. Spence was single-minded about certain things. Promises in particular. The world bears witness to all manner of addiction, but Spence's addiction was an obsession with not breaking his word. A flaw garbed in the robes of a virtue is perfectly camouflaged.

If he were as honest as he was hopeful, Spence could have acknowledged his own stubbornness and the dread that his wife might suffer a relapse. And he, once more, would succumb to the daily chaos that marked the hours of Serenity's addiction. It was not even the effects of the heroin he feared, though they could be lamentable. It was the constant quest for a fix and the obsessive madness induced by withdrawal. It is a simple thing to sip wine all day, or to graze on comforting little lies. But securing a steady supply of smack was to lurch from one crisis to the next like a hammer swinging inside a bell.

He had spent the summer of Serenity's residence in the treatment centre working as the day manager of bar called Dillinger's. He would drop six-year-old Clara at Blossom Daycare weekday mornings and pick her up late afternoons. On Saturdays, he would take her to visit her mother at Pacifica. He had given up his own apartment and now lived with Clara in her mother's little basement suite. Serenity was discharged in time to allow Spence to attend his Professional Development Program classes at Simon Fraser University: initial academic course work followed by the six tedious weeks of appeasing Fernsby's damp blend of self-importance and insecurity.

And so, on Christmas Eve, having survived the fall term, and with Clara asleep, Spence felt, finally, relaxed and relieved as he and Serenity sat on the sofa gazing at the soft lights on the Christmas tree. Together they had made a little artful pile of the gifts they'd purchased for Clara. More than, strictly speaking, they could afford. Serenity leaned against Spence. He shifted his position and put his arm around her and she sank back into him a little farther. To his surprise, she began to sing the first few lines of "Silent Night" in a sweet, almost whispered voice.

He could not remember having ever heard her sing.

Quietly, he added his voice to hers.

She stopped.

"Go on," he said. "You sound good."

"I can't sing."

"Sure you can. You have a lovely voice."

Serenity looked over at the row of a couple hundred vinyl albums she had gathered over the years. The collection was book-ended by two plump gold-coloured Buddhas that Spence had bought for her in Chinatown, back before they were married. She had admired them in the window of one of those shops filled with a wonderland of bric-a-brac. Spence bought the pair the next week, lugging them to her place cradled, like twins, one in each arm.

"I always dreamed of being a singer," she said. "So stupid."

"You can learn," Spence said.

"It's too late."

Spence kissed her on her forehead.

"It's not too late. I'm a decade older than you and, with luck, I'll be starting a teaching career in a year or so. Look at me. I'm pushing forty. You're still in your twenties. Maybe in ten years one of your albums will be in that collection."

She laughed.

"Everything we create starts as a dream," Spence said. "I survived Fernsby and that absurd practicum. You survived treatment. Clara has survived—"

"Both of us," she said.

"Six months clean, Serenity. Learning to sing will be a breeze compared to all that."

She said nothing.

Silent night, holy night. All is calm, all is bright.

They sang slowly and softly, in unison.

Round yon virgin, mother and child.

"Lovely," Spence said. "Keep to the melody and I'll put a harmony over it."

Holy infant, so tender and mild.

Serenity's eyes glistened and she smiled.

Sleep in heavenly peace. Sleep in heavenly peace.

Then she began to sob. Her whole body shuddered. Spence was not alarmed. He could tell she was liberating something that had been held captive for a very long time. Perhaps her whole life.

"It's all right." Spence said softly. He held her and, with the palm of one hand, traced slow circles over her back. She sobbed for several minutes. Crying and laughing in turns. He kept his hand moving, as if he could polish her woundedness into something bright and luminous and whole again.

"It's all right. Everything is going to be all right."

For Serenity, the night arrived too soon; for Spence, the morning of January 6th dawned too late. He was wakened by Clara urgently shaking him. He reached over to touch Serenity but she was not lying next to him.

"Daddy, Daddy, Daddy. She won't wake up. Mommy won't wake up."

It took a moment for Spence to take in his surroundings. He glanced at the clock: just after eight. Faint light from the window. Clara took him by the hand and led him down the hallway to the kitchen.

Serenity was lying on her back on the kitchen floor. She was wearing the dressing gown Spence had given her for Christmas— white with cherry blossoms. It had fallen open at the waist and her panties were visible.

Her eyes were open. The glasses she seldom wore were slightly askew.

Spence got down on his knees beside her. Her arm was cold and strange to the touch. Like something alien. A thing that no longer belonged to her. He touched her cheek. It was cold and drained of colour.

"No, no, no, no . . . " he kept repeating in panicked groans. He placed a palm on her chest and pressed, desperately hoping he was mistaken. That against all the evidence, with a little encouragement, her heart might take up its rhythm again.

The pressure produced only a ghastly croak. Spence's own breath escaped him in anguished wails. Clara sat down on the floor on the other side of Serenity's lifeless body. She shook her by the shoulder.

"Wake up."

Spence swept up his daughter and plopped her on the sofa in the living room.

"Don't move, sweetie. Don't move. Here, hold this." He scooped up a plush toy from under the Christmas tree and handed it to her: a chocolate-coloured dog with a squished nose that his mother had sent as a gift.

He called 911. Absurdly, he could not remember his address and had to search for it among a pile of bills. Then he sat, quietly moaning next to where Serenity lay. He reached over and closed the folds of her dressing gown. Shortly, he heard the siren of the approaching ambulance. A little later, the police arrived. On the kitchen counter were a syringe, a spoon, a Bic lighter and a little sachet of white powder. An officer donned latex gloves and carefully arranged them in evidence bags.

Spence had gone to sit with Clara, holding her tightly on his lap and absently looking about the living room as if he were searching for something. Some fresh threat, perhaps. Or an escape route. A portal to yesterday. He got up and slumped against the wall at the entrance to the kitchen as the paramedics lifted Serenity onto a gurney. The body bag was zipped to her chin. One of the medics removed her glasses, carefully folded them, and placed them on the table. Spence sucked in a quick breath as the bag was fastened closed over her face.

The police were solicitous. Their questions seemed to come from somewhere far away, as if they were above the surface of the sea and Spence was floating at the bottom. He answered them distractedly. But wherever it was in his mind that language resided, it seemed like some jumbled landscape where he had to dig to dislodge the simplest of words.

Soon a woman arrived. So tiny that at first Spence thought she was a child, with her large brown eyes. A social worker. She sat with Clara, asking her about the stuffed dog she was holding. They went to Clara's bedroom to look at some other toys. Spence called after them, "Please, she should put her socks on." His own feet were bare. The exterior door was open and he finally registered that the floor was freezing cold.

One of the officers asked Spence if he used heroin. He shook his head.

"Could you just roll up your sleeves, sir?"

Spence drew back the sleeves of his pajamas. He was crying. Crying and softly groaning.

"Is there someone you can call? A friend? A relative?"

"My sister," Spence said. He was staring at the Christmas tree. Usually he unplugged the lights at night. A custom he remembered from his childhood when Christmas lights were usually larger and multi-coloured. They burned hotter. But Spence had left these on through the night. They twinkled like tiny stars. Cold and faraway stars.

"I'll call my sister."

The service was in the little chapel adjacent to the Rainforest Memorial Services funeral home. Spence's family came: his mother, his sister, Babs, and her husband, his brother Ian, whom he seldom saw. His father had died some years before. A few of his friends from university attended. Some of Serenity's friends from the treatment centre came as well, but none of her family. She and her mother had been estranged for many years, and Serenity had spent most of her childhood in foster homes. Spence didn't know where her mother lived or if she were even alive. Serenity had once told him that she had a half-brother who, maybe, lived in Seattle. But they had never met.

Everyone knew their marriage had been tumultuous. And the turmoil of those years had left both Spence and Serenity isolated. What mutual friends they had cultivated had slipped away. Long-time friends had either tried to stay above the fray or, from an abundance of loyalty, taken up allegiances. No one seemed positioned to deliver the eulogy, so that final tribute fell to Spence.

He got through the first paragraph of what he had written but stopped short at the words, "She was twenty-eight." He could go no further. His expression did not change but he stood stricken and mute as tears began to fall freely down his face.

"I'm sorry . . . " he whispered. His sister had been sitting with Clara. She came next to him, took the papers from his hands and read the rest aloud. Spence picked up his daughter and stood beside his sister while Clara applied tissues to his face.

In the weeks following the funeral, he busied himself with settling Serenity's affairs, such as they were. He was grateful to learn that he was not responsible for the student loan she had taken out for the one unsuccessful term she had spent at college. It was less encouraging to discover that he was not eligible to receive the subsidy for Clara's daycare. That arrangement had been an extension of Serenity's treatment. But more disturbing was receiving a legal document from one of Serenity's old friends applying for custody of Clara.

"This is ridiculous," Spence complained to Babs. "This fucking woman is on welfare and already has three children. I'm pretty sure by three different men."

He came to the portion that described him as an "unfit father" and tore the papers into pieces. A few weeks later, he received another document, likewise applying for custody of Clara. This from a woman who had spent time with Serenity in treatment.

"She's a junkie. Ex-junkie. I'm unfit? I'm ten years sober. I've never been unemployed. If you consider the time Clara has spent in daycare, I've cared for her more often than Serenity. How am I unfit?"

Despite the absurdity of those applications, Spence felt beleaguered. And alarmed that the law permitted anyone to apply for custody of any child, however slim the chances of success. Single fathers were not exactly unheard of in the nineties, but a single father with a seven-year-old daughter seemed a bit of a leap for even a few of his own friends to accept. A single mother was qualified to raise boys—how was it that a single father was incapable of raising a girl?

Babs suggested these women were simply projecting their own childhood trauma onto him. Spence knew that Serenity had been a survivor of childhood sexual abuse, and he had always assumed that her addiction, her struggles with mental health, had been a consequence of that abuse. Awareness of childhood sexual trauma had begun to gain recognition in society, but with this had come a sort of hyper-sensitivity. Spence began to feel his every decision concerning Clara was under intense scrutiny.

A warm day in March. Spence and Babs sat watching their children clambering over the maze-like apparatus in the park. Clara was chasing her four-year-old cousin, Martin, repeatedly contriving for him to achieve narrow escapes. The boy squealed with pleasure each time she closed in on him. It was a game that Clara called Sharks. She and Spence had played it together when she'd been that age.

"Let me help, Lyle," Babs said. She could see what he could not. He had lost weight. From the dark circles under his eyes, it was evident that he was not sleeping. He had taken no time off work.

"You're a bit of a mess," Babs said.

"Where's Clara?" He stood, suddenly panicked. Clara had disappeared from view.

"She's there. She's right there," Babs pointed to where Clara sat in the sand with her back to them both. She was helping Martin scoop the sand into a little pile. Spence sat.

"I'm okay," he said. "I'll be okay. I just need . . . "

He wasn't sure what he needed.

"You need a break," Babs said.

Clara and Martin came running toward the bench where the adults sat. Breathless, they half threw themselves onto Babs' lap.

"Do you want to come and stay with your auntie for a couple of days?" Babs asked.

Clara nodded happily. Spence took his handkerchief from his pocket and wiped Martin's runny nose.

"All right," he said.

It seemed to him that Babs could be—would always be—the one thing he could never be. A mother.

At home alone, that evening, Spence was restless. He puttered around the kitchen, cleaning and rearranging. From the bottom cupboard, he dragged out the crockpot that Serenity had asked for on her last birthday, but used only once. Maybe he would make a soup tomorrow. He lifted the glass lid and saw a little stack of twenty-dollar bills. It took him a few moments to realize that Serenity must have stashed the money. An emergency heroin fund, maybe. He picked up the bills and a carefully folded paper sachet fell onto the floor. It was about the size of a nickel. Spence pried open the tiny flap. It contained a pinch of white powder.

He sat staring at it listlessly for half an hour. From the neighbour's yard he heard a dog barking. The refrigerator in the kitchen abruptly stopped its incessant hum. The kind of sound you don't really notice until it stops. And then you realize. And it is as though some tremendous burden has been lifted from your shoulders. Spence poured the white powder onto the kitchen table. He folded one of the twenties and divided the powder into two neat lines. He rolled the bill and snorted both lines.

Sleep, he thought. Sleep at last.

"It's not fancy, but it will get you from A to B. And it climbs well."

After Spence had been released from the hospital, his brother had secured one of his old bicycles onto his car's bike rack and made the trip from Victoria to Vancouver.

"It's more of a commuter bike, really. A hybrid, I guess. I'm not even sure why I bought it."

Ian had several road bikes and used to race a little. "Take it for a spin."

Spence rode it down the block and back. Ian walked to his car and brought back a little set of Allen keys. He lowered the saddle slightly.

"Try now."

Spence took another spin.

"Perfect." He stood straddling the bike. "Thanks, Ian."

"Okay."

The brothers stood a little awkwardly. Then Ian spoke.

"What were you fucking thinking, Lyle?"

A cat that Spence had seen around the neighborhood a few times padded up to him and rubbed its back against his pant leg. It was skinny and black with a white blaze on its chest. Spence laid the bike down on the lawn and picked up the cat.

"I wasn't thinking anything, Ian. I just felt . . . I don't know . . . "

Ian picked up the bike and lay it on its opposite side.

"A bike that's lying down can't fall over," he said. "But don't lay it down on the side with the derailleur."

"Got it," Spence said.

"Babs said you nearly had a heart attack."

"Look, I just wanted to sleep. I wanted one good night's sleep, that's all. And it wasn't a heart attack. It was, I don't know, some sort of arrythmia. Irregular heartbeat."

Spence put the cat down but it continued to circle his legs and brush up against him.

"Just sleep?"

"I called a fucking ambulance, for Christ's sake."

A stout woman in a yellow sleeveless shift came out of the house next door and disappeared around the side. There was the squeak of a tap being opened. She came back with a hose and began to water her flowers. Spence and Ian walked to the house and sat on the steps that led to the main floor. The cat settled on Spence's lap.

"Does Mom know?" Spence asked glumly.

"No," Ian said. "She doesn't know about the hospital. She doesn't know about the social workers. She thinks you're leaving Clara with Babs so you can focus on school."

"It's temporary," Spence said. The cat leaped off his lap and found a spot to roll in the grass near his new bicycle.

"According to Babs, the Ministry decides that." Spence had been given a choice: voluntarily turn custody of Clara over to Babs or Social Services would place her in foster care.

The brothers were silent for a few minutes. The cat wandered over to the yard next door but the woman aimed a little spray of water at it.

"Maybe she's better off without me."

Ian stood up. He walked down a couple of steps, turned, and punched Spence in the shoulder as hard as he could.

"What the fuck! That really hurt!"

"That hurt? That hurt? That's nothing. Hurt is what Clara is since her mother died. More hurt is what she is going to be if you don't get your shit together."

Spence rushed at his brother and knocked him down onto the grass. The cat was startled. It hissed and leaped into the air. He straddled Ian and rained down mostly ineffectual punches until he exhausted himself.

Ian pushed him off and sat up. He ran his tongue along his teeth then rubbed his hand over his mouth, checking for blood. Two brothers. Grown men. How was it that in an instant, they could be transformed into the boys they once were? The stout woman with the hose stood looking at them disdainfully. Ian waved at her and she shot a little spray of water in their direction, as if it were a warning.

"You still punch like a girl."

"Fuck off."

After a moment, Ian stood and walked over to where Spence lay in the grass, breathing heavily. He offered his hand. Spence took it and Ian hoisted his brother upright.

"Sorry." Spence massaged his hand.

Ian walked to his car and came back with a bicycle U-lock. He picked up the bike and locked it to the railing of the porch.

"The landlord going to mind this?"

"He's hardly ever home," Spence said. "Maybe I'll keep it inside."

They both stood staring at the bike. The cat ran up the steps to the top of the porch and poked its head through the railings. Spence picked it up again.

"You know who owns this cat?" he called to the woman who was now dousing her lawn. She shrugged.

"Listen, Lyle. I'm not a doctor but I think it is fairly safe to assume you are depressed."

"Who do you belong to?" Spence said to the cat.

"Are you listening?"

"Yes," Spence kept his attention on the cat. "I'm depressed, you say."

"I say it. Babs says it. If you had any real fucking friends left, they would all say it."

"I have friends," Spence said.

"Who? Father What's-His-Name? When was the last time you talked to him? You didn't even invite him to the funeral. What was the point of becoming a fucking Catholic, Lyle, if you can't reach out to someone for help?"

"Desmond," Spence said. "Father Desmond." It was true. He had lost touch with Desmond. Perhaps he was ashamed that his marriage had been such a dismal failure. Or that Desmond would suggest something sensible. Like an annulment. They hadn't spoken for several years. He thought, briefly, of his old AA sponsor, Normand, who had finally succumbed to AIDS.

"Anyway, I brought the bike so you could get some exercise. Endorphins. Just trust me on this. If you ride that bike. If you ride that bike every day. It will help. I promise."

"You promise?" Spence looked at his brother. Ian made a fist as if he wanted to punch Spence again. Then he smiled and tossed him the keys to the bike lock.

"I fucking promise."

"Okay then." Spence said. "I promise I'll ride it."

"Every day."

"I promise I'll ride it every fucking day."

Spence rode the bike every day. When his classes started that summer, he rode it up the long, steep hill to SFU. When his second practicum started that fall, he rode it to school every day. He reconnected with Father Desmond, and at his suggestion he rode it to the 7:15 am Mass nearly every morning for weeks. He rode it across the bridge into Richmond to his sister's house to visit Clara as often as he could.

She was home again with Spence in time for Christmas. He bought her a bicycle. It had a little basket on the handlebars and sometimes she would put Black Star, the cat Spence had befriended, in the basket and give him a ride. Clara named him that. Because he was black with a white star-shaped blaze on his chest.

Thierry has had free run of the place for more than a week. I was hoping the terms of our arrangement might promote a peaceful coexistence—man and mouse. I like Thierry and I'm genuinely sorry for his recent loss. But so far, it's been a week of chaos and mouse poop. And all I have to show for it is twenty bucks, a handful of laundry tokens, some stick matches and a blood-specked trinket. Oh, yes—a used paperback copy of *L'Etranger*.

He means well, but these haphazard contributions are not paying his share of the rent. I'm living on a modest pension and it might be years before I have mastered enough French to manage some part-time employment. What if Clara and Gabriel decide to get married in France? Where will I get the money? I need Thierry to hold up his end. So far, he mostly eats, poops, swills booze and smokes a prodigious amount of weed.

I'm thinking of sweetening the pot to keep Thierry reasonably sober and to encourage him to step up his game. To that end, I've fashioned a little rope ladder from the edge of the table to the floor. That way we can share a civilized meal once in a while instead of him always eating detritus off the kitchen floor. Also, I've dusted off a little Toshiba notebook that I never use. It's old but it still works. That way he can have his own internet access. I get it—a mouse has needs.

I'm also going to ask him about maybe using the toilet instead of leaving a trail of disgusting droppings wherever he pleases. I know his friend, Jean-Guy, met his fate in a toilet and I don't want to stir up bad memories, but damnit, mouse poop can cause illness in humans! I don't think I'm being unreasonable here.

I ride my bike over to Clara's place to water the plants. Three days into spring and it is still below zero. As I encounter the warmer air of her apartment I must contend with the steady drizzle from my nose. No toilet paper in the bathroom. None under the sink. I open the hall linen closet. There are a few rolls on the bottom shelf.

Higher up, I see that she has stored several smaller canvases. I am a little startled to realize that one of them depicts me. The painting is clearly based on the school photo taken when I was in Grade 8. Why is it hidden here? Was it intended as a gift? Is it unfinished? She has captured a certain guardedness in my thirteen-year-old eyes. Not fear, exactly. The eyes are wary; strangely, she has painted shadows and lines under those eyes. My eyes as they are now, as if she is depicting the child and the man.

I decide that I am flattered, both pleased and a little confused. As though I've inadvertently intruded upon myself. I stand looking at the painting for a long time trying to recognize the boy I once was. Then I blow my nose.

THIRD SUNDAY OF LENT

Thierry has a plan. It involves stealing cash from the landlord's office. I'm not sure how I feel about it. But it would certainly solve a lot of my money problems and more than cover his portion of the rent.

"*Écoute, camarade, il y a des propriétaires et des locataires.* We work our 'ole life to put bread on de table. Dey just own shit and collect de rent an' get rich. *C'est qui le vrai voleur?* Who is de real thief?"

Evening. We are sitting at the table. Actually, Thierry is sitting *on* the table, nibbling a hazelnut and talking between mouthfuls.

"But why do so many *locataires* pay their rent in cash?"

"*Voyons!*" Bits of hazelnut fly from his mouth. "So de *propriétaire* dun 'ave to claim de income, Einstein! You was a teacher? *Incroyable*! What you teach, by de way?"

"Drama."

"*Comme Trudeau?* Okay. Dat explain a lot."

"You're pretty cocky for a guy who puked on my Josh White album a few days ago."

"Mice dun puke, man."

"No?"

"*Non*. Look it up. Dat stain you is upset about is blood. I bite my cheek, man. Look." He opens his mouth wide. Hazelnut mush and an ugly red gash.

"Whatever. I believe you. So. You were saying. Landlords can conceal cash payments in order to get a tax break and tenants co-operate so they can save a little on rent."

"Bingo!" He finishes his hazelnut, reaches for another, then changes his mind.

"Don't put it back in the bowl, Thierry! That's rude."

"You tink 'cause I'm a mouse I'm dirty? I got germs? Dat what you tink, brudder?"

"No. I mean . . . can't you just stuff your cheeks and, you know, eat it later?"

"Dat is 'amsters, man. What? We all look de same to you?"

"No. Sorry, man."

"So, you in or out? We gonna do dis or no?"

"When?"

"De first week o' April, man, after peoples pay dere rent an' before Nick spend dat money 'cause he not gonna put it in no bank. You sure you was a teacher?"

"Let me sleep on it."

"*Câlisse*. Okay. You sleep. I gotta go case de office."

He takes another hazelnut from the bowl, licks it and puts it back. "*Ciao*."

SOLEMNITY: FEAST OF THE ANNUNCIATION

"What you readin', brudder?"

"*Le Petit Prince*."

" 'ow come you got dem 'eadphones?"

"It's a recording of the book. I can read quite a bit of French but

I have trouble with pronunciation and I usually can't understand people when they talk. This is a learning tool for me."

Thierry is sprawled on his back, leaning on a cushion on the other end of the sofa. Sometimes I worry I'm going to sit on him. He lets loose a stream of fast French.

"*T'as compris?*"

"*Rien.*"

He laughs. "Yeah. And when you talk French, man, you sound like a lil retard kid."

"Retard is not a nice word, Thierry. Please don't use it."

"*Ta yeule. Retard* just mean slow in French."

"No. '*Retard*' is a French noun used to express a temporal circumstance, a delay or lateness: *Je suis en retard.* You clearly used the word as an English adjective as a pejorative term for a person who is developmentally delayed or who has a profound intellectual disability."

"*Comment?*"

"*Tu m'as compris.*"

"You must 'ave been a pail of laughs as a teacher." He yawns.

"Barrel."

"*Quoi?*"

"A barrel of laughs. *Ça ne fait rien. Comment va ta surveillance?* When are we going to put down the mighty from their seat and exalt the humble?"

"I dun know nutin' about de 'umble but everything else is goin' good. All I need now is de combination to de safe."

Safe?

Tuesday, Eighteenth Day of Lent

Suddenly I'm awake. It takes me a moment to get my bearings. I reach over to my night table and check my phone. 3:37 am. What is that sound?

My bedroom window is open a crack. All my curtains are usually drawn open even at night and the street lamps yield enough light to softly illuminate the whole apartment.

That sound again. No. It's not coming from outside. A steady squeak, squeak—like bedsprings.

The guy next door?

Not likely. He has all the charm of a moist handkerchief and none of the wherewithal to seduce anyone, man or woman. And anyway, Thierry reports he still hasn't fully recovered from his gastro-intestinal episode.

Squeak, squeak, squeak.

A steady rhythm. Thierry? If he were a pet in a cage, I'd guess he was burning some calories on the exercise wheel.

Squeak, squeak, squeak.

In my bare feet I creep over to my bedroom door, quietly pull it open and peer into the gloom of the living room. There is a strange mouse leaning against the leg of the table that supports the stereo. It's standing with its front hands gripping one ornately carved wooden leg. Eyes closed. Lips parted to reveal long yellow teeth. *Merde!* It's wearing that stolen faux-pearl earring in one ear.

Squeak, squeak, squeak.

Now I see him. It's Thierry. He's standing behind, sightly obscured, his hips thrusting rhythmically. Our eyes meet. He winks and puts a finger over his lips. Shhhh.

I slink back into bed. Wide awake. Staring at the ceiling. A truck rumbles past outside. What is this feeling?

Dégoût? Envie?

EVENING . . .

"*Pour hier soir.*" Thierry climbs the rope ladder to the table. He helps himself to a slice of cucumber from my salad. "*J'm'excuse.* I tawt you was asleep. Preddy loud one, eh? *Pour sûr.* We jes meet. One thing lead to anudder . . ."

"*C'est correct.* It's your place, too. We made no rules about overnight guests. *C'est les enfants qui m'inquiètent.*"

"*T'inquiète pas.* I always take precaution, man. *Toujours.*" He inspects the cucumber.

"So how come you never 'ave a woman? You a *fifi?*" He tears off a hunk with his teeth and chews loudly.

"No, I'm not gay. And I'm pretty sure *fifi* is not a polite term."

"*Désolé.* M'bad. Okay. Yer not gay. Got kids?"

"*J'ai une fille. Elle est enfant unique.*"

"Only one? Something wrong wid yer dick?" He gulps the rest of the cucumber and filches a piece of yellow pepper.

"*Non. Ma femme est morte. Content?*"

He is about to bite into the pepper. He stops. Mouth open.

"*Je suis désolé. Vraiment.* Sometime I make sex and den I get all macho. Is a mouse thing. *Comment on dit les hormones en anglais?*"

"*Le même chose.* Hormones."

"Okay. So, when de man mouse make sex, he gotta be, like, way more sexier den de udder man mouse. *Tu sais? Instinct animal?* It take some time to wear off. *Les hormones.* Sorry 'bout your wife, man. 'ow she die?"

"She died of sorrow, Thierry."

He nods solemnly.

"Can we please talk about something else?"

"*Pas de problème. Je suis désolé. Je suis un trou d'cul, des fois.*" His ears droop.

Oui, Thierry. Sometimes you're a real asshole. *Moi aussi. Nous sommes tous les deux des hommes.*

"I'm pregnant."

Spence kept his gaze on the flotilla of cargo ships that sat anchored in English Bay, waiting to be piloted into the harbour. Hulls all the same nautical red. Containers piled on deck. It was spring and a huge raft of scoters and goldeneyes were assembled a quarter mile from shore, preparing to head north.

"Did you hear me?" Serenity asked.

"You're pregnant," Spence said. Serenity had asked him to meet her after work at Second Beach. Spence sometimes brought Clara here to play on the swings or to clamber over the old red firetruck that had been there since before Serenity was born.

"I want a divorce," she said.

Spence took a deep breath and released it slowly. "We've been separated for nearly three years. You don't need me to agree in order to file for divorce. I thought you said he was a lawyer."

"Doctor," Serenity said.

"Anyway," Spence said, "I won't contest a divorce but I won't consent to it, either."

"Do you want . . . what? An annulment?"

In the distance, several thousand sea birds rose out of the water, as if prompted by some unseen cue. They flew just above the waves for a few hundred meters, circled back, and then settled again.

Spence turned and looked at Serenity. "You would need to be interviewed for an annulment. Typically, you get asked if, when you made your vows, you understood them and if you truly intended to honour them. Which are you? Incapable of understanding a promise? Or just a liar?"

Neither said anything for a minute.

"That's not fair," she said. "I was young."

"Joan of Arc was younger when she was leading an army. Mary Shelley had written *Frankenstein*."

"Yes. And the fucking Virgin Mary had been raped by God."

"What the fuck are you talking about? You don't even believe in God."

"No, but—"

"So how can a God who doesn't exist rape a girl? You can't have your fucking cake and eat it too."

"I hate you," she said.

"Fine. We're even. I hate you, too."

They were sitting on a bench along the seawall. Not wanting people passing by to be privy to this conversation, Spence walked down to the beach and idly threw a few stones into the waves. Shortly, Serenity joined him.

"How many months?" Spence asked.

"What?"

"How many months pregnant?"

"I don't know."

"Are you planning on getting married?"

Serenity didn't say anything.

"You know what? I work double shifts four days a week so that I can take Clara for three days. I give you enough money to pay your rent. You collect welfare. You have free daycare because why? Because your fucking therapist says you need it. Let's see, Serenity. When Clara's not with me, she's in daycare while you're off fucking your lawyer or doctor or some fucking bass player in a fucking punk band for Christ's sake. So tell me, because I'm curious. Where do you find the time to be a fucking mother to our daughter?"

"That's cruel."

Spence had meant to hurt her. He wasn't sorry.

"Does he have kids?"

"He has a son," Serenity said.

Spence looked at her.

"He lives in Kelowna with his mother."

"Perfect," Spence said.

"What?"

"Nothing. Give me his phone number."

"Why?"

"I want to talk to him."

Spence telephoned that evening. Dr. Anthony Palk seemed reasonable. Almost professional. The sort of man, it seemed to Spence, who understood that life was a game and who had figured out how to play it.

"Lyle," he said almost kindly, "It's my understanding that your marriage has been over for years."

Spence had made a point of asking for Mr. Palk when he telephoned. Not Dr. Palk. But he didn't like this man calling him by his given name.

"My marriage isn't over just because you've arrived at an understanding for yourself. What I need to know is if you are planning to marry Serenity. And how a man who has given up his own son plans to care for my daughter."

"Is that what she said? We are getting married?"

Spence stayed silent. She had not said that. Not in so many words.

"Look, Lyle. I have advised Serenity to get an abortion. I've told her I will pay for therapy afterwards. Her real challenge at the moment, though, is getting off of heroin."

After the word "heroin," Spence didn't hear anything else. Palk kept talking in the same measured tones, as if Spence and Serenity were both patients and he was explaining some course of treatment.

Spence hung up the phone without saying another word.

Heroin. I must be the stupidest man on earth.

For nearly three years he had failed to see what should have been his first guess. Ignorance had not been bliss. It had been near daily agony. And now that he knew, now it was sheer hell. A few weeks later, Serenity called and told him it had been a false alarm. She wasn't pregnant. She seemed almost disappointed.

In retrospect, Spence should have immediately taken custody of Clara. Done whatever was necessary. Gone on welfare if he had to. Maybe things would have turned out differently. Better. But he didn't. Spence decided he needed a regular job. A decent income. Not the transience of the theatre or the vagaries of slinging liquor. He would become a teacher, he decided. About the time Clara started school, he would start too.

That was his plan.

Dusk. I turn on the lamp near the sofa so I can see to read. Thierry appears from under the sofa. He's just woken up. He yawns then crawls up my leg to sit next to me.

" 'ave a good, day?"

"Hmm." I turn a page.

"*T'as fait quelque chose d'intéressant?*" he asks.

"Mmmm."

"What you do all day, man? *Presque tous les matins, ton bicyc est parti.* Where you go every day on dat ol' bike, brudder?"

"I have French classes."

"You teach French? Dats a laugh."

"No. I learn French." I show him the text I am reading.

"I tawt you say you were a teacher? You kenna teach yourself? I learn English, *pas de problème.* I dun go to no school."

"Perhaps you have an aptitude for languages."

He is silent for a minute. I read.

"Why you do dat, man?"

"Pardon?"

"Use dos big word? Aptitude? *Quessé ça veux dire?*"

"Aptitude? *La même chose qu'en français, je pense. L'aptitude. La disposition.*"

"More big word dun 'elp, brudder."

"Talent, Thierry. Maybe you have a talent for learning languages."

"Okay. Tanks. Jes say dat. *Tu es capable.* Something like dat. You keep talkin' wid de big word you not gonna have a lotta friend."

Another long silence.

"*Au fait, j'ai jamais vu tes amis.* 'ow come nobody visit you, man?"

"No offence *mais je dois étudier. J'ai un examen sur le subjonctif, demain matin.*"

"*Subjonctif.* Dere you go again. You know de big word in two language but you never got nutin' to say."

Another long silence.

"Okay den. *À bientôt, mon chum.*"

He runs down my leg and disappears under the sofa. I reflect, for a moment, on his remarks about big words. Plenty of six-year-old kids in the neighbourhood speak French better than I. How is it they absorbed that knowledge without knowing *l'indicatif, le conditionnel, le subjonctif, l'impératif*? None of them had attended, say, walking school. Yet, before long, they are running everywhere. Lower a baby into the wading pool. How do they know to swim? Experience. Discovery. Have I forgotten how to learn?

THURSDAY, TWENTIETH DAY OF LENT

Thierry scampers into the kitchen from under the stove. I am startled and burn myself slightly on the edge of the frying pan. Damn! How many ways are there into this bloody apartment?

"Got it, brudder! I got it!" A pause. "Hey, dat smell good."

"You got what?" I run my fingers under some cold water.

"De combination to de safe, what else? *Épais.*" He stands up on his hind legs. "Dat smell *really* good. " He clambers up my leg and makes a little leap onto the counter, hands me a crumpled slip of paper, and then gingerly picks a piece of butter chicken from the pan.

"Ooo . . . ooo . . . ooo . . . *Chaud! Chaud! Chaud!*" He juggles the chicken for a moment then pops it into his mouth. Scrawled on the scrap of paper are three crudely drawn numbers: 11-22-33.

"You sure this is the combination?" It seems doubtful. But then maybe someone really wanted an easy combo to remember. Or, maybe, it is someone's birthday.

"*Je l'ai regardé trois ou quatre fois, mon chum.*" He fans his tongue with his hand. "First you spin *à droite* an' den stop at dat pair of dicks."

"You mean 11?"

"Whatever. Den you go *à gauche* to dos numbers *comme deux canards*."

"Two ducks? 22?"

"Den *à droite* to dos two sideways tit. Or mebbe dey is ass? Tit an' ass?"

"You mean 33?"

"I mean dos shapes what I draw! *Ostie!*"

"Thierry, can't you read numbers?"

"I ken read nutin' man. Who tol' you I ken read? I never tol' you dat."

"You can't read?"

"'ow I gonna learn to read, Einstein? Mouse school? No such thing."

I think back.

"So . . . how did you find mouse porn on my computer?"

"What? *T'es fou*! I dun watch no—"

"First week you were here, Thierry. I saw. I wish I could unsee it."

"Okay. *Je l'avoue*. 'ow I do dat? Watch."

He makes a pretty impressive leap to the table and deftly opens my laptop. He goes to my history and scrolls down until he finds the word *sex*.

"I know what dis word mean, okay? *Tout le monde* know dat. Dat get me to de porn page. *Pis*. I know de word mouse *à cause de* Disney. Mickey Mouse? I ken put two and two togedder."

"Really? What's two plus two?"

He glares at me.

"Bedder question. 'ow come you got chicks wid dicks porn?"

"What's two plus two?"

" an' dos schoolgirl in de lil skirt? Dats jes sick, man."

"What's two plus two?"

"Shut up, man! NO WONDER YOU DUN GOT NO FRIEND!"

A silence. He flicks his tongue to retrieve a droplet of butter sauce from the corner of his mouth. More silence.

"So, what you say, Spence? You in or out? We gonna rob de safe or no?"

He called me Spence.

"*C'est la première fois que tu m'appelles par mon nom.*"

He holds my gaze.

"*Alors*, Spence?"

Deep breath.

"*Tabarnac!* Let's do this thing!" I say.

FRIDAY, TWENTY-FIRST DAY OF LENT

"Are you eating your own poop?"

Thierry pauses, his mouth agape. He has a brown pellet in his hand.

"*Non . . . peut-être . . . pis?*"

"*C'est de la merde, Thierry! Merde. Personne ne mange sa propre merde.*"

"Lotsa animal do. *C'est normal.*"

"*C'est dégoûtant!*"

"*Tu te prends pas pour du 7Up flat.*"

"*Quoi?* I don't take myself for flat 7Up? What the hell does that even mean?"

"*Quessé ça veut dire?* It mean you is a fuckin' snob, man. It mean you tink you too good for me, *hein?*"

"*Non. Je suis un peu choqué. C'est tout.*"

"You is shocked? *J'ai regardé dans l'armoire de cuisine hier.* You know what I see in dat cupboard? You know what I see? I see a big box with an hundred mousetrap, man. *Une centaine de pièges!* You plannin' to murder me, *hein?* An' who else? *Toutes les souris qui vivent ici? T'es un tueur en série?*"

"Wait. Thierry. I can explain. *Attends! S'il te plaît!*"

"*Mange d'la marde!*"

"Attends."

"Crisse de câlisse de tabarnac d'ostie de sacrament!"

He is gone.

SATURDAY, TWENTY-SECOND DAY OF LENT

I'm not a mass murderer. I mean a mass mouse murderer. It is true I have exactly one hundred mousetraps in a cardboard box stored in a cupboard next to the kitchen sink. For a mouse who cannot count, Thierry appears to have a gift for estimating quantities. But there is a good reason I have one hundred mousetraps.

They were on sale. *Pas cher.*

The members of the Improv Club at Queen of All Saints were fans of the television show *Whose Line Is It, Anyway?* They had watched an improvisation in which two barefoot and blindfolded actors were on a stage strewn with mousetraps. I am told it was hilarious. I advised my students that it sounded like a lawsuit waiting to pounce. They assured me no one would be hurt. They had already found mousetraps on sale from Amazon for twenty cents each. So, twenty dollars for a hundred. I thought, you know, for twenty bucks we'll give it a shot. That's the truth.

The only reason I still have a hundred mousetraps is that I didn't notice the delivery would take six weeks from someplace in China. They arrived in June during exams and the Drama Queens never used them. I'd paid for them, so I kept them. I thought inspiration might strike and I'd work up some sort of mousetrap routine and go busking on the street in my retirement. Actually, that's not a bad idea. Montréal is a great town for street performances in the summer. I had done a little of that with friends right after university.

Damn. How am I going to explain this to Thierry? *Et est-ce qu'il va rentrer à la maison?*

I have made a breakfast of toast and a little fried bacon but I have no appetite. My neglected coffee has gone cold. I decide to walk to Clara's place this morning to attend to the plants. I need some time to think. As I round the corner of the building, I just catch a glimpse of a vehicle, *une voiture,* slip under the door to the parking garage. Had I not noticed the distinctive putt-putt of the Volkswagen engine I might not have seen the back end of an emerald-green Karmann Ghia. But there was no mistaking the long curve of the rear end with the engine vent on top. They were not a mass-produced car. They were lovingly sculpted—as close as they come to a handcrafted auto. I had only ever seen one up close as a kid. At an auto show with my dad. I was nine. No, ten. I remember because it was the same year that he took Ian and me to visit the Confederation Train. It was a sort of museum on wheels celebrating the Canadian Centennial. Not exactly on the same scale as Montréal's Expo 67—but something. Strange, the things we remember. Or forget. For certain no one living in my building could afford a vintage Karmann Ghia. Was my landlord a collector?

Fourth Sunday of Lent

"I'm supposed to find dis funny? You tink a fuckin' minefield is funny jes 'cause nobody you know get blowed up?"

We are watching the mousetrap episode of *Whose Line Is It, Anyway?* on YouTube.

"No. But if you think about it, Thierry, humour is about other people's pain."

"*Vraiment?*"

"Really. It is a well-established comic principle."

"*Ah ouais?*"

"For example, if I have a hangnail, that's a tragedy. But if Wile E. Coyote falls off a cliff, that's comedy."

He walks behind my laptop and slams it shut.

"You ever been in a lab where dey do dem experiment on mice? You tink dat is funny?"

"No."

"But, *mettons*, a science guy in a cage wid a mouse stickin' a needle in 'is ass. Dat is funny?"

"Well, yeah. That could be hilarious. Because it is a reversal of expectation. And a status swap."

"*Alors* if de guy got it coming, dat is funny?"

"*Exactement*. Though a lot would depend on the context."

Thierry holds up an alarmingly large pellet of dried mouse dung.

"So, if I eat dis, is disgusting. But if *you* eat it . . . ?"

Plus tard, je vais me brosser les dents vigoureusement dans la salle de bains.

Thierry shouts through the bathroom door: "Some time you gotta eat something twice in order to digest, man. You want vitamin an' shit? You gotta follow yer instinct. Like liver, brudder. Nobody like it, but it good fer you."

Merde.

PAST MIDNIGHT . . .

An unfamiliar sound through the wall wakens me.

Snap! Snap! Snap! Snap!

The bedroom of the guy next door is right next to mine. If he goes into his closet, I hear the wire hangers jostling as they slide along the rod. When he changes into his pajamas at night, I can hear his belt buckle hit the floor as he drops his trousers. Sometimes he eats dinner in bed and I hear the fork scraping the plate.

Screams. They are the high-pitched screams of a man falling into madness.

Snap! Snap! Snap!

I get up and rush to the cupboard. The one next to the kitchen sink. The box of mousetraps is empty.

Thierry.

"De last thing 'e always do before 'e leave de office is tug de handle o' de safe to make sure it closed."

"Well, that's that. It's impossible." We are reviewing the proposed heist. It is exactly one year since I retired. April Fool's Day. Fittingly, for one being beguiled, I choose an apple from the bowl on the table and take a bite.

"*Ben là. Rien n'est impossible. J'peux pas faire ça tout seul. Tout ce que je te demande, c'est d'ouvrir le coffre-fort.* You know de combination. Open de safe. Close it again. Den turn de dial a couple o' numbers an' bingo. De safe *seem* lock but I only gotta nudge de dial a bit an' *voilà*. I seen 'im do dat."

"Me?" A little juice from the apple dribbles down my chin, and I wipe it with my sleeve. "You're the professional. I'm not a thief."

"Everybody a thief, *mon chum*. You tink yer shirt were not made in a sweat shop? You tink you no stealin' de wage o' some migrant worker when you eat dat apple? Gimme some."

I bite off a piece of apple and hand it to him.

"De bourgeois take from de poor an' give to dem self. De rich take from everybody an' put it in a tax shelter." He gnaws his piece of apple to nothing.

"Stealing from the *propriétaire* doesn't make us Robin Hood and Friar Tuck."

"No. But it mebbe pay de rent. Mebbe cover yer dentist bill, man."

He is talking about the small fortune I'd spent on a root canal that became an extraction. I ended up paying for both procedures and my insurance covered a very slim fraction of the cost. Thierry thinks it is weird that my teeth don't keep growing as his do.

"Mebbe if yer daughter get married in France, like you said you is worried about, den you got de money to buy de ticket."

"How much cash are we talking?" I hand him what is left of the apple.

"I dunno. I kenna count, remember, Mister-what-is-two-plus-two?" He tears into the apple core, spinning it like it's corn on the cob.

"I can teach you to count, Thierry. We'll start with the numbers one to ten. It might come in handy."

"Cool."

I step on the foot pedal to open the lid of the garbage can. He tosses in the remnant of the core.

"Threy! An' mebbe I ken teach you to talk French so you dun sound like a lil kid who memorize some shit from a book."

"Is that what I sound like?"

"Worse, brudder. Way worse."

Tuesday, Twenty-Fourth Day of Lent

Thierry seems restless. He's on his way out now.

"*J'ai besoin d'exercice, mon chum,*" he tells me. "Also, I need a lil piece o' dat church mouse ass. Dos religious one act all proper, man, but dey is wild when dey get wid Thierry."

I go out to the balcony and stand there in slippers and a sweater. Steam rises from my cup of tea. A minute later I see Thierry streak across Boulevard Décarie. A couple of crows leave their perch and circle. Thierry slips as he crosses a patch of snow, then gains the cover of some grass. The crows climb higher and settle on the bell tower.

That's when I notice a squirrel scuttle head first down the trunk of a still barren tree. He's followed by another. And another. They advance toward the spot where Thierry has taken cover in the grass and arrange themselves in a circle, poised on their haunches. A breeze stirs the grass. Bare branches sway. The sun is low in the sky. I shiver.

Cours, Thierry! Run!

On my way out the door I grab my hiking stick. *Je l'ai utilisé*

96

tout l'hiver pour rester debout sur les trottoirs glacés. It might come in handy again. A siren wails. Traffic has stopped for an ambulance coming down Avenue Notre-Dame-de-Grâce. I sprint across Décarie and slip on the same mound of frozen snow as I enter the park. Two boys, maybe eleven or twelve, are sitting on a nearby picnic table sharing a cigarette. They laugh.

Je vois Thierry maintenant. The squirrels have backed him up against a stump. *Il attire mon regard.* He reaches up behind his head with both hands and grabs the protruding stub of a branch. Two of the squirrels advance on him. The third sees me, turns and leaps. Thierry hoists himself up and delivers a double leg kick that connects with the noses of both his assailants. They are briefly stunned. He bobs and weaves like a boxer and lands a couple of good shots. One of the squirrels bounds away.

The squirrel challenging me evades my hiking stick as I swing, then grabs hold of it and scampers up the whole length to my right hand. Fearing that he will bite me, I throw the stick in the air and catch the opposite end with my left hand. With the squirrel now clinging to the far end, I pivot like a muscleman in a hammer throw contest and launch. Squirrel and hiking stick sail across the park and land with a clatter near a baby carriage. The startled mother picks up my stick and furiously stabs at the retreating squirrel. I turn and see Thierry. He has sunk his teeth into his remaining opponent's bushy tail. The squirrel twists and turns in a fury. Thierry crawls onto its back. With one hand in the air, he rides like a bronco buster at a rodeo. Finally, he leaps off. The squirrel races to the top of the nearest tree, its weight sending the tip teetering. He lets loose with a high-pitch stream of squirrel gibberish.

"*Crisse de câlisse de tabarnac d'ostie de sacrament!*" Thierry spits. The mother with the baby carriage drops my hiking stick and hurries away. There is a priest standing on the steps of St. Augustine's. I wave. He shakes his head and goes inside. Thierry is grinning.

"Hey brudder. *C'est le fun! Hein?*"

"Fuck, Thierry." I'm breathing hard. "Those squirrels are lunatics. Aren't rodents supposed to stick together?"

"*C'est ça. On est tous des chums.*"

"Is this like some territorial thing?"

"No, man. Dey is jes 'ungry. *Comment ça tu portes des pantoufles?*"

I look down at my ruined slippers. One of the boys from earlier swaggers up and hands me my hiking stick."

"*Hé monsieur. C'est votre souris?*"

"*Non, il n'est pas à moi. Nous sommes des amis.*"

"*Cool. Ils sont fous ces écureuils, hein?*"

"*Non. Ils ont juste faim.*"

Wednesday, Twenty-Fifth Day of Lent

"Okay. Tell me again what you gonna do. Dun leave anything out." Thierry holds a matchstick. He paces the floor with it and swings it a few times like a major league slugger determined to hit a home run.

"Four o'clock, just as Nick is leaving, I go to his office and ask if I can have an urgent word with him. Wait . . . what am I supposed to talk about?"

"It dun madder, man. Tell 'im you got a problem wid mice. When you lie, try to stay close to de truth." He holds the matchstick laterally in both hands behind his back and stretches extravagantly. The fur at his throat feathers out as his head goes back.

"But what if he believes me and starts setting traps and poison? Won't that put you at greater risk later?"

"Ahh, my 'eart is touch dat you care." Thierry tries to make that sound sarcastic, but I can tell he is pleased. "Dun worry 'bout me, *mon chum*. Beside, Nick is not dat kind o' *proprio*. He not gonna spend money unless 'e see de mice for 'imself. And 'e never 'ere at night so 'ow 'e gonna do dat?"

"Okay. Once I'm in the office, you are going to create a distraction down the hall in the lobby."

"*Check regarde.*" He performs a series of athletic thrusts and feints as though the matchstick were a fencing foil. With a flourish he swirls and strikes the tip of the match on the floor. It flares briefly and sputters out.

"That's your distraction?"

Annoyed, he snaps the matchstick in half, pulls off a sliver and sticks it in his mouth like a toothpick.

"No, de distraction is all de mail an' shit dat nobody collect from dat mailbox 105 'cause nobody livin' dere. Tanks for teachin' me de numbers. It already come in 'andy. *Crois-moi.* When it catch fire it gonna make a lotta smoke and stink. 'is office is jes 'round de corner. 'e gonna smell dat sucker fer sure."

I give him a doubtful look.

"Dun worry. I gonna 'ave an 'ole box o' matches. Nutin' ken go wrong."

"Right." I take a deep breath and continue. "When he leaves to investigate the distraction, I open the safe. Then I close it and turn the dial just three numbers to the right. Just enough to make the door feel secure when Nick returns and gives it a tug."

"*Pis plus tard dans la nuit.* I get into de office de usual way and turn de dial three number to de left. *Voilà!*"

"I don't think the Ranger is going to like this, Yogi."

"*Comment?* "

"*J'ai dit, voilà!*"

"*C'est ça. Boo Boo.*" He smiles.

Thursday, Twenty-Six Day of Lent

I'm in Nick's office, sitting across the desk from him. The landlord. *Le propriétaire.* He can tell I'm lying. I'm sure of it.

"Spence, Spence. I'm not saying you're imagining things. But I got to tell you, you're my only tenant that's told me he's seen a mouse." Nick is Montréalais, born and raised, but his family is Greek. He speaks English with one of those Montréal accents that sound like a jumble of Italian, Yiddish and New York. Sort of Brooklyn-lite.

"Two mice," I say.

He's actually a lot like a New Yorker inasmuch as he comes off really aggressive and suspicious when you first meet him, but once he trusts you, you're suddenly his best friend. He's friendly like a gangster is friendly. Until you cross him, I imagine. Then he would probably come off as the kind of guy who explains how sad and disappointed he is while he breaks your legs with a baseball bat.

"Two mice?" he says. "What? Like—they're a couple?"

I'm not sure if he is asking me if they are a couple or there are a couple. I consider telling him about the mouse coitus I had witnessed. *Now would be a good time for the distraction, Thierry.*

"Do you smell that?" I say.

"I don't smell anything." Nick frowns. Then, "Fuck!"

Smoke drifts down the hall past the door to the office. *Merci, Thierry!* Nick bolts out the door and down the hall into the lobby. The safe is surprisingly small. It sits to one side in the kneehole of the desk so I must get down awkwardly on all fours. My hands are trembling. 11-22-33. Nothing. This whole thing is crazy. 11-22-33. Still nothing. I wipe the sweat from my palms on my shirt. 11-22-33. I hear the whoosh of a fire extinguisher being discharged. 11-22-33. Shouts from the lobby. Panicked, I straighten up and bash the back of my head on the bottom of the desk.

Then it occurs to me. 77-22-33. Click. Thierry and I need to review our lesson on numbers. I close the safe and carefully set the dial at 36. Straightening up, I bash my head again. I hope I'm not bleeding. I just settle back into my chair as Nick returns. He is holding a fire extinguisher in one hand and a huge key ring that resembles some kind of medieval torture device in the other. I can feel my eyes watering from the pain in my skull.

"Look, Spence. I got a problem. Those fucking dope-smoking kids in 207—I'll bet any money. They think this kind of shit is funny? I warned them. They will find out. They will learn."

I imagine Nick breaking their thumbs so they can no longer ignite matches. Or maybe they'll get off easy. Just a beating with a sock full of oranges, like in that movie. Oranges don't leave any visible bruises. Just internal bruises. He goes behind the desk. I watch him reach under and give the handle of the safe a tug.

"We'll talk another time, okay?"

Right. Another time. While you're crushing my safe-cracking fingers with a ball-peen hammer.

Friday, Twenty-Seventh Day of Lent

4:00 am. Nearly twelve hours later. No sign of Thierry. Maybe I've been duped. Maybe he's been stringing me along for a month just so that he could use me for this heist. Maybe that was the plan all along. I'm just a patsy.

I jump. My phone is ringing.

"Hello?"

"*Dieu merci! Ostie!*"

"Thierry? Where the hell are you?"

"*J'suis enfermé dans le coffre-fort!*"

"Locked in the safe? This was not part of the plan, Thierry."

"*Câlisse*! I know dat! You tink I dun know dat? *Tu penses que je l'ai fait exprès?*"

"Wait. If you're in the safe. How are you on the phone?"

" 'e come back man. I jes got in de safe an' 'e come back. 'e knocked de door close when 'e move de chair. 'e open de door. ' toss dis phone inside an' lock up."

"Wow!"

"Wow? All you gotta say is wow? Lucky I learn de numbers. I get de password for dis phone right away 'cause it 1234—*crétin*—but I been callin' all over for hours!"

"Calling who?"

"*Tout le monde!* All kinda people, man, 'cause I kenna remember *exactement* yer phone number what you taught me."

"I'm surprised you've got a connection."

"It's crazy. I even got wifi, man!"

"You probably picked up MTLWiFi from the park across the street. It's free."

"Dats real nice, brudder. But I runnin' outta battery an' runnin' outa air."

"On my way, *mon chum. J'arrive!*"

The connection falters. Then fails.

SOMETIME LATER . . .

It is an hour before I am through the office door.

Thierry is dead when I find him. When I open the safe, he falls face first to the floor. I see faint scratch marks on the inside of the steel door. I turn him on his back. His eyes are open. His mouth is open. I place my finger on his chest. He is not yet cold. A mouse's heart can exceed eight hundred beats per minute. A mouse can take more than two hundred breaths per minute. This mouse has no life. No breath. But he still has a heart. A lot of heart.

I drum a rapid tattoo on his chest with my finger and bring my face close to his. I purse my lips and send a gentle, steady stream of air into his open mouth. A minute passes. Nothing.

I pray.

Hail Mary, full of Grace . . .

Nothing.

. . . pray for us sinners now and at the hour of our death. Amen.

He blinks. A sudden breath.

"Thierry! Thank God!"

"De money . . ." he croaks. "Get de money, *tabarnac!*"

EVENING . . .

"You some kinda 'oudini or something?"

"Houdini was an escape artist, not a burglar."

"*La même chose.* You know 'ow to break out den you know 'ow to break in. *C'est juste logique.*"

Thierry is sprawled on a fairly substantial pile of mostly $20 and $100 bills. He is sipping Don de Dieu beer through a paper straw. The same bottle I bought for him a week ago and it is still half full.

"Before I was a drama teacher, *mon chum*, I was an actor."

"*Vraiment?* For real, man? You in any movie I seen?"

"I wasn't in any movies, Thierry. I was an actor in the theatre."

"Dats lame."

"Hey, I saved your life, man."

"I know, man. *Le baiser de la vie.* You give me de kiss o' life. I not gonna forget." He burps.

"Anyway. I was in this play called *A Pair of Deuces.* I played this hardboiled Philip Marlowe-type detective."

Thierry folds a $100 bill into a paper airplane and launches it.

"*C'est fascinant, ton histoire mais . . .*"

"All right, all right. Long story short. My character had to pick a lock in the play. So, in the interest of authenticity—"

"Big word. What I tell you?"

"In order to keep it real—"

"Bedder."

"I practised picking a lock with a real locksmith."

" An' it take you an hour to pick de lock an' I almost die?"

"No, it took me an hour to find two bobby pins. *Salle de lavage. La poubelle. Le recyclage.* It took me two minutes to pick the lock. And you didn't almost die. *Tu étais mort.* You can thank Our Blessed Lady for your miraculous resurrection."

"*Oui, oui. Avé Maria. Sacrament.*" He makes a hasty sign of the cross and then performs a little whoop-de-doo with his finger. "*Alors.* You dun got no 'air. Where you find two bobby pin?"

"Where I should have looked in the first place. Outside the entrance to 302. The guy who lives there is a drag queen. He's always shedding bobby pins."

"*Notre Dame* and a drag queen. *Mes sauveurs.*"

"And *A Pair of Deuces.*"

Saturday, Twenty-Eight Day of Lent

"*Cinq mille huit cent quatre-vingt-dix-sept . . . Cinq mille huit cent quatre-vingt-dix-huit . . . Cinq mille huit cent quatre-vingt-dix-neuf . . . C'est ça.*"

Thierry has learned to count. He carefully arranges all the bills in order. Quite a few hundreds, a handful of fifties, a lot of twenties, some tens and fives, and two tidy little piles of loonies and toonies. $5,899. *Exactement.* With my help, he has counted it four times. Slowly. Deliberately. Twice in English and, so that I could practise, *deux fois en français.* It is like watching a bilingual episode of *Sesame Street,* sponsored by the letters I and O. Indictable Offence. Theft over $5,000. Up to ten years imprisonment.

"*T'inquiète pas . . . tu connais mon chum, Jean-Guy?*"

"Your friend who died?"

"*Non. C'était un meurtre. Il a été assassiné.*"

"*Je m'excuse.*"

" 'e spend a year in de big 'ouse."

"What was he in for?"

"Nutin'. Mice dun get no trial, Einstein. Jean-Guy live in Drummondville when 'e were young. Right next to de prison. He made some good friend dere. Inmates get lonely and mice is good company. Jean-Guy used to smoke up wid dem guys all de time."

He turns away from me. I give him a moment.

"So, you're saying if I get convicted, you and I can spend our time stoned in Drummondville Penitentiary?"

"No way, man." He laughs and rubs his nose with the back of his hand. "*Drummondville c'est trop loin. Peut-être*, we ken talk on de phone."

"That's a real comfort." He flips a loonie to me. "*C'est extra.*"

"*Tu fais des maths, maintenant?*"

"*Facile, mon chum.* So, what you doin' wid yer half?"

"I'm not sure. What are you doing with yours?"

"Mice dun really use money. *Mais, j'penserai à quelque chose.* I ken keep dis envelope, *hein?* The one from de safe dat de money was in?"

"I'd rather destroy it. It's evidence."

"Dun worry. I not gonna keep it in our place. I jes want it. Okay?"

"*Oui. D'accord. Mais fais attention.*"

FIFTH SUNDAY OF LENT

Me: *Ça va?*
Thierry: *Bien. Toi?*
Me: *Ça va.*
Thierry: *Bien.*
Une pause.
Me: *Alors . . . qu'est-ce que tu fais ce soir?*
Thierry: *Rien.*
Me: *Rien? Vraiment?*
Thierry: *Ouais. Tu sais. Comme d'habitude.*

It is evening. He scrambles up to the stereo with a Steely Dan album in his teeth: *Can't Buy a Thrill.* Thierry is surprisingly adept with things you might imagine are cumbersome for a mouse. As the long instrumental intro to "Do It Again" begins, he jumps onto the album cover and rides it like a surfboard as it floats to the floor.

It worries me that Thierry has told me he isn't doing anything tonight, just the usual. The vocals to the song begin—guns, water— and Thierry stands up, supporting himself on his tail. Like a cowboy in a western, he mimes firing a pair of six-shooters and then blows some imaginary smoke from his fingertips and smiles.

What's he up to now?

Monday, Twenty-Ninth Day of Lent

Early afternoon. A knock at the door. I peer through the peephole.

Le propriétaire.

He's wearing a tool belt: pliers, claw hammer, utility knife, gaffer tape. Your basic Mafia torture starter kit. I briefly consider hanging off the balcony and dropping from the third floor to the sidewalk below. Instead, I open the door.

"Hey, Spence." Nick is chewing gum. Peppermint. I stammer something half English and half French. Nick nods. He gives me a look. He can tell I'm hiding something.

"I . . . I . . . I . . . just got back from French class," I say. "My brain . . ." I point to my head in case he doesn't know where a brain is located. "*Mon cerveau. Il est confus.*"

"You'll get the hang of it. Look, I just wanted to tell you I'm sorry if the noise next door disturbed you. In a few days I got a new tenant moving in."

He rests one hand on his tool belt, on the head of his hammer. I swallow hard. I say nothing. I wonder, briefly, if the guy next door is getting evicted. Nick shifts the gum from one side of his mouth to the other. He holds it delicately between his front teeth and chews some more.

"Okay. Later. I got some repairs."

I close the door and watch his retreating figure through the peep-hole. He takes the hammer out of his tool belt, tosses it in the air one full rotation, then catches it expertly by the handle. He suspects.

EVENING . . .

"You've got a hat!"

Thierry is sporting a Buster Keaton-style pork pie hat.

"What you tink?" He smooths his whiskers with one hand.

"*Très beau.* Where'd you get it?"

"Renaissance. Dey got an 'ole section of miniature stuff."

Renaissance is a non-profit that accepts used goods that it sells to support job training for new immigrants and marginalized people. Their slogan is *Merci de faire du bien avec vos biens!* Thank you for doing some good with your goods.

"Thierry! You didn't steal from Renaissance?"

"No way!" He flicks his tail indignantly.

"Okay. *Désolé.*"

"I mean—I steal it fer sure. But on de way out I leave *dix piasse dans la caisse.* It were only five bucks. *Garde le change. De rien.*"

He flips the hat down the length of his arm and gives it a little pop with the back of his hand. It lands squarely between his ears.

"Nick came by to see me earlier today," I say.

"*Ah ouais?*"

"He knows."

Thierry spins his hat into the air and catches it behind his back. "*T'inquiète pas.* He dun know nutin'. Anyway. I took care o' dat. 'e gonna be off de scent. Trust me."

TUESDAY, THIRTIETH DAY OF LENT

Last Friday I missed my morning French class for the first time. That was the morning I found Thierry after he'd been trapped in the safe for hours. Today I miss class for the second time. Thierry spent yesterday evening practising fancy moves with his new pork pie hat. His dexterity is truly impressive. This morning I notice he has left the hat on the table. I suppose he forgot it. Then I recall that I have exactly the same hat. Except much bigger. I used to wear it almost daily but I haven't worn it for over a year because of my recent devotion to cycling. I pick up his tiny hat and I am, inexplicably, overcome with a sense of panic. I rush to the closet to confirm that my hat is still there, that I'd not forgotten it in the move from Vancouver.

After a little hunting around I find it tucked into a white plastic bag on the top shelf. I can't explain my reasoning—it is not rational—but for a moment I suspected that Thierry had stolen my hat.

Crazy, I know. But what is crazier? When I found the hat I fainted. At least I think I fainted. Because I don't remember what happened, exactly. One moment I was holding my old pork pie hat and the next I was slumped on the floor of the closet. And what is stranger? I didn't care. I just lay there. It must have been for quite a while.

I have no recollection of thinking about anything during that time. It was as though my mind went utterly still. In some sense, I was aware. But it was as though I wasn't really present to myself. As though I'd wandered off and left my body, as a hermit crab abandons its shell. I was the shell. But I was also . . . somewhere else.

The noon bells from St. Augustine's rouse me from that state, and I have missed class. I make another cup of coffee, sit at the table and gaze out the windows to the west.

At 6:00 pm the bells toll again. I am still at the table. It is almost dark.

WEDNESDAY, THIRTY-FIRST DAY OF LENT

Après-midi. Il pleut.
Just got home from French class. I'm outside the building, a

little sweaty from cycling. Still breathing hard, I hoist my bike up the steps and through the glass doors of the entrance. In the lobby, the elevator opens and two cops emerge. *Un homme et une femme.* Slumped between them, the guy from next door.

He's in handcuffs.

I position my kickstand and leave my bike upright by the windows, then hold the glass door open to let them out. The guy next door looks stricken.

"*Merci, monsieur,*" says the woman cop.

"*Bonne journée, madame.*"

I stand in the lobby and look at the rows of bronze mailboxes. There is a dark, strangely beautiful starburst around box 105, blackened by the escaping smoke. Thierry's distraction. In the apartment I leave my bike dripping over the entranceway mat and strip off my rain gear. I'm miserable. Wet and miserable.

"Thierry!" I sit and pull off my shoes, they land with a clunk. "Thierry!" My socks leave the wet shape of my feet on the floor. "Thierry!" I'm startled as he squeezes under the door of the hall closet right near my damp socks. He's yawning.

"You mind? For mice dis is like three in de morning, *mon chum*." His new hat is askew.

"*Qu'est-ce qui se passe?* "

"What 'appening? You stinkin' up de joint with dos socks. Dat what 'appening. Phew."

"I just saw the guy next door being dragged out of here in handcuffs."

"Oh dat? I 'eard *les cochons* got a tip about some *cambriolage*."

"Our *cambriolage*, Thierry! Ours!"

"*Les cochons ont trouvé des preuves.*"

"What evidence?"

"*Une enveloppe du coffre-fort.*"

"An envelope you planted! The money, too?"

"*Bien sûr. Alors?* What a mouse gonna do wid money?"

"He could go to prison!"

"Boo hoo."

"You framed an innocent man!"

"*Un homme innocent?* He fuckin' drown Jean-Guy in de toilet!"

I stare at the ceiling. My head hurts.

"*Écoute. Le fils de pute* got an alibi. I check. 'e gonna spend one night in jail. Max. Jean-Guy gonna spend de rest o' his life bein' dead down a toilet, *tabarnac.*"

I pick up his hat and hand it to him. He covers his face.

"*D'accord. Ça va. Ça va. Okay. Mais, Jean-Guy a été vengé, non?*"

He nods. His face is still buried in his hat. A pause.

"*As-tu faim?*"

He shakes his head.

"*Tu veux une bière?*"

He shakes his head again.

"I goin' back to sleep." He slips under the closet door like a shadow.

"Okay," I say, stripping off my wet socks. A little helplessly I add, "*Fais de beaux rêves.*"

LATER . . .

Now that the weather has warmed up a little Thierry is spending time outdoors. Near a reliable food source, your average house mouse rarely ventures more than twelve feet from their nest. And your average house mouse can travel that distance in under a second.

Thierry is not average.

The world record for the hundred-meter sprint is just a hair under ten seconds. On even ground, Thierry can cover that distance in less than thirty seconds. If Usain Bolt were mouse size, he'd be eating Thierry's dust. We can leave our third-floor apartment at the same time and Thierry is consistently on the sidewalk before I am. He won't talk about his route. Secrets of the trade, he says. Magicians and thieves.

Thierry says magicians steal their ideas from pickpockets and grifters. And according to him, every trick and every con was originally invented by a mouse.

"Dats why *les cochons d'anglos* call it an MO, brudder. Dats de first two letter o' mouse."

I am mindful that mouse is among maybe six or seven words that Thierry can read and the teacher in me doesn't want to discourage his impulse to speculate. But I cannot resist disabusing him.

"*Je suis désolé, mon chum, mais MO signifie Modus Operandi. C'est Latin.*"

"*Oui. Le même en français!* Dats where de word mouse come from *en anglais.* Des Anglos always stealing de French word, man. Look it up. You guys steal everybody language."

I did look it up. Mouse comes from the Old English *mus.* Plural *mys.* I keep that to myself. But Thierry is essentially correct about English stealing words. Though, to be fair, French was thrust upon the English by conquering francophone Normans and lingers there so utterly that English is a sort of chimera tongue.

Nous étions deux Montréalais. Une paire de voleurs. Partners in crime.

I am like the slave in Matthew 25 who receives one talent in silver from his master and simply buries it in the ground. I have hidden my share of the loot under the bathroom sink. There it squats, like a reproach. Nothing ventured; nothing gained.

Have I stolen from Nick? Or stolen something from myself?

I suppose we all keep much of who we truly are hidden from ourselves. We bury gifts that we secretly fear are unworthy of being offered. Efface transgressions that we cannot confess; attenuate our own suffering. Perhaps Thierry is right, though, when he observed we are all thieves. In every transgression there is a kind of theft. Truth goes missing. Trust disappears. Innocence is lost. Even the mystery of life is a larceny of sorts. No creature can exist without thieving life from fellow creatures. We all prey or become prey. Often, we do both.

A beautiful balancing act? Or a cruel con? And how can one illiterate rodent move my thoughts to these mysteries? I suppose if it could happen to Robbie Burns, it might happen to anyone.

THURSDAY, THIRTY-SECOND DAY OF LENT

Printemps. Spring. Sounds in the corridor. Someone is moving into the apartment next door. Maybe our neighbour was evicted. Or maybe he'd had enough of suffering Thierry's punishments. Thierry wakes. It's too noisy for him to sleep. It's just noon but he rolls a joint and we share it.

"Where do you find all this weed, Thierry?"

"You dun wanna know, brudder." He coughs.

From time to time, I go to the peephole. For a while I spy only one man in blue overalls. He wields a dolly, loading in boxes and whatever furnishings he can manage alone. Later, another man joins him and the two of them maneuver a large filing cabinet and a table. They exchange remarks in *joual*. The only word I recognize is *tabarnac*. By now I am thoroughly stoned.

Then she appears. Her hair is white. Silver white. Luminous. As she moves down the corridor the walls seem to draw back a little in deference. Two rows of courtiers would not have seemed out of place. She removes two crisp twenties from her handbag and bestows them on the movers. *Ce ne sont plus de ouvriers simples, mais de vrais acolytes.* Did they just bow? It is as though she has conferred knighthood upon them. I watch all this through the peephole.

Who is she that looks forth as the morning, fair as the moon, clear as the sun, and terrible as an army with banners?

"Excellent weed, *hein?*" Thierry calls from the living room.

"Amazing," I say.

I have a new neighbour.

Returning from class and walking past the apartment next door, I can hear music playing. My new neighbour. The woman with the silver-white hair. I recognize Django Reinhardt's unmistakable guitar and the melody of his jazz composition "*Nuages.*" Then she begins to sing. I didn't even know the song had lyrics. She is singing in French. A little off-key. The sound is muffled and I can scarcely understand a word. I put my ear to her door.

Un jour croyant trouver l'amour / On fait un beau rêve / Mais l'orage emporte votre bonheur.

Something about one day believing, finding love—a beautiful dream but a storm carries away your happiness. Something like that. A door opens farther down the corridor and a little girl holding a stuffed bunny emerges. She stares at me. I still have my ear to the door. Her mother follows, grabs her hand, and they head to the elevator.

Later, in the evening, I persuade Thierry to help me a little with my French in exchange for a bit of a reading lesson. *Le Petit Prince.* Thierry sits on my shoulder. I read aloud : "*J'ai de sérieuses raison de croire que la planète d'où venait le petit prince est l'astéroïde B 612.*"

Thierry grabs the book from me. "*Attends une minute. Le prince vit sur un astéroïde?*"

"*Oui.*"

He points to the illustration. "*C'est impossible.* I like de lil guy an' all. But dat planet—"

"Asteroid."

"—dat asteroid no bigger den dis *appartement*. Dat not really believable, man. You sure dis book is famous?"

"I'm sure. It's been translated into three hundred different languages. Still sells two million copies a year. It's a classic."

"So, dis guy who never trust *les grandes personnes* meet dis *petit bonhomme*? Dey become friend in de middle o' de Sahara?" He frowns. "*Pas très croyable.*"

"I agree. It's not a very plausible premise." I put the book aside and go to the kitchen. Thierry is still on my shoulder. "*Maintenant, mon petit bonhomme,* what shall we have for dinner?"

SATURDAY, THIRTY-FOURTH DAY OF LENT

Our apartment is a mess. Thierry likes to chew the paper I lay along one side of the living room for him and bits float about. He smokes a lot of weed, which I gave up at the same time I stopped drinking more than thirty years ago.

But now? I'm retired. It's legal.

So, I must confess I am pretty stoned when I head down to the parking garage to dispose of the recycling. When I arrive, I am not particularly surprised that one of the pipes in the ceiling has sprung a substantial leak. Today, there is a wide puddle in the middle of the garage floor.

I am startled when I hear the clatter of the garage door opening. An engine revs. It is an unmistakable sound from my childhood, the big throaty growl of a V8. Being high, I think at first I must be imagining what emerges from the entrance tunnel. It is a 1960 metallic green Ford Fairlane. I recognize the distinctive chrome molding that runs the length of the body before flaring out at the rear. It stops just before the puddle. A man wearing oversized sunglasses gets out, leaving the engine idling. He removes his flat, wool cap, revealing a scalp that has the sheen of a carefully shaved head. When he takes off his sunglasses, dark eyes and thick black eyebrows are revealed. He surveys the puddle before getting back behind the wheel and then drives cautiously through it to the far end of the garage and expertly backs the big Fairlane into a parking spot. He gets out, lights a cigarette and watches me skirt the puddle to get to the recycling bins.

A while later, I return with a plastic bag of trash. He is gone and the car is concealed under a grey dust cover. I glance about me, still high. There are more than a dozen vehicles similarly shrouded. Ghost cars, I think to myself, like the 1960 Ford Fairlane, cruising from out of my past to haunt the dreary damp of the parking garage.

I am way too stoned to ride my bike to Clara's apartment to water the plants. I missed last Saturday, the morning after our little heist. After counting the loot with Thierry, I'd gone to bed and slept most of the day away. I suppose I could have gone sometime this week instead. But what with the unsettling visit from Nick, that strange episode looking for my damn pork pie hat, missing class and the new neighbour, it has been an eventful week.

At Clara's apartment, I open all the windows and the door to the balcony to let in some fresh air. I keep my coat on while I water the plants, none of which seem to have suffered too much in my absence. I take a moment to look at the collage that hangs in the hallway leading to her studio. It was something I'd had mounted and framed behind glass more than twenty years ago. The last activity that Clara and Serenity had shared before her mother died. Just bits of thread and buttons and sparkles glued to a large piece of brown craft paper. They had coloured with crayons and had cut out pictures from a fashion magazine and from the liturgical calendar I had bought at the cathedral the previous year. I'd picked it up from the floor of Clara's bedroom the day her mother died. Over the years, a few of the buttons have come loose and settled on the bottom of the frame.

The absurd clank from the solitary bell from St. Raymond's across the street breaks my little reverie. Sometimes it seems that half my life has been spent listening to bells sounding . . . what? Invitations? Warnings? Premonitions?

I take out my phone intending to send a quick "thinking of you" message to Clara but I realize it must be four in the morning in Paris. I don't want to wake her. Idly, I tap the photo icon. The face that appears stops me cold.

It is the photo of the priest I'd snapped at St. Raymond's. When . . .

a month ago? The day that band was practising country tunes in the basement. In the photo his name is not in focus. What was it again? Why had I even snapped the photo in the first place?

I close the windows and secure Clara's apartment. Out of curiosity I cross the street to St. Raymond's and check out the photograph of the priest in the vestibule.

Mallory Parent OSM 1968–69.

I note the name. I'll look him up. Just out of curiosity.

A few people are entering for the five o'clock Saturday Mass. In terms of fulfilling the obligation, it is considered Sunday Mass. I can't remember why. Maybe something about the Sabbath starting at sunset. An old woman stands beside me. She is scarcely five feet tall and could be ninety. It is hard to tell because she is wearing one of those old-fashioned lace veils that women traditionally wore to Mass decades ago. It is black and obscures much of her face. She looks at the photo and says something to me in Italian. Then she shakes her head. Taking tiny steps into the church, she blesses herself at the little font of holy water by the entrance and carefully performs a deep genuflection to the altar despite her aged knees.

Mallory Parent OSM 1968–69.

SERENITY, 22

Serenity's contractions began just after midnight. It was July, on the day that was to be hottest of the year in Vancouver, the hottest for more than twenty years. CUPE had been on strike for three weeks and garbage was piling up in the alley behind the apartment. Spilling out of the dumpsters and spoiling in the heat.

Spence and Serenity had occupied their renovated two-bedroom, second-story apartment since February. The building was situated on a busy commercial street comprising small businesses, grocers, cheap eateries, and coffee shops. Their apartment was just above Vito's Italian Bakery, a shop that manufactured tofu and a little hole in the wall café.

Spence telephoned their midwife, Anna, who arrived within a half hour. Her presence was reassuring. She was a tall woman with strong, no-nonsense hands the size of a man's. She took Serenity's blood pressure and temperature.

"You're doing beautifully," she wrapped an arm around Serenity and gave her a little squeeze of encouragement. "You're in early labour. Everything is normal. It will be hours yet, so I am going home to get some sleep. I'll be back around seven."

Spence and Serenity sat up in bed, their pillows propped against the headboard. Spence would close his eyes for a few minutes but he kept his hand on Serenity's belly. Every time he felt a contraction, he would consult his watch, measure its duration, then make a note of how much time had passed since the last one. A vigil is the surest way to prolong the night.

By five o'clock the sound of birdsong drifted through the open windows of the bedroom, and Spence made some toast and raspberry jam. Serenity claimed she wasn't hungry but he sat next to her on the bed, coaxing her to take a few nibbles.

"I can smell the garbage from the alley," she said.

"I'll light some incense."

"Can we close the windows?"

"The cross-breeze is the only thing keeping the apartment cool."

Serenity nodded. In another hour, the sound of delivery trucks starting their rounds and the first stirrings of Monday morning traffic began. It seemed surreal to Spence that the world was carrying on at its usual pace. For him, time had slowed. Lack of sleep fogged his mind. The scent of sandalwood from the wisp of smoke rising from the stick of incense. Refuse spoiling in the alley.

He brought the two gold-colored Buddha ornaments from the living room and set them on the night stands on either side of the table. They made Serenity laugh.

"Take a picture," she said. She crossed her legs as well as she was able, cradled her belly in her hands, and adopted the same serene expression as the two Buddhas flanking her. Spence snapped a photo.

"Are Catholic boys supposed to be setting up shrines to Buddha?" she teased.

Serenity drew a quick breath. With each contraction her eyes seemed to be gazing through the walls at some point far in the distance. Someplace Spence could not go. He felt what so many men before him had experienced.

Awe.

Helplessness.

At seven, Anna arrived. Once again, she measured Serenity's vital signs and cheerfully declared everything was going well. By late morning, Serenity came to the living room and sat next to where Anna had taken up a position on the sofa, calmly knitting a tiny sweater suitable for a newborn.

"So hot," Serenity said. Spence had been regularly plying her with ice chips and arranging cool, damp cloths on the back of her neck. He ran a shallow bath of cold water and soaked several bed sheets in it. He drew up the bamboo blinds and fastened the sheets to the brackets, arranging them like sails over the four tall windows in the living room. They billowed softly in the breeze, diffusing the sunlight, and cooling the room, a little, as the moisture evaporated.

"We're inside a womb," Anna said, looking around. The whole room seemed to be softly breathing.

By eleven o'clock that evening, Serenity had had enough. They had hoped for a home-birth, but now they piled into Anna's car and headed to Children's Hospital. Serenity's water broke while they sat in the car and her labour intensified so swiftly that Spence wondered if the baby was going to be delivered somewhere on route.

Just before midnight, their daughter, Clara, arrived on a wave from her little captive sea and everyone in the room burst into tears. They stayed for another couple of hours before the doctor agreed that they could go. Back home, Serenity and Clara immediately fell asleep. Spence snapped a photo of them curled up together. He looked out the bedroom window. The nearly full moon hung not far above the horizon, the same familiar moon that Spence had seen traversing the sky on thousands of nights. But it felt as if he were seeing it for the first time. And it was though a great burden had been lifted from his shoulders even as a tiny bundle was delivered to his care.

Anna had fashioned a length of Clara's umbilical cord into a knot, like a pretzel, and given it to Spence.

"Once it has dried it will make a good teething ring," she said.

Spence carried the little token to the kitchen. He placed the neatly tied cord in a saucer and returned with it to the bedroom. He chose a spot for it on the bedroom window sill under the soft light of the moon.

"How long has she been crying?"

"All evening. Hours. She won't stop." Serenity burst into tears as well. Spence took his daughter from his wife's arms and cradled her with her head resting on his shoulder. It was nearly midnight. He had worked a double shift, trying to keep up with all the new expenses occasioned by Clara's arrival nearly seven months ago.

"I can't do this anymore," Serenity said. "I feel like I'm going crazy."

"You're doing wonderfully," Spence said, though he knew this was not true.

Serenity had been attending a weekly support group that their midwife, Anna, had recommended for mothers with postpartum depression. Spence, likewise, had tried attending a support group for husbands of women with postpartum depression. The doctor who led the group had explained that post-partum depression could be further complicated if a woman had a previous history of mental illness, or of drug addiction, childhood abuse or sexual abuse. He inquired if any of the men's partners had experienced these things. Spence was the only one who raised his hand.

"Which?" the doctor asked.

"All of them," he said.

After that, the other men seemed to distance themselves a little, as though the complexity of Spence's situation might suck the momentum out of their own progress. He stopped attending after a few weeks.

"I wanted to throw her out the window," Serenity said.

"No, you didn't." Spence shook his head.

"Yes. I wanted to throw her out the window. She won't stop crying. I'm going crazy. I'm a bad mother."

"You're not a bad mother," he said. "Clara is colicky. That's all. Some babies are colicky. It's difficult. It would be difficult for anyone."

Being a new parent is stressful, he reasoned. Emotions weren't a sign of failure.

"I'll take her for a walk," he said. He handed Clara back to her mother and fitted the corduroy baby carrier over his head. Serenity arranged Clara's feet into the openings.

"I'm sorry," she said.

"It's not your fault."

"I'm useless."

Spence cupped her face in his hands and tried to smooth away some of her tears. Her eyes were tired. He kissed her. Then he kissed both her hands. Her fingertips were red and inflamed from compulsively chewing her fingernails.

It was a warm night. Within half an hour, Clara stopped wailing but her breath still came in soft little sobs. Spence walked as far as St. Francis of Assisi, the little Italian church in his parish. He had only attended Mass there once. Inside, it was dark and musty and garishly ornamented but it had a lovely garden. He followed the path to the sheltered area behind the church and sat on a bench near a little shrine to the Virgin Mary. A new moon hung cradled in the branches of an oak.

He woke just as it was getting light. Clara opened her eyes briefly and smiled at him. She fell asleep again on the way home. Later Spence lay down on the bed next to Serenity, fully clothed with Clara still in the carrier on his chest. He stayed like that for a couple of hours until Clara woke again, then passed her to Serenity who nursed her. They all slept for a while longer.

"*Bonjour, tout le monde. C'est la fête de la Saint-Jean-Baptiste.* Well, not exactly. That was last month. But we is going to get this little girl sprinkled today. *On y va.* I is not parked legal. Bad luck to get a ticket, today."

It was the morning of Clara's baptism, and it was big Normand LaBelle who drove everyone to Holy Rosary Cathedral. Anna, the midwife who at Clara's birth cried to Spence, "Catch your baby," had consented to be godmother. Normand would serve as Clara's godfather. They all squeezed into his Volkswagen Beetle.

"This is a 1979, the final year they rolled off the assembly line," Spence said.

"How you know these things about cars?" Normand asked.

"It was the only interest my father and I shared when I was a kid.

He would buy me and my brother those little Meccano toy cars. Car magazines all over the house. His father—my grandfather—had been a mechanic."

"I am sort of a god-grandfather," Normand joked. He was at the first Alcoholics Anonymous meeting that Spence ever attended, the designated greeter that evening. Later, he would serve as Spence's sponsor when he was baptized and confirmed in the Catholic faith.

Normand and Spence were, on the surface, unlikely friends. Normand was twenty years Spence's senior. He had come to the west coast as a young man, eager to escape the little rural Québec town of his childhood where he had been raised in a strict Catholic home, the ninth of ten children, and where he had been educated by priests and a small army of sisters and brothers from a dizzying variety of religious orders. Normand had even considered becoming a priest, himself. But he had been swept up by *la Révolution tranquille* and, like much of Québec, had forsaken a church that thought the route to redemption required strict adherence to traditions that no longer made sense. Maybe never made sense. That is the trouble when you are possessed of the Truth—there are no more questions.

"First I move to Montréal," Normand had explained in his musical Québécois accent. "But even there, I can't find no romance. You know why there is so many stairway on the outside of building in Montréal? Because the Church want to make it harder to sneak into the next apartment for a little hanky-panky. You got to climb the stair outside for the whole neighbourhood to see."

Normand joked that he had come to Vancouver because he fell in love with a west coast Anglo. He stayed for the scenery. It was self-acceptance and, maybe, those vistas of sea and mountains that gradually restored his faith.

Serenity had been slow to warm up to Normand. He was a big bear of a man with a full rust-colored beard that seemed a little incongruous given his almost black locks and the mat of black fur on his chest. Normand was gay and HIV positive. Spence had seen acquaintances that he knew from the theatre wasting away from AIDS over the past several years, but Normand's robust health seemed unassailable. The first time Spence placed Clara in Normand's beefy palms, she immediately reached up and buried her tiny hands in his thick beard. Her affection for him seemed to reassure Serenity.

As Clara was about to receive her baptism, Spence positioned himself on the opposite side of the font from Father Desmond. From his vantage, he had a view of the stained-glass window on the east wall of the Sanctuary, next to the ornate shrine to the Blessed Virgin. Sunlight flooded through a depiction of the Risen Christ in crimson robes. Surrounding him, depictions of Mary, draped as always in blue: Annunciation, Birth, Visitation, Presentation in the Temple. Above the crucifix over the altar, light poured in through a half dozen of the apostles in the tall clerestory windows. Particles of dust sparkled in the air below the dome.

The previous week, Clara had celebrated her first birthday. And just as at her birth, every hand within reach now joined to support her over the font as Desmond pronounced: "I baptize you in the Name of the Father, of the Son and of the Holy Spirit."

She blinked as Father Desmond poured a little water over her forehead. He scooped it from the font with an ordinary shell which he held in one hand. In the other he awkwardly held open a little black, leather-clad volume. Her eyes went suddenly wide as the cathedral bells began to sound.

"Tuesday," Desmond said.

"What?" Spence leaned closer to hear.

"I forgot. It's Tuesday. They practise ringing the bells every Tuesday morning." Desmond raised his voice above the din. Clara looked around her. She was curious but not alarmed.

"It's a good sign," Spence shouted.

Desmond performed the final rites—the anointing with oil sweetened with balsam, the lighting of the candles, the blessings—over the clamour of the bells. They fell silent just after the final "Amen" and everyone laughed. They gathered around Clara and Serenity, exchanging hugs and drinking in the scent of the oil.

"The Balm of Gilead," Anna said.

Father Desmond had another baptism scheduled that afternoon, but everyone else climbed back into Normand's Volkswagen. The plan was to have brunch. A block from the cathedral, Spence glanced to his right in time to see a red blur hurling through the intersection toward him. There had been no time to shout a warning. The little VW Beetle was struck soundly on the passenger side and both cars screeched to a halt on the sidewalk opposite. Spence and Normand turned immediately to check out the backseat. Anna sat, looking stricken. Serenity was hyperventilating. Clara was in her car seat between them. She was smiling. Apparently oblivious. She reached forward and tried to touch Normand's beard.

There are times we drift peacefully through life, Spence thought, and times when the daily dread of life's hardships makes each moment feel unbearable. And there are times when lightning strikes. A single spark sets your world ablaze and the flames consume everything in their path.

Serenity was not severely injured in the accident: a case of whiplash, painful for some weeks but not permanent. Within a year, the lawyer that Spence had engaged to handle her personal injury claim presented her with a very substantial cheque. Enough so that she could afford to leave Spence for a new lover and the exhilaration of new love that seemed to lift her out of her depression. Enough so that she believed she could provide for Clara, so long as Spence would contribute his share, and so long as the welfare cheques arrived each month.

Nearly three years a husband and two years a father. All of Spence's adulthood had been, otherwise, directly or obliquely, connected to the theatre. How was it that now he no longer understood his role?

Spence could not bear to be present the day Serenity and Clara moved out. He left that morning and spent the entire day walking aimlessly. He returned to an apartment stripped of almost everything. Serenity had left the sofa but had taken their bed. On the window sill of the bedroom he saw the saucer with what remained of the little length of Clara's umbilical cord. He had placed it in that exact spot the night Clara was born. It was dry now and as hard as a shell. Spence lifted it to his lips. The faint scent of Clara, as a newborn. The smell of the sea that, for days, had clung to her scalp. The salty fragrance every parent must know when they gather their newborn in their arms, kiss their brow, and breathe a long sigh of gratitude.

So faint. So far away.

Palm Sunday

"*Crisse de câlisse d'ostie de ciboire!*"

"What the fuck, Thierry?"

"Where you get dis . . . dis . . . *abomination?*"

Thierry is pointing to the little traditional palm cross that parishioners fashion from the palm fronds provided at Palm Sunday Mass. One of the little kids at St. Monica's had given it to me. He holds the little cross upside down with the sort of disdain one might reserve for a used tissue.

"Big words, Thierry."

"Fuck you. Where you get dis?"

"*De la messe, Thierry. De l'église.*"

"*La messe.* You go to church?"

"Only on Sunday. I'm not some sort of fanatic."

"You tink you fuckin' know someone an' den . . ." He flings the little palm cross at me. I pick it up from the floor.

"Thierry, why is this a surprise? I told you I prayed the Hail Mary when you died in the safe."

"Yeah. But I jes tawt, you know, no atheist in a foxhole, man."

"Where you going?"

"Back to bed! *J't'en tabarnac, ostie!*"

Holy Monday

"Why you never tell me you go to church?"

"You never asked, Thierry. And you're always still asleep Sunday mornings."

"You dun really believe all dat bullshit, *hein? Un ami imaginaire dans le ciel?*"

"It's not a question of belief, Thierry. Believing doesn't make something true."

"I tawt you religion nuts gotta have fate."

"Fate?"

"No, fate."

"*Fête?*"

"Fate!"

"Fate?"

"FATE! *La foi, tabarnac!* Clean yer ears!"

"You mean faith."

"How many time I gotta say dat? Fate. *La foi.*"

"I don't think faith is certainty, Thierry."

"Non?"

"*Mais non.* It's more like trust. *La confiance.* Doubt is actually the starting point."

"Mebbe. *Mais faire confiance à quoi?*."

"It's hard to explain, Thierry. It's kind of like saying . . . like . . ."

"*Comme quoi?*"

I take a deep breath. "*Comme . . . le monde est ma maison. Notre maison. Je m'empêche d'avoir peur. Comme ça.*"

"I won't be afraid?" Thierry snorts. "Easy to say when you at de top o' de food chain, *ostie*."

"Thierry. *Ce n'est pas facile à dire pour personne*—man or mouse—*et ostie?* The Host?"

"I know what it is, man. *Maman était catholique.* An' once I stay in a church for a week. I stole some off de altar when *le prêtre* were kneelin' and sayin' some mumbo jumbo."

"Thierry."

"I tawt you guys was all about feed de 'ungry. *J'avais faim.*"

"*En tout cas, ostie, l'Eucharistie, c'est un moyen de comprendre que Dieu fait partie de la chaîne alimentaire comme nous tous.*"

Another pause.

"God is in de food chain wid de rest o' us? *T'es plein de marde.*"

A ping from my cell phone. A message from Clara. Followed by a photo.

"Notre-Dame is burning," I say.

"*Quoi?*"

"Notre-Dame. In Paris. There's a fire." I show him the photo Clara sent.

I search for news on my computer. For an hour we sit in silence and watch the flames growing.

"I like what you said tonight." She was standing beside him at the coffee urn.

"I can't remember what I said. I'm always so nervous." It was Spence's turn to tidy the kitchen area, one of the several volunteer positions he had taken on at The Door since his first AA meeting, two years ago. She was standing close to him. Close enough that he could detect a trace of perfume.

"About acceptance. About accepting that what is happening is actually happening. Like when you said you missed that bus and you felt like smashing the glass of the bus shelter because you were late for an audition. But then you realized that you were in a kind of denial. You hadn't really accepted the situation. That the bus was gone and you weren't on it." She spoke quickly, her sentences jostling one another as if each new phrase was racing to overtake the last.

"Ah, yes." Spence watched her stir three teaspoons of sugar into her coffee. "I have a quick temper. But I'm starting to learn that I can get angry without having to stay angry."

"You like to control things," she said. "Maybe because your life is out of control?"

That struck Spence as a bit of a presumptuous remark. He had seen her at a few previous meetings. He noted she had stirred a bit of interest among the lesbian contingent in the group. Something in the way she dressed, he wondered? The leather motorcycle jacket over a girlish white dress. Black army boots. A little too much black eyeliner.

"I don't think anyone controls their life," he said. "We make choices, I think. But we can't control the outcomes. Hence, acceptance."

She looked amused. Spence wondered if that had sounded a little pompous. She stood closer to him. He noticed she was not wearing a bra.

"So, you're an actor?"

"Sometimes. Most of the time I'm a bartender," Spence said. "You know the joke. I'm an actor. Really? Which restaurant?"

"You're an alcoholic bartender. That is crazy. Don't you ever worry that you'll have a slip?"

"No," he said. "Anyway, people don't have slips. We make choices. Sometimes we make the wrong choice."

"Serenity," she said and offered to shake hands. Her wrist extended out of the stiff leather sleeve of her jacket. It was wrapped in a white gauze bandage. Spence took her hand.

"Sorry. I'm Spence."

"I know," she said. "'I'm Spence and I'm an alcoholic. Hi Spence.'"

"Right."

She laughed and looked up at Spence over the lip of her paper cup as she took another sip.

"Sorry I just have to . . . " Spence picked up the coffee urn and took it over to the sink to rinse it. "So. You are new to AA? I've seen you a couple times but . . . "

"Not really. I've been going to NA and AA off and on since I was fifteen."

"Narcotics Anonymous," he said. "What's that like?"

"Like AA," she shrugged. "But a bit of tension between the junkies and the potheads. Like the potheads aren't really addicts. But actually, NA is mostly potheads if you want to know the truth."

"Which are you?" Spence set the coffee urn in the corner of the counter. He fussed a little getting the basket in position and then replaced the lid. Serenity was silent.

"Sorry," he said. "None of my business."

"It's okay." She tossed her cup into the garbage bin. "Heroin."

She looked at him steadily. Spence's hands were wet. He wiped them on his shirt.

"Is that a deal breaker?" Serenity asked.

He blushed. He was a little taken aback by her boldness. The place was nearly empty. Normand was by the exit saying goodnight to the stragglers.

"How are you getting home?" he asked.

"Walking."

"I'll walk you home if you like."

They passed Normand on the way out. Spence usually caught a ride home with him.

"Be good," he said and winked. Spence rolled his eyes.

Serenity turned twenty that evening, asleep in Spence's bed. He treated her to a birthday breakfast the next morning. That afternoon he walked her to the clinic where a nurse changed the bandages on her wrists. It was another two weeks before she showed him the scars.

Weeks later, when Serenity had not returned his calls, Spence tracked her down through one of her friends. Normand dropped him off at UBC and Spence wandered, lost, for nearly half an hour in the gloom before he finally arrived at the reception desk on the UBC Psychiatric Ward. He was escorted through a series of locked doors before arriving at a quiet, softly lit area on the third floor. He saw Serenity sitting with her back to him in an open lounge supplied with several comfortable sofas that he noted were bolted to the floor. Wordlessly, he sat down next to her. It seemed to take her a moment to become aware of his presence. Finally she turned and looked at him. Without speaking, she reached for his hand and linked her fingers around his.

"I'm a screw up," she said, finally.

"Nearly a year clean and sober," Spence said. "How is that screwing up?"

She closed her eyes. For a moment her chin rested on her chest. Spence wondered if she had fallen asleep. Abruptly she lifted her head and looked around startled.

"It's okay," Spence said. "I'm right here."

"Sorry. It's the medication. They like to keep us calm." She managed a little smile and then her face was serious again.

"I don't want to go to sleep," she said, gazing out the window. It was now dark enough that they could see a few faint stars despite the soft lights surrounding them. Spence thought of the times they had slept together. How she would thrash about in her sleep as if she were battling phantoms. Sometimes she might cry for several minutes without waking. Or waking, she might suddenly start pummelling him with her fists.

"You should go," she said.

"I just got here."

"I mean you should go. You shouldn't be with me. Shouldn't stay with me. I'm not going to get better. I'm just going to cause you a lot of pain."

In the row of windows, Spence could see his own reflection with Serenity leaning against him on the sofa. They seemed to be floating among the nearly bare branches of the trees and the soft lighting gave them the appearance of a Renaissance chiaroscuro painting.

"You don't know anything, Spence. You don't know anything about me. Because I haven't told you anything, really."

"You've told me some."

In his mind, Spence had a thumbnail sketch of Serenity's childhood. Bounced from her mother's care into the hands of relatives whom she vaguely recollected might have been her father's family—though she had no memory of her father, didn't even know his name. Foster homes. Back to her mother. Then living on the streets and the day-to-day chaos of that existence.

"Turning tricks by the time I was fourteen. Did I tell you about that?"

Spence felt a brief wave of almost panic. It was the sort of knowledge that leaves no place to escape. He had not exactly led a sheltered life, but this was outside his experience. This was not some sort of confession, he understood. It was Serenity trying to push him away.

"That wasn't your fault," he said quietly.

"Whose fault was it then?"

From the distance came the dull thud of fireworks exploding. It was Halloween. Through the windows, a little barrage lit up the trees from behind and Serenity was startled. Spence put his arm around her. She was trembling.

"I can't do this anymore. I'm afraid to be alone."

"You're not alone. You're with me."

"I can't go home."

"You don't have to go home. You'll come live with me. You need looking after. You need to be loved, that's all."

He thought of the children that he and Normand had passed while driving down 10th Avenue. Their masks and painted faces. Zombies and monsters and skeletons lurching out of imaginary graves. Whatever frightful garb they might muster for the evening always disguised an innocence. If there was any real presence of evil, it was almost certainly hidden in the smiles of those adults looming in the warm glow of their doorways, bright candy slipping from their fingers, beguiling as the polished beads of a rosary. Trust always preceding a betrayal.

More fireworks in the distance and the black branches of the trees through the window were starkly illuminated, like veins painted on the night sky. Then darkness again. Once more, their reflection appeared in the window, like a Caravaggio. And stars reappeared faintly. Ancient martyrs dragged across a canvas of sorrow. This time Serenity was not concerned.

She had fallen asleep.

"Okay. *Je l'admets.* I never seen nutin' like dat before. Dat were preddy awesome."

Thierry and I are exiting the Basilica of St. Joseph's Oratory. After the tension of the past couple of days, I thought I'd invite him to see some positive aspect of the Church. He came grudgingly. Maybe he was curious. Maybe, like me, he wanted to do something to acknowledge yesterday's fire at Notre-Dame de Paris. Maybe he just wanted to get out of the house.

"I live 'ere most o' my life, brudder. I never knew dat were in Montréal."

"It's a big tourist attraction, Thierry. Come summer, the tour buses will pull up here like caterpillars on milkweed."

"*Attraction touristique?* I tawt dis were a shrine?"

"Well, it's that too."

It is my turn to be the jaded one. Clara and I had seen scores of churches and cathedrals in Europe when we visited a decade ago and, though the Oratory is sublime, let's just say I admire its austere beauty. Thierry is gobsmacked. Except for a young woman silently praying her rosary, we'd had the place to ourselves. It was so quiet you could hear her lips moving. Thierry had not spoken a word the whole time. He'd even taken off his hat.

We reach the bottom of the first set of stairs.

"What's dat?" he whispers.

"That's a reliquary. It displays a relic." We are both whispering.

"Like Indiana Jones?"

"Not exactly. That's the heart of Frère André."

"Dey murder 'im?"

"No, no. He died at age ninety-one of natural causes. Removing his heart was an act of reverence, Thierry. Frère André was revered for his holiness, his devotion to St. Joseph, and for many miracles of healing."

"*Des miracles? Vraiment?*" A little too loud.

"Shhh. This basilica wouldn't be here were it not for the devotion he inspired. There was only a little wooden chapel before this. That's got to count for something, I guess."

Thierry is peeking out of my coat pocket. He nods solemnly. I don't tell him Frère André's heart was stolen and held for ransom back in 1973. I don't want him getting any ideas. Through a plate glass window, we regard a Madame Tussaud-style display—a life-size wax effigy of Frère André in a restoration of his tiny office. For years he had been the doorman at Collège Notre-Dame just down the hill in Côte-des-Neiges.

"Lil guy, *hein?*"

"Five foot," I whisper. "He had a stomach ailment. Likely he suffered malnutrition. I think he lived mostly on flour stirred into a glass of water."

"Yummy."

We walk past a glass display case.

"Hey. Dats de Olympic Stadium!"

He is pointing at a framed photograph. I read the English description: "October 30, 2010. Monsignor Jean-Claude Turcotte presides over a Thanksgiving Mass at the Olympic Stadium in Montréal in honour of the newly canonized St. André with close to 48,000 people in attendance."

"De Pope make 'im a saint? 'e is *Montréalais* like me?"

I am about to add that he was illiterate like you, too. But I think better of it. I say instead, "The stadium's half empty."

"Yeah. 'ow come?" We are still whispering.

"Maybe the Habs had a home game that day."

" 'ave some respect, *ostie.*"

"I'm just saying." Then I add, "Pink Floyd sold out the stadium in 1977."

Thierry says nothing. Two days ago, he called my Palm Sunday cross an abomination. Yesterday, I was full of shit for trying to explain my thoughts about faith. Today, I'm an apostate for making a lame joke about Frère André's canonization.

"If it's any consolation, more than a million paid their respects back in 1937 when he died."

Before we leave, we visit the Votive Chapel adjacent to the Crypt Church. Thousands of candles: green, red, white. Earlier the basilica had been empty. It is busy here as people offer prayers for Paris. Thierry bums a toonie off me and scrambles away. He drops it with a clank in the box and lights a white votive candle.

"For Jean-Guy," he says. "Also Notre-Dame." He shrugs. "I still dun believe all dis superstitious bullshit. But it can't hurt, *hein?*"

He takes one last look at the hundreds of dark walnut-coloured crutches and canes that line the walls. Silent testament from those who'd found healing. In Paris, Notre-Dame is still smoldering. *Autour de nous, mille chandelles brillent en hommage silencieux.*

"I got shivers," Thierry whispers.

On the way out, at Thierry's suggestion, I buy a little book chronicling the life of Frère André.

"I'm a bit interested in dis lil guy an' all dem miracles."

Who's the superstitious one now?

Holy Wednesday

"Who paint dos pictures?"

"My daughter." I don't look up. I am studying irregular French verbs. I am trying hard to step up my game. I am pretty sure the woman next door, with the beautiful silver hair, is a francophone. If I get a chance to meet her maybe I can make a bit of conversation in French.

"She got talent."

"Uh huh."

"Mice dun look at de painting too much."

"Why is that?"

"Colour blind, man."

I look up.

"You see in black and white?" He's on the top of the sofa staring at a triptych that is among my favorites of my daughter's work.

"No. I can see some faint colour. But I dun see red. Whatever dat is. Also, I gotta be up close to see good."

"Well, those three have quite a subdued palette with very little red. So, you're probably not missing much."

He is sitting absolutely still.

"I tink I like things what are beautiful. I never knew dat before."

Perhaps our visit to L'Oratoire Saint-Joseph has stimulated Thierry's aesthetic sensibilities.

"Help me with these verbs and I'll take you to Le Musée des beaux-arts de Montréal tomorrow."

He stands and turns. "*Vraiment?*"

"We can go after my class. One condition. You help me with these verbs." I hold up my *Bescherelle*. He slumps.

"You know I kenna read."

"Frère André couldn't read before he became a monk."

He perks up. "*C'est vrai?*"

"Not until he was in his twenties. He was such a sickly kid he scarcely went to school. The brothers of his order taught him."

He nods. He's thinking. Is it possible Frère André has inspired him?

"You ken teach me?"

"*C'est ce que je fais.*"

He hops down from the sofa and joins me at the table.

"*D'accord.*" He stops. "But we not readin' no Bible."

"Hell no!"

Spence had been sober for nearly two months. He had just closed a show, *A Pair of Deuces*. It had been an equity co-op production. Everyone shared in the box office and everyone made a little money. Not much, but better than minimum wage, all things considered. At the age of twenty-seven, Spence was again in the position he found himself in most often as an actor. Between jobs.

Spence was friends with the author of *A Pair of Deuces* and had helped workshop the play. The lead role had been written with him in mind, but he got the job under the strict condition that he stay sober for the rehearsal period and for the run of the show.

Now the show was over. And now he wanted a drink.

That morning Spence had stopped by the theatre to pick up his final pay cheque. It was enough for him to meet his rent and to buy a few groceries. Next week, he would see about doing some bartending. Likely Dillinger's would hire him back.

It was December, three weeks before Christmas. Spence sat on a bench in the square across from Holy Rosary Cathedral, his hands in his coat pockets. A man was asleep on another bench nearby him. He was lying on some newspapers and had spread an old wool blanket over himself. Parked near his head was a shopping cart bursting with a heap of detritus—a sad parody of Santa's sleigh. A row of white plastic shopping bags hung off the cart like chicken carcasses in a butcher shop.

The bells in the cathedral began to toll. The man lying on the other bench growled "fuck off" and threw something in the direction of the sound. It was a plastic bag. Spence got up to leave. As he walked by the bag, he nudged it with the toe of his shoe. It was both soft and heavy, like a towel soaked in water.

"That's mine," the man said, lifting himself up on an elbow.

Spence shrugged. It was starting to rain. He walked across the street to the cathedral. Looking up he caught a glimpse of the bells in the tower. They appeared to be swinging in full circles. They were not musical, exactly, but neither were they discordant. There was some sort of blundering melody in progress.

Without really thinking about it, Spence mounted the steps to the cathedral and entered the vestibule. It was just a place to shelter from the weather. Idly he began to read the notices on the long cork bulletin board. They included an appeal for volunteer bellringers. Practices were Tuesday mornings. This morning.

Spence pushed through the heavy door into the cathedral. He had seldom crossed the threshold of a church—weddings mostly, sometimes for a concert. He found Catholic churches more unsettling than the Protestant sort. But he preferred the aesthetics of a Catholic church, what with the stained-glass windows, the luridly painted statues, the Stations of the Cross and everything dominated by a large crucifix looming above the altar. It was a little like entering an exultant torture chamber.

He stood in the back. The now muffled sound of the bells gradually settled and stopped. Some distance away, at the communion rail, there were two women kneeling in prayer. Spence saw them make the sign of the cross and stand. They left by a side door that gave out onto the alley from the transept. He heard the door slam shut. Spence was alone and, briefly, everything was hushed. A single candle flickered in a red lamp in front of the tabernacle, just to the left of the altar. Spence stared at it. After a moment, he was startled by a flash of movement on the floor near the pew to his left. Just a blur. Maybe a church mouse, he thought to himself and smiled. If there is such a thing.

And that is when it happened.

Spence could feel himself losing his balance and he reached out to grab the back of the pew on his right. He could feel he was touching the wood but it was as if his hand had entered into it. He wasn't touching it. He was connected. The sensation overwhelmed him. He could no longer feel a clear distinction between himself and everything that surrounded him. The floor, the walls, the pillars, the high arched ceiling—everything lost its density. They became his habitation and he became theirs and everything felt as though it were connected to the same weave of fabric suffused with a luminous flame. At first, he was intensely alarmed. Spence wondered if he was dying. But, after a moment, he was filled with such an irresistible sense of utter well-being that he didn't really mind. Because it didn't matter. Nothing mattered. No. That wasn't quite it. He had simply stopped judging things. Nothing had a category. Nothing was reduced to some purpose or to some definition. Everything just, ineffably, was.

Half an hour later, Father Desmond found him slouched in the pew at the very back of the nave, crying. Not crying in the usual sense. He was not making any noise. But his body was shaking and his tears flowed freely. The front of his shirt was wet. Desmond touched his arm. Spence turned and looked at him.

"I'm sorry," he said.

"It's okay," Father Desmond said.

"Thank you," Spence said.

And then he fell asleep.

For several weeks Spence spoke to no one except Father Desmond. He woke early, attended the 7:15 Mass and, rain or shine, he began walking. Mostly along the seawall circling Stanley Park. Sometimes he walked to Granville Island and then as far as Spanish Banks. Occasionally he would hike up to the university. He had been careful with the little bit of money he had set aside after *A Pair of Deuces*. Not spending anything on liquor helped, but he knew he would have to start working before the end of January. No theatre work seemed to be forthcoming and the only other thing he knew how to do was to tend bar.

"Did you used to drink on the job?" Father Desmond asked.

"Never. Well, almost never."

"Then just do the job and leave by the service entrance so you don't have to deal with walking past the bar at the end of your shift."

Spence nodded. They were sitting in Desmond's little office at the Catholic Centre. Spence had come to understand that Desmond, with his shoulder-length hair and his casual attire, was a bit of a curiosity in the Diocese. He was a Jesuit who had spent most of the seventies in El Salvador, learning Spanish and trying to make himself useful. But eventually the government there decided he had worn out his welcome and obliged him to return to Canada. It was rumoured that he was an old friend of the archbishop and had been given this tiny office and a free hand to do more or less as he pleased.

Desmond handed Spence a pamphlet.

"What's this? More prayers?" he asked.

Desmond had included a little booklet of short scriptural passages to accompany the rosary he had given Spence. He had suggested Spence attend Mass as often as possible. Spence interpreted that as every day.

"It's a list of all the AA meetings in the Lower Mainland. Times and places. I think you should go."

Spence turned the pamphlet over in his hands. He looked up at Desmond.

"I've decided I want to convert," he said.

"I think you should spend some time attending AA before you make that decision."

"I don't think I'll change my mind."

He looked at Desmond steadily.

"I don't think you will either. At first, I thought the experience you described to me might have been a psychotic episode. I no longer think that, particularly since it was so brief and has had such a positive outcome. I feel convinced you had a genuine mystical experience. You described a profound sense of unity with . . ." Desmond hesitated.

"Everything." Spence shrugged.

"Everything." Desmond nodded. "That is consistent with stories other people have shared with me. About their, um, experiences. My concern is that you seem to be an all-or-nothing sort of person, Spence. If you are capable of one extreme, then how can you be sure you are not capable of the opposite? The middle road is—"

"I used to have these dreams," Spence interrupted. "Lucid dreams. Do you know what those are?"

"That's when you are asleep and you are aware that you are dreaming?" Desmond looked at him quizzically. What had this to do with anything?

"Exactly. I can remember several things from when I was really just a baby. I remember the little yellow ducklings painted on the headboard of my wooden crib. I told my mother this, not long ago, but she didn't believe me. Then I told her about the little jagged lines I'd left on the wooden headboard from teething. She was pretty taken aback. I would have been six months. Maybe a year."

"Okay . . ." Desmond stood and opened the tiny window near his desk. He lit a cigarette. "That's a bit unusual but I'm not sure I understand."

"I also remember my umbilical cord. I liked touching it. I liked the way it smelled."

Desmond blew a stream of smoke toward the ceiling.

"I know that sounds improbable and a bit weird. Very weird. What I'm saying is I have some unusually strong memories from infancy. I may have been about two years old when I had my first lucid dream. I can remember the dream, but I can't really remember my age except that I was no longer sleeping in the crib with the yellow ducks. I remember floating above my bed. I stayed there for a while, near the ceiling. I was aware that I was floating. But I was also aware that I was sleeping, just below myself. Then I floated through the roof of the house. I could see the whole neighbourhood from above. I have a very clear image of that in my mind. I suppose I could have constructed that image later after, you know, repeatedly revisiting this memory. There was no hill, no vantage point near my house where I could have seen the neighbourhood from above. But I have a strong memory of that."

Desmond nodded. He cleared his throat as though he were going to say something. But he simply tapped his cigarette on the edge of the ashtray.

"I started to float up. Not flying. Though I did quite a bit of flying in later dreams. But this time I just floated. I knew I was dreaming, so I wasn't really afraid, at first. I was ascending so fast that I was approaching the stars. Then I remember being frightened by how many stars there were. I wouldn't have known the concept of infinity, back then. But I'm pretty sure infinity is what scared me. I became really quite alarmed. So, I closed my eyes and rolled over. I had the intense sensation of falling very fast. And then I woke up."

"I'm not sure—" Desmond began.

"The experience in the cathedral was a bit like that. Not the same, exactly. But when you are lucid dreaming, you are not really afraid. I mean, I experienced fear, but I knew that I couldn't really be hurt. Like in a scary movie. The difference in the cathedral, I suppose, is after a few moments I wasn't even afraid. I knew that whatever happened, no harm would come to me. And it was inconsequential whether I woke or not."

"I still don't see . . ." Desmond crushed his cigarette out in the ashtray.

"I have this regret." Spence was growing more animated. "I regret being afraid when I was a baby floating among those stars. Well, maybe not a baby. But no more than three. I've always felt that if I had just stayed calm then something immense would have happened and maybe my life would have been different. I would have seen everything differently. I'd have grown up with a different perspective."

Desmond leaned back in his chair and linked his hands behind his head. They were both quiet for a moment.

"Do you still have those dreams?"

"No. They stopped when I was ten or eleven. I don't really dream much, anymore. Or at least I don't remember my dreams. And I'm not saying my experience was like, you know, an angel appearing to Joseph or something. I just think I've been living my life and . . ." Spence looked down at his hands.

"And?"

"And not really paying attention."

Father Desmond nodded.

"And there is something about the Mass that makes me want to pay attention. And there is something about the Eucharist that is very . . . I don't know what. Very compelling and very ordinary at the same time. Like when I was a kid and everything ordinary seemed new and interesting. It's like I have a chance of becoming that person again. A person who knows when he is dreaming and when he is paying attention."

Desmond scribbled something on a notepad.

"All right. Here is what you do. Stop by the front desk and give them this note. Ask them to register you in the Rite of Christian Initiation Classes. They are Tuesday evenings, once a week. You're too late for the first session of the year. The second session starts sometime after Easter. But I really impress upon you how important it is to go to AA. Mystical experiences, dreams, all those sorts of things, those are gifts. But they won't keep you sober. The spiritual life involves a lot of very practical considerations. It's hard work. Do you remember the miracle of the loaves and fishes?"

"Yeah. The loaves and fish multiply and feed five thousand."

"The Gospels don't tell us the loaves multiplied. Only that a few loaves and fishes were offered and everyone ate their fill with plenty left over. Miracles aren't magic, Spence. We offer ourselves to God— our insufficient selves—and God takes our paltry lives and shapes them into something that can serve others. You understand?"

Spence nodded. He looked down at the note Desmond had given

him. It said, "Du Maurier King Size." Beside those words he had drawn a little heart. Spence looked up.

"Alice at the front desk knows where to get cigarettes cheap," Desmond explained.

"What? Like smuggled?"

Desmond shrugged.

"Nobody's perfect."

Jeudi saint. Lavement des pieds. Washing of the feet.

We take the 24 Sherbrooke. There is a bus stop directly across the street and our route takes us right by Le Musée des beaux-arts. At the entrance a young woman indicates the cloakroom.

"*C'est nécessaire?*" I ask.

"*Non. Mais c'est gratuit.*"

"*Merci, mais je préfère garder mon manteau.*"

"*Bien sûr.*"

A security guard glances over at me. For a moment I think maybe he's going to frisk me. As we pass into the museum another guard holds the door open. She has only to peer into the hood of my jacket to discover Thierry.

"Dun be so paranoid, brudder."

"They take security seriously here, Thierry." I try to talk like a ventriloquist, without moving my lips. At the elevators I discover the third and fourth floors are temporarily closed for maintenance. So much for the Middle Ages, Renaissance, Golden Age and the Enlightenment. We still have the Impressionists, the Romantics and the Modernists. I turn left toward the Impressionists Gallery. I can feel Thierry's whiskers next to my ear. Cézanne, Matisse, Monet . . .

"*Ces gars-là sont français, comme moi!*"

I try to imagine what he sees. Lots of blues and greens here. That's probably a good thing. I try to stand as close as possible without attracting a scolding from security. We pass a small bronze version of Rodin's *Le Penseur.* The Thinker.

"Dat guy havin' a dump?"

"Very funny." Sometimes Thierry has all the wit of a twelve-year-old. "We can go if you want."

"*Non, non.* I like dis. But de paintings is a bit fuzzy."

I cross the hall into the Academic Gallery. The aesthetic there tends more toward realism.

"What you mean by real, man?"

"I don't even know anymore."

One of the galleries has a lighting effect that makes the walls and ceiling seem like a forest moving in a breeze.

"Cool," he says.

We stand in front of Gabriel Max's "*La Résurrection de la fille de Jaïre.*" I can see Thierry is intrigued. The figure of Jesus is shrouded in darkness, his face turned away. Only his palm is in light. The girl's pale hand nestled there, also palm up. The gesture suggests vulnerability, as though an invisible nail has pierced both their hands and fastened them eternally together. Her sheets are white. Her skin pallid. A fly has settled on her forearm.

"*Talitha koum,*" I say softly.

"What dat mean?" Thierry is right next to my ear.

"Little girl, get up."

This is my favourite painting here. And I am intrigued by the sound of *talitha koum*. It is, I think, the only clear record in scripture where Jesus speaks in Aramaic. There is something tender in this instance that preserves what is certainly his mother tongue. Like half our world—and half of Montréal—Jesus was likely bilingual. Maybe trilingual.

While I am lost in my little reverie, Thierry has crawled behind my neck to get a better look at the painting to our left. "Street Child" by Fernand Pelez. A visual record of the cruelties of industrialization. A boy of ten, maybe, seated on the ground. He has rolled a cigarette from the discarded butt of some gentleman's cigar. His match is poised to light it. Dirty face. Dirty hands and feet. The dirt under his nails rendered lovingly but with no sentimentality.

"Mebbe when Jesus finish bringin' dat lil girl back to life 'e ken come 'ere an' wash dis lil kid feet. Dats 'ow 'e get 'is kicks, right?"

Part of me feels like grabbing Thierry and flinging him across the room. The other part is just weary. I am trying to understand his hostility toward Catholicism, but crass insinuations I can do without.

"We're going," I say.

"I'm stayin', *mon chum*." I am alarmed to feel Thierry crawl down the inside of my shirt, squeeze under my belt and into my boxers. He slides down one leg of my pants and perches for a moment on my shoe. I look down. He gives me a brief thumbs up and disappears through the tiny space between the wall and the floorboards.

Gone.

GOOD FRIDAY

7:00 am. No class today. I sit at the kitchen table. My coffee has gone cold. No sign of Thierry. I consider knocking on the door of the woman next door. Asking her if she has seen a mouse. So stupid. Yet, she reminds me of someone I used to know. Someone I could trust. Who?

Noon. Across the street, a single bell in the tower at St. Augustine's briefly tolls. I get dressed. Still no Thierry. The temperature has dipped below zero. Well into spring and it is snowing, softly but steadily.

I walk the two kilometers up to St. Joseph's Oratory. As I did on Tuesday with Thierry, I climb the one hundred wooden steps to the entrance. Halfway up I pass a woman on the stairs. She is old. Old without being elderly, exactly. A scarf over her head. She is climbing the stairs on her knees. I remember that Gabriel said he had climbed these stairs on his knees when he was a boy.

Once inside, I take the escalator to the basilica on the fourth level. I'm in a hurry. Inexplicably I imagine I might find Thierry there. Or maybe one floor down, venerating the heart of Frère André. Or in the Votive Chapel, lighting another candle for Jean-Guy. I don't know why I imagine this. I should be looking for him at Le Musée des beaux-arts. But they're closed for Good Friday.

Inside the basilica the altar has been stripped of candles, as is customary. Any ornamentation not carved or painted or nailed down has been removed. The door to the empty tabernacle is wide open. Above, the red candle indicating the presence of the sacrament is extinguished.

Silence.

I sit.

I leave.

Outside, the old woman is nearly at the top stair, still on her knees. There is a layer of snow on her back. Once she achieves the final step, I hold out my hand to help her stand. She takes my hand but doesn't look at me. The snow is swirling around us. She goes.

At the foot of the stairs a brown leaf flutters past my feet. For a moment I think it is a mouse. I wander for a while. When I get home, it is evening. Thierry is on the sofa smoking a joint. Next to him, an empty bottle of Don de Dieu.

"Hey man! It were so cool. I were settin' off de alarm all night in *le musée*. Only way to get de guards to turn de light on. Lucky fer me de No. 24 still gettin' tru dis snow. What de fuck, *hein?* Supposed to be spring, *ostie.*"

I go to my room and shut the door.

"So, Original Sin is Augustine's excuse for why he couldn't keep it in his pants when he was young?" Spence watched Tadla light another cigarette from the butt end of the one she had been smoking. Perhaps it was this custom of chain smoking that had given her voice the husky quality that was among several attributes that kept her in demand as an actor. There was, as well, her striking beauty. And though she was nearly the same age as Spence's mother, she possessed a spark of what used to be called glamour. Her brown eyes were so dark that they appeared almost black. When she was onstage, her gaze was so penetrating she was all anyone could look at.

"Augustine was always a bit obsessed with his 'little man'," she said, and her eyes flashed amusement when Spence blushed. "How could he, the great orator and intellectual, allow himself to be led about by his, let us call them, involuntary arousals? Why would God create such a passion if all it served was to lead people astray? His conclusion? This was a consequence of Original Sin. Had Adam and Eve not sinned, then their conjugal relationships would have been sober, reasoned occasions. Strictly for procreation. Like so many saints, Augustine sublimated his sexuality."

She took a long drag of the fresh cigarette poised between her jewelled fingers. Both her hands were bedecked with rings and her collection of silver bracelets jangled delicately when she moved. She set the spent stub of the other cigarette upright on the step behind her like a tiny guttering candle. There were already two others balanced there on their filters.

"You must become accustomed to paradox if you are to find anything in philosophy that might feed the spirit," Tadla said.

She and Spence had been sitting, talking on the steps leading into the theatre for nearly an hour. The day's rehearsals were done. *Righteousness* was scheduled to open in a little over a week. His contract stipulated "as cast." Spence was playing a variety of smaller roles, but the most significant was Adeodatus—the illegitimate son of Augustine of Hippo. It occurred to him that every role in his life, in or out of the theatre, had been as cast. While other people seemed to be born with a sense of their own destiny, Spence felt swept up by a stream of events over which he had no real control.

Tadla was playing Monica, Augustine's long-suffering mother. In the hands of a lesser actor, the character might have come off as a bit of a scold. And though Monica was a secondary role, Tadla's calm presence seemed to keep the whole sprawling mess of a play somehow grounded.

After last summer's tour of Saskatchewan, Spence had been invited to work for several weeks workshopping a new play based on the life of St. Augustine. By spring, the play was substantially finished and Spence was rehired for the premier production. He had spent the interval reading Augustine's book, *Confessions*. Perhaps "reading" was something of an exaggeration, because it was a bit of a slog to get through. The translation was in a somewhat elevated style that was intended to be reverent but was simply a bit tedious. Spence had skimmed rather a lot, pausing to puzzle through the passages that caught his attention.

He shifted his position on the steps. By now the sun was partly obscured by a grove of trees in the little park across the street. He sat back down in the patch of sunlight that remained. Tadla moved a little closer to him to stay in the warmth, as well. Normally at this time of day, Spence would be in The Kettle, the local watering hole frequented by the actors. But he was flattered that Tadla had expressed an interest in his questions and seemed to take him seriously. She reached out and touched Spence's hand for a moment.

"Where is your little paperback *Confessions*?"

Spence rummaged through his canvas shoulder bag and produced the copy he had found, months ago, in a used bookstore. Tadla took it from him and flipped through the pages. She read: "So was I speaking and weeping in the most bitter contrition of my heart, when, lo! I heard from a neighbouring house a voice, as of boy or girl, I know not, chanting, and oft repeating, 'Take up and read; Take up and read'."

Tadla tapped the page with the tip of her fingernail as if to emphasize a point.

"This comes at the climax of the first act of the play. He hears the children's voices and opens his Bible at random. I think there is even a word for that. Bibliomancy." She looked at Spence and her eyes crinkled with mischief. She continued reading: "I seized, opened, and in silence read that section on which my eyes first fell: Not in rioting and drunkenness, not in chambering and wantonness, not in strife and envying; but put ye on the Lord Jesus Christ, and make not provision for the flesh, in concupiscence."

"A bit corny," Spence said.

"Yes. But it is the story everyone tells because it marks the moment of his conversion. She flipped ahead in the book and read: "She and I stood alone—"

"Who are we talking about?" Spence asked.

"Augustine and his mother, Monica."

She continued reading: "'We were discoursing then together, alone, very sweetly. And when our discourse was brought to that point, that the very highest delights of the earthly senses were not worthy of comparison, we did by degrees pass through all things bodily, even the very heaven whence sun and moon and stars shine upon the earth; yea, we were soaring higher yet. Where life is the Wisdom by whom all these things are made, and what have been, and what shall be, and she is not made, but is, as she hath been, and so shall she be ever...' and so on at ecstatic length."

She closed the book and tapped Spence playfully on the head with it.

"Wisdom is always depicted as a woman, you may wish to note," she said.

Spence nodded.

"A little bit Oedipal don't you think?" she added. "This mother and son mystical experience? Freud should have written about this. Interesting that two foolish men, obsessed with their mothers, could have such a profound influence on Western culture."

"I had a very similar experience," Spence said. He looked at Tadla earnestly.

"You and your mother were close?" Tadla teased.

"No. That 'passing through things bodily' and 'soaring higher'. All that stuff about the sun and the moon and the stars. That happened to me when I was a little kid. In a dream."

As Spence told her about his curious recollections and lucid dreaming, Tadla listened intently. Spence could feel her dark eyes searching his own.

"I think I will buy you dinner tonight, Lyle Spencer," she said. "You are an interesting young man. You can tell me more about those strange, childhood dreams of yours."

She stood and stretched extravagantly. Spence watched the curve of her small breasts rise and settle again like a pair of kittens yawning in their sleep. She stooped and plucked the little collection of cigarette butts from the step behind her. Taking Spence by the hand, she placed them in his palm.

"Be a dear and put these somewhere safe," she said.

Spence could feel a growing infatuation with Tadla. Had she instructed him to swallow her discarded cigarette ends, he might have done so. He walked up to the entrance of the theatre and dropped then into the sand of the ashtray just inside the glass doors. He joined Tadla on the sidewalk and stood facing her. He was nearly a head taller. She reached up and with two fingers she brushed his hair off of his forehead. Spence wondered if she were bestowing some sort of blessing on him.

"No drinking," she said. "Tonight, you will be like St. Augustine and you will give up 'rioting and drunkenness'. But a little 'chambering and wantonness' might do you some good."

And so Spence became Tadla's lover for the duration of *Righteousness*. Because of their age difference, the rest of the cast did not guess their relationship. It was their little secret and keeping it made Spence's ardour more keen. He did not mind one bit that he was, in every sense, her pupil and she his mentor. Tadla was enormously well-read and Spence was not sure which he relished more, making love or listening to her talk of science, philosophy and religion. Once the play had opened, they could lie in bed until noon. Sometimes she would play her little nylon-string guitar and sing to him.

"What language is that?' he asked.

"Tamazight," she said, setting her guitar beside the bed. "It is one of the languages of the Berbers."

"I don't know anything about Berbers," he said. Spence was lying on his side, naked. She slapped his bare buttocks.

"Foolish boy!" she said, playfully. "Augustine was a Berber. Monica is a Berber name. Tadla is a Berber name."

"Tadla." He said her name as if it were a sweet he was rolling round on his tongue. She kissed him.

"What does Tadla mean?"

"What does Lyle mean?" she countered.

"Island, I think. Like the French, isle."

"Tadla means branches. Now I understand. You are a lonely island and I have gathered you in my branches."

"Sing me another song," Spence said.

"Make love to me first."

Over the course of a month, Spence had not once had a drink. Tadla had told him that she did not want to see him if he had been drinking. And though staying sober caused him some anxiety, Spence was more than intoxicated with Tadla. Her beauty. Her searing intelligence. Her passion. But mostly her kindness. Spence did not mind that he had, perhaps, been used. Even if that were true, he had been used gently. In just a month, Spence felt she had made him a better man than when she had found him.

Tadla seemed delighted that Spence had tears in his eyes when they parted.

"Oh wonderful son, that can so astonish a mother," she laughed and kissed him a final time.

"Hamlet," Spence said.

"Well done, my prince. May flights of angels . . ." she caressed his cheek.

On the plane home to Vancouver, Spence ordered only one beer. Then he fell into a deep sleep.

Tadla. She reminds me of Tadla. The woman next door. She's a little older but has the same ageless beauty. I am sixty-two. Tadla must have been what? Nearly fifty when we met. I have scarcely visited my Facebook page for the last couple of years. Maybe I can find her. I take out my phone and realize that was more than thirty years ago. Thirty-five. She would be eighty. About my mother's age.

I should call my mother. I haven't spoken to her since Christmas. No, not true. She called me in February, on my birthday. I sit staring at my cell phone. Instead of calling my mother, I tap the photo icon.

Father Mallory Parent OSM 1968–69.

I open my laptop and type. To my astonishment I am led to something called Cynthia's Blog, a site chronicling cases of sexual abuse within the Catholic Church in Canada:

Father Mallory Parent OSM. Priest, member of the Servites de Marie. Ordained 1941. Sexually abused three brothers ages 11, 10 and 8.

There is a photo. An old man: thinning lips, sagging skin where his neck meets his clerical collar, the right eye strange, as though he'd gone blind in that eye. I scroll down, skimming the dates.

1967 Chaplain, Belmont Park, Galiano Crescent, Victoria, B.C.

I still remember our old address and phone number: 620 Galiano Crescent, Granite 8-6848

1968–69 St. Raymond Roman Catholic Church, St. Jacques St., Montreal, Q.C.

The Church next to Clara's apartment building. The church with the photo.

21 December 2011: Died, age 94, at Francicsan Infirmary, Montreal, Q.C.

I scroll further down. There is a newspaper article. I read:

It has been more than 20 years but it is no wonder that

Michael Simard will still not step across the threshold of a Roman Catholic Church. As an 11-year-old altar boy in the late 1970s, he was, on countless occasions, sexually abused by a priest named Mallory Parent. Michael's brothers confirm that they, too, were abused.

I would have been in my early twenties in the late seventies.

In 1997, Parent was charged with a number of sexual offences involving the boys. He pleaded guilty to some of those charges and was sentenced to four concurrent six-month terms. Normally, our editorial policy forbids us from identifying those who have been sexually abused, but the Simard brothers say the public should be aware. It has been a long time and a difficult process, but Michael says they've come to terms with the past. "This is part of the healing process," he adds.

In 1997, I was in my first year at Queen of All Saints.

Police were informed of the abuse in 1978. Shortly afterward, Church authorities transferred Parent and no further action was taken. It wasn't until 1997, after the brothers once more told their story to police, that charges were laid.

I close the laptop. I can't read anymore. I can feel my heart racing. I'm shaking.

I try to piece together the past. As a child, all the adults I knew seemed unpredictable. And certainly, their motives were entirely inscrutable. For me, childhood had seemed a kind of chaos where you never knew if you were going to suffer a thorough thrashing from your father's belt or be handed ice cream on a stick.

LATER . . .

"So tomorrow de big day, *hein? La résurrection. La magie et le mystère?*"

I am washing the dishes.

"The Resurrection is not magic." I glance at Thierry's wavering reflection in the window. "I resurrected you, didn't I?"

"*Quoi?*"

"That safe in Nick's office could have been your tomb."

"*Touché.*"

I turn to look at him briefly. *Touché* doesn't really sound like something Thierry would say. It sounds like something *I* would say.

"*Le lapin de Pâques* find de empty tomb?"

I can't quite remember the meaning of *lapin*, but guess it means rabbit. I set a plate on the drying rack.

"*La Vierge Marie dépose des œufs de Pâques dans la crèche?*"

"*Fais attention, Thierry.*" I set down a glass. I have a real affection for Our Blessed Lady and I don't feel kindly disposed toward Thierry having her distributing Easter eggs in a stable.

"All de angels have de orgy in heaven tomorrow?"

I turn away from the sink and give him a hard look. He is sitting on the table playing solitaire with a ragged deck of cards. He meets my gaze.

"Okay. Okay. M'bad. So, you been to confession?"

I take a deep breath.

"Things change, Thierry. These days, we rarely or never go to confession."

I had never really gotten anything out of confession. So many minor lapses that any sensible person could forgive themselves. And for one's serious failings? The absolution. The ten Hail Marys and an Our Father. It was childish. And for me, it never seemed to help. I could always find ways to continue to punish myself.

"Well, it is Hell for you, brudder," Thierry laughs.

A part of me wants to give him a good slap. But he isn't wrong. How many cringeworthy occasions had I heard some priest remind the congregation that Holy Communion was for those in a "state of grace"—as if the eucharist were a reward reserved for the nice, and the naughty could go hungry?

"Besides, Thierry," I add, "I am unlikely to go alone into a closet with a priest."

"*Pourquoi? Un prêtre pervers* pinch yer little dick when you were a kid?"

He laughs again. Then he ducks. A coffee cup smashes against the wall behind him. It takes a moment before I realize I have thrown it.

"*Tabarnac de fuckin' crisse!* You could o' . . ."

A long silence.

"Hey, *mon chum*," he says.

I am leaning over the sink. I watch my tears falling into the dishwater.

"Were it something I said?"

DAD

Spence was in a dreary motel room in Dundurn, Saskatchewan when he got the news of his father's death. He was touring with a children's theatre company, performing in schools around the province: two short plays in the morning for primary and intermediate students, Tennessee Williams in the afternoon for secondary students. Monday to Friday, on the road on Saturdays. Sundays off. Despite the monotony and the numbing cold, Spence was grateful for the opportunity.

It was the stage manager, Teresa, who gave him the news. When Spence opened the door, he was surprised to see she had already changed into her pajamas though it was not yet six in the evening. It was late January. The sun had disappeared. She had slipped on her snow boots and parka over her pajamas. When she spoke, her words hung in the air like a little cloud of dread.

Teresa was kind. The news she had was already more than a week old because it had taken several days before Spence's mother was contacted and several more before she could recall what theatre company Spence was touring with. Teresa offered to cancel the next day's performances but she seemed almost relieved when he shook his head no. The show must go on.

The last time he'd seen his father was at the Red Lion, a faux-English-style bar in Victoria, shortly before Spence graduated university. Two years ago. His father's trips to Victoria were few. According to Spence's mother, he was now shacked up with some woman in Abbotsford. "God knows what he is doing for money."

They drank rye and gingers for several hours. Spence was thankful for the cover band on the pub's little stage that rotated through a repertoire of mostly CCR tunes mixed with some Eagles. It meant they didn't have to talk. At one point, his father turned and shouted, "Johnny Cash," and they obligingly went into their rendition of "Fulsom Prison Blues." Halfway into the song, Spence's father got up and weaved his way to the washroom. When he got back, the band was on a break and he sat back down heavily into his chair.

"What are you doing after?" he asked.

"Actually, I have rehearsal in the morning."

"No, I mean after you graduate."

A waiter passed and Spence's father leaned back and gestured for two more.

"I suppose I'll start auditioning. I'm moving to Vancouver this summer."

Spence's father nodded with an exaggerated gravity, as though he were turning over some serious question in his mind.

"Why not LA? Hollywood?"

The waiter arrived with two more rye and gingers on his tray. Spence's father made a great show of searching for his wallet. Once he produced it, he spent another few moments fumbling through the several folds. The waiter gave Spence a dubious look.

"I got this, Dad."

Spence paid and they both drained what was left in their glasses. There were four empties in front of them. The waiter dropped Spence's change on the table and plucked up all four with his fingers, like a bowler. He nodded a grudging thanks when Spence folded a dollar bill and slipped it onto his tray.

"He should check his fucking attitude," his father remarked when he'd gone.

Gordon Spencer was in his early fifties but he looked older. Years of hard drinking had exacted a price. A couple years earlier, he'd been diagnosed with prostate cancer. It was unusually aggressive, and unexpected in a man his age. The medication he was taking suppressed the production of testosterone. Spence noticed that the usually lush bed of black hair on his father's forearms had completely disappeared.

"I think I'd rather stay in Canada, Dad," he said, observing his father closely. Spence could see his father had reached the point of drunkenness where he could be a little unpredictable. But the medication seemed to mellow his mercurial moods. A decade earlier, Spence would never have contradicted him.

"How's your mother?" his father asked suddenly.

Shortly after Spence left home, his parents separated. His mother rarely had a drink, his father was rarely without one. The last few times Spence and his dad had met, it was always over drinks and on each occasion his father appeared increasingly maudlin, sometimes even tearful. These episodes made Spence uncomfortable. He had no experience of his father expressing any emotions beyond a kind of amused joviality that could easily turn into rage. He was the kind of man who burned with a low, seething anger that made living with him like living on the slopes of a volcano.

"Mom's fine. I saw her at Christmas, after I saw you. Babs, too."

The band was reassembling on the little stage. Spence's father shouted "Johnny Cash" again. He saw their waiter shake his head and say something to the bartender, who nodded.

They stayed until closing time. When his father drove him back to the ramshackle bungalow on Fern Avenue that Spence shared with a group of fellow students, Spence did not invite him in, even though he suspected his dad might pass the night asleep in his car. They shook hands while seated in the front seat of the old Vauxhall Viva that was still, miraculously, clinging to life. Spence got out and walked around to the driver's side. His father rolled down the window. He had turned the radio on as Spence was climbing out and said something over the music.

"What?" Spence turned.

"I love you, son."

His father looked away and reached up to adjust the rear-view mirror.

"I love you, too, Dad," Spence said and tapped the roof of the car a couple times as a final send off. The grinding of gears and the car lurched away. He stood in the street and watched the taillights disappear up and over the steep hill a few blocks down the avenue. It was the first and only time Spence heard his father say, "I love you."

A part of him was glad that they had finally spoken the words they had always carefully manoeuvred around. And part of him wanted to throw a stone at the car as it climbed the hill and slipped from view. What do you do when the gift you wanted on your third birthday arrives when you are twenty-three and have given up on it? Getting what you always hoped for never seems to be exactly what you expected.

Spence called his mother from his Saskatchewan motel room. She seemed philosophical about it all and said she was grateful that no one else had been hurt in the car accident that had killed her husband. Though separated, they were not legally divorced. Spence's father had fallen asleep at the wheel. Drunk. His twenty-year-old Vauxhall Viva had flipped three times and had come to rest on its crushed roof at the side of the highway.

"It's a wonder he and that ridiculous car both lasted this long."

Spence's father was cremated and his mother kept his ashes in a squat, bronze urn on a side table next to the hall closet for several months. Spence's mother would give the lid a little pat as she came and went. Her unruly husband was finally tamed and sleeping it off for eternity.

For a time, Spence carefully monitored his own drinking, resolving to stick to beer to better control his intake. Even so, for the remainder of the tour he kept to his usual pattern. Drunk one evening. Hungover the next morning. The following evening, just enough to take the edge off. Next morning restored and sufficiently recovered to get drunk again that evening. The ebb and flow of hangovers was like having a perpetual flu that came and went every second day.

His father's son.

Easter Sunday

Thierry went to Easter Mass at St. Monica's with me this morning. Moral support. He mostly stayed in my coat pocket. I had to wake him up three times. He was snoring.

"Eleven o'clock is preddy late for a mouse. Also—no offence—preddy borin'. I tawt dat priest never gonna shut up."

I am frying up bacon and eggs for breakfast. Thierry lights a joint and passes it to me.

"Mind you, when dem Eritreans was singin' wid dem drums. Dat were preddy cool." Thierry is talking about a small Eritrean community that have attached itself to St. Monica's ever since the parish sponsored a family of refugees who were fleeing political persecution.

A pause.

"So. You wanna talk about it?"

I take a second drag and shake my head.

Pas encore, I think to myself. He yawns and after a while he begins nodding off. A notification from my phone briefly wakes him. He looks around bewildered and falls asleep again. It is a message from Clara. It must be early evening in France.

Happy Easter! I love you, Daddy!

Happy Easter! I love you, too!

And our Easters *had* been happy occasions for her. Even before she was old enough to read, I would hide Easter eggs in little clusters and leave a note with each. We would read them together. They were simple riddles written in rhyme that provided hints about where to find the next collection of eggs: "You can find me on the wall, who's the fairest of them all?"

She told me, years later, those were among her happiest memories. A bit of chocolate and some silly rhymes.

Miss you!

Miss you, too!

More tears.

THE ROMANIAN

The cast had come downtown to party after the closing performance of *Love's Labours Lost*. Spence had played Longaville and had understudied the part of Berowne. The male lead had been performed by an alumnus—now a professional—who had been hired through some sort of special grant. Spence was not impressed since he knew the experienced actor's dialogue more thoroughly and, on several occasions, he'd had to bail him out in performance by feeding him a line. It was Spence's habit to memorize all the lines of every scene in which he appeared. It reassured him, as if he could only experience risk if he knew he, ultimately, had a certain control.

Spence's second year of university had been even more chaotic than his first. He had applied late for a student loan and had spent much of September picking up shifts at the bookstore until it was finally processed. He longed to quit his other menial job, washing dishes at Little Caesar's where the eternal damp of steam and spray enveloped him in a rancid cloud of sour tomato sauce and garlic.

When his loan and bursary finally arrived, it was less than what he had applied for but enough to release him from drudgery. Spence was free. With renewed energy, he threw himself into his studies. Theatre had become a sort of temple where he could pay homage to the muses. No sacrifice seemed too great if only he could be a part of this ancient tradition. The cruel tragedies of classical Greece. The frenetic plots of Commedia dell'arte. Hamlet's searing intelligence; Lear, naked and mad, flailing at the storm. Burbage, Kean, Irving, Olivier. Spence burned to feel a part of it all.

But beneath this exhilaration, he was a seething mess of impulses that he could not understand. His limited budget, to some extent, restrained his drinking. But without this daily solace he found it difficult to sleep and sometimes went for days with only intermittent naps. He was constantly on edge, given to sudden flashes of anger followed by bouts of contrition. But his mercurial temperament was coupled with considerable raw talent and Spence found himself constantly in demand for plays or scene studies or someone's experimental hybrid of forms.

Whenever there was some little respite in these near constant endeavours, Spence would get drunk. Afterwards he might do little but sleep for days until the whole relentless cycle began again. And in the midst of it all. During his periodic bouts of drunkenness, Spence allowed himself to be drawn into a number of encounters that left him with a jumble of emotions, lashed by both lust and self-loathing.

Always older men.

Spence met him near the outskirts of Chinatown. He was drunk and had become separated from his friends.

"Are you lost, young man?"

Spence looked up at this stranger. There was something familiar about him. Not so much his appearance. It was his gaze. Almost amusement. As though he understood something. Was there some chalk mark, some symbol scrawled on Spence's face that only certain men were able to detect? Spence seemed to wear a target under his skin that, when drunk, emerged like a faintly glowing tattoo: This boy is vulnerable.

"Are you lost, young man?" Spence repeated the words back to the stranger in a passable imitation of his accent. "Not quite Italian and not quite Russian," he added.

"Well done," the man smiled. He had several gold teeth and Spence could not decide if this were an affectation or if it were simply some custom about which he knew nothing.

"Some people say that Romanian is like hearing a Serb speak Italian. You have a good ear."

"Romanian. Are you a vampire then?" Spence said. He was feeling reckless.

"That is a regrettable stereotype," the man pouted a little, as though his feelings were wounded. "I live near here. Would you enjoy a drink? I promise I will not suck your blood."

Though Spence knew where this exchange was leading, he pretended to himself that he did not. On other occasions he had told himself that he was an actor now, open to all experiences for the sake of the art. But mostly, he just tried not to think about it. It was not even that he was allowing himself to be seduced. It was not desire. It was a compulsion that went against his natural inclination. It was submission to something he did not want but felt helpless to resist.

The sex was always the same. Spence didn't even have to do anything. A quick blowjob from some older man. They never even removed their clothes. A professor who had expressed admiration for the poems Spence had written for Creative Writing 210. A stranger in an alley where Spence had, drunkenly, paused to pee. The well-known Stratford actor who had delivered a guest lecture and then consented to join a few enthusiastic students for a drink in the SUB. Tonight, this Romanian, with his urbane smile and gold teeth.

Spence was not a child. But in every instance, the men were some twenty or thirty years his senior. And to their credit, they seemed content to simply enjoy observing Spence submit to their attentions. Maybe the satisfaction of successfully seducing drunken straight boys was fulfilment enough. Perhaps there was some sporting code that Spence was unaware of that stipulated catch and release: small fry must be tossed back, unharmed, into the sea. In Spence's case, despite the inappropriate age difference, they behaved like gentlemen, one and all. He believed he had no one to blame but himself and even fretted, a little, that it was he who had led them on.

The sun had just begun to rise as Spence trudged home. He was not cheered by the sound of birdsong emerging from the branches above him along the street. Nor by the pink petals that drifted down from the cherry trees and lay heaped against the curb like confetti on the steps of a church. He had the wherewithal to pause over a storm drain before throwing up. Standing hunched over for some minutes, his hands on his knees, he prayed that the sick heaves that produced almost nothing would finally stop.

Please let me die.

This was as close to a prayer as Spence had ever come in his life. But to whom was he praying? He stood up straight at last.

There had been something familiar about the Romanian. His cologne, perhaps. Or the incense he had set to smoldering after they had arrived at his apartment. Or maybe the odour of some old-fashioned hair pomade. Camphor? The sun rose behind him and Spence followed his own long shadow toward home.

It was then it occurred to him.

Father . . . what was his name? Something French. Parent?

Spence had scarcely given the priest a thought for years. But as the day began to warm and the dazzling light of dawn flooded the tree-lined boulevard, it occurred to Spence that, without being consciously aware, he had been repeating a decade-old experience he had been too young to comprehend. He stopped walking and took a few deep breaths to suppress a renewed urge to vomit.

Was it all as simple as that? It seemed ridiculous. Nothing had happened, really. Spence had trouble recalling exactly what had transpired between him and Parent. Just some stupid games. Nothing more. Like wrestling. Like a father teaching his son to wrestle.

A series of blurred images came into his mind. An old-fashioned bottle of coke and a glass of ice. Colourful fish swimming in an aquarium.

There were some daffodils in a nearby garden.

"Yellow ducklings." Spence said this aloud and wondered why. An odd sensation overcame him and he pondered, for a moment, if he were actually inside of a dream that he could not escape. He experienced a strange urge to leave his own body behind. Spence leaned over and put his lips to one of the daffodils as though it were the mouthpiece of an old-fashioned telephone.

Hello. Hello.

As though he were a character in his own play, Spence absorbed these insights. If that is what they were. In any event, they were enough to help him understand that his drunken encounters with older men were not erotic attraction, but compulsion. As though he had been knocking on the bedroom door to his own memory and calling.

Wake up. Wake up.

EASTER MONDAY

The Easter Octave refers to Easter Sunday and the following seven days, ending on what used to be called Quasimodo Sunday but is now referred to as Divine Mercy Sunday. In music, an octave is an interval of eight notes in the major scale: do ri mi fa sol la ti do. These aren't random sounds. They come from *Ut Queant Laxis*. "Sounds like a wet fart to me," Thierry remarked, when I explain that it is a well-known medieval hymn. The do ri mi scale markings were created by a Benedictine monk named Guido d'Arrezo early in the eleventh century.

Quasimodo. Guido d'Arrezzo. I like saying those words. They've got music. An octave might also describe the number of days left in my French classes before I complete *niveau six*: eight days remaining. I decide to quit.

The majority of the students at my school are sponsored by Emploi-Québec. For many, their employment benefits will run out when they finish this class. After six months, most of them speak and understand French about as well as I. Hardly at all. Most will have difficulty finding work in Montréal if they are not bilingual. And for some reason I feel responsible. I mean, I know I'm not responsible for what other people experience. But somehow, I think it is my responsibility to *do* something to ease their suffering. Maybe "suffering" is the wrong word. Anxiety. Frustration. Envy. Impatience. Hostility. Boredom. Fear. I am sure my own students experienced similar feelings.

Sometimes.

Often.

Most of the time.

But as a teacher, at least I had some things I could do to help. I could, as JF advised me, love them. But as a fellow *étudiant* with these younger students in their twenties and thirties, no one needs me. I am not certain anyone really sees me. I am just the old guy.

The old guy who sits in the corner: Invisible. Dispensable. Incapable. *Le vieil homme. Le même en français: Invisible. Dispensable. Incapable.*

MARDI, OCTAVE DE PÂQUES
Lacune. Gap.

MERCREDI, OCTAVE DE PÂQUES
Lacune

JEUDI, OCTAVE DE PÂQUES
Lacune

VENDREDI, OCTAVE DE PÂQUES
Lacune

SAMEDI, OCTAVE DE PÂQUES
Lacune

DIMANCHE DE LA DIVINE MISÉRICORDE

I open my eyes. Above me the ceiling is spinning. It takes me a long time to realize I am in my own bedroom. I am thirsty. Everything hurts. I roll over onto my side.

"Please let me die," I mutter.

"No chance o' dat, brudder. You is too stubborn."

Thierry is sitting in my doorway, balanced on his tail, exactly as he was the first time that I saw him. Except for the hat. *Déjà vu.*

"What happened?" I sit up, think better of it and lie back down.

"What happen? You been on a bender. Dat what happen."

"Thirty-four years. Nearly thirty-five. Sober thirty-five years." I groan.

Thierry takes off his hat and scratches an ear with his hind foot.

"*Un jour à la fois.*"

"*Tais-toi.*"

"You remember anything?"

"I hope not,"

I have a vague memory of a hotel bar called Les Soeurs de la Miséricorde. The Sisters of Mercy. I recall (thanks to a Medieval Studies course taken as a lark in the fourth year of my degree) that in English "misericord" has several meanings, including a long narrow blade that a comrade-in-arms might use to dispatch a mortally wounded knight on the battlefield. A mercy I can relate to just now.

I go into the bathroom and search under the sink. All my share of the heist is gone: $2,950 of ill-gotten gains squandered. It appears I am not the man who buried his master's talent. I am the Prodigal Son. I make my way back to bed, my hand on the wall for support.

"I used to get de black out, *mon chum. Je comprends.*"

"Please get me some Tylenol. Or Advil. Both. Just bring the bottles."

"*Pas de problème. Tu veux une bière?*"

"*Non. Un café, s'il te plaît.*"

"Comin' up."

"*Merci.*"

LUNDI

Il pleut.

Noises in the corridor. I look out the peephole, hoping I might catch a glimpse of my silver-haired neighbour. It's the guy who used to live next door. He is in the hallway, carrying a box. I open the door. The guy puts down the box and says something in rapid French that I can't understand. I take a few steps back. I'm not sure what a mouse-murdering ex-neighbour ought to look like. But if I were casting a play, it wouldn't be this guy. I suppose I had seen him a couple of times without really registering him. He is about my age and as nondescript as a paper lunch bag. A no one, really. For Thierry's sake, I wish I could hate him a little. Instead, I mumble my apologies.

"*Je suis désolé. Je suis juste . . .*"

I am just what? I'm not even sure why I'm apologizing. I am a little surprised when he gestures to something on the floor between my feet. I look down. It is a dime. Picking it up, I realize that it is the 1957 silver dime that Thierry had left on the threshold of my bedroom weeks ago. It could have fallen out of my pocket, I suppose. When I reached for my keys, maybe?

"May I?" he says in English. He has an unusual accent. Not quite French. I pass the coin to him and he examines it. He nods and raises his eyebrows, making a kind of exaggerated grimace. Maybe the date surprises him. As he hands it back, I realize I am wearing only a pair of pajama bottoms and a T-shirt.

"*Je suis désolé,*" I say again as I start backing in through my own door. He reaches out his hand to shake mine. I hesitate for a moment, then take it. He shakes my hand in one quick motion, the way you might flick your hand to shake off some water. Without a word he picks up his box and goes to the elevator.

I am strangely disconcerted by the whole encounter, as though I may have dreamed it. Truthfully, recovering from my little bender, it almost feels as though I am trapped in a dream and can't awaken.

I won't mention this to Thierry.

Mardi

The last day of April.

"Something weird goin' on in de parkin' garage."

Thierry is on the kitchen counter having a bath. His first, as far as I am aware. He is reclining in a wide mouth coffee cup. The sort you might use for a latte. The soapy water splashes over the lip of the cup and into the saucer as I add a little more hot water from the kettle.

"Take it easy, brudder! I jes wanna bath not a scuba lesson."

I hand him a Q-Tip and he uses it to scrub his back.

"All right. What's happening in the garage?"

"Nick change all dem shitty *lumières fluorescentes*. It so bright down dere now I gotta squint to see anything." He briefly disappears below the surface and spits a little fountain of water as he re-emerges.

"Why would he do that?"

Thierry gathers an armful of soap suds and fashions himself a snowy beard. "Regarde! Je suis le Père Noël."

"*Thierry. Pourquoi il a fait ça?*"

"*Sais pas.* Mebbe he gonna clean up down dere." He climbs out of the coffee cup. I'm a little surprised when he gives himself a vigorous shake, like a puppy, releasing a fine spray into the air.

"Use the towel, Thierry." I hand him a facecloth.

"Hey. You got some cologne? Big date tonight."

I drain the coffee cup into the sink and pour a few drops of vanilla extract onto the saucer.

"Try that."

"*Qu'est-ce que c'est?*"

"*Eau de boulangerie.*"

He dabs a little behind his ears then runs his fingers through his whiskers.

"Okay. *À tantôt!*" He disappears into the cutlery drawer. A moment later the bottom cupboard swings open. Thierry stands between a bag of oatmeal and another of rice.

"*Où est mon chapeau?*"

I hand him his pork pie hat and the cupboard slams shut. A muffled *bonne soirée!* and he's gone. Grabbing the half empty bag from the garbage bin, I head down to the parking garage. I need to see this for myself.

Thierry was right. All the fluorescents have been replaced. A cold, relentless light has transformed the garage. What was once a gloomy, mysterious den is now a stark, cheerless bunker. I lower the bag into the large garbage bin and quietly close the lid. I can see Nick's Subaru parked in the farthest corner. In this harsh illumination it is easy enough for me to see the two men deep in conversation. They do not notice me. Behind the wheel is Nick. In the passenger seat, a man who seems vaguely familiar. He is bald—with jet black eyebrows. Behind them in the back seat, a flash of silver hair.

ELLIE

"I love you, Spence."

Ellie was among a handful of people who called him Spence rather than Lyle. After classes, outside the rehearsal hall while waiting for him to walk her home, she had heard the other kids in the school play call him that. So, the boy who had been Lyle adopted the name and rechristened himself Spence. He couldn't remember the last time anyone had spoken the words "I love you." Certainly, his father never uttered them. His mother? She must have. Sometime. But he was Spence, now. And he was loved by a girl named Ellie.

By Grade 12, Spence had left home, as his brother had done the year before. Neither he nor Ian could manage to survive both the demands of high school and the increasingly erratic behaviour of their father. Spence had two part-time jobs on the weekends and struck out on his own. His apartment was a cramped attic above a garage, accessible only by the fire escape. A beaded curtain replaced the door to the bathroom and he had to duck to access his little collection of vinyl records and books assembled where the sloping ceiling met the wall. His gas guzzling Pontiac Parisienne, as long as a sloop and with an odometer that was only a couple hundred miles from rolling over, was parked outside. The capacious back seat was almost as wide as Spence's bed. It was there, and in his attic apartment, that Spence's fumbling affections with Ellie grew more impassioned.

"I love you. I love you. I love you."

She met his eyes briefly then closed hers again. It had always been this way between them. A willingness, but always coupled with the subtle stipulation that she was somehow acquiescing to him. As though to completely surrender to her own desire would be improper. "I love you" always seemed to be some desperate permission Ellie gave herself in order to experience what she desired but could not acknowledge. And, for Spence, he felt a twinge of guilt.

Not so much for his lack of mastery as a lover. It was something else. He could not quite fathom his own confused feelings. Why did he always feel he must reach out and wrap the darkness around him like a fistful of fig leaves?

"What are you going to study at university?" Ellie asked one Friday evening. The comfortable bench seat of Spence's Parisienne was upholstered with some sort of faux leather and Ellie always slid right up next to him while he drove. His arm was around her.

"English, maybe. Or theatre. I'm not sure," Spence said. He had given it some thought and was leaning toward theatre. Maybe even movies. But that seemed like some near-impossible fantasy. It was as though he did not really recognize that he had choices. His brother, the first Spencer to ever attend university, was nearly finished his first year at the University of Victoria.

"Theatre is more of a hobby, isn't it?"

Her head had been leaning on his shoulder. Now she lifted it and looked at him earnestly. Spence glanced at her face in the rear-view mirror.

"Okay." He shrugged. "Maybe English, then. I could be a writer. I like writing. I could even write plays." Spence was slightly annoyed that he so often found himself subtly adjusting his own expectations in order to keep the peace in their relationship. He stopped at the intersection just before the turnoff leading to her place. He kissed her on the cheek.

"That's not a very realistic plan, is it?" Ellie said.

"Some people have plans, some people have dreams," Spence said.

"What does that mean?"

"Nothing." Spence was not certain what he meant. It was not that he had ambitions, exactly. He felt hurt that she seemed to belittle something he took seriously. The light turned green. Ellie slid out from under his arm and positioned herself against the passenger side door. Neither spoke for several minutes.

"Where are you going after you drop me off?"

"I might go for a beer," Spence said and immediately regretted it.

Ellie said nothing. She looked out the passenger side window. They passed the little grove of trees where they used to stop on their route from school last year, when they'd started dating in Grade 11. When Spence would walk her home. The grove was a secret chapel fragrant with the spicy citrus of tree resin and the muskiness of crumbling logs and fallen needles. Hours of kisses and wandering hands. So much had already changed.

"What?" he said. "School all week. Two jobs on the weekend. This is my only night off—it's not my fault your parents want you home by eleven."

At eighteen, he was not of legal age but he was never asked for identification. Perhaps it was the wispy beard and moustache he had grown. He usually sat alone, nursing his beer and negotiating with a fatigue that left him weary but, somehow, reluctant to sleep. He was rarely very drunk. He hadn't enough money to get drunk every night, anyway. Just enough to take the edge off, he told himself.

After rehearsals, or studying, or making love with Ellie, he always seemed to find the music, the chatter, and the general cacophony of a pub a welcome distraction. He was rehearsing the part of the Stage Manager in his school's production of *Our Town* and he would sit to study his lines while enjoying a few cold ones. He reasoned that if he could remember his lines despite the noise and despite a few beers, then he would certainly not forget them on stage.

On the evening of their graduation, Spence and Ellie argued bitterly. She brought up his drinking and what she saw as his increasingly eccentric interests—the poetry he read, the art films he sought out, even his taste in music, as if Leonard Cohen or Dylan were somehow subverting the very fabric of society. His recent, unrealistic dreams for a career in the theatre and the erotic poems that he had written for her—Ellie's mother had angrily confronted her with them, tearing them to pieces and declaring them obscene.

Spence ridiculed the banality of her middle-class aspirations. He accused her of living a life manufactured by advertising. He reminded her that he had written most of her term essays for English so that she could concentrate on Math and Physics. Told her that her ambitions aimed no further than a comfortable home in the suburbs and a cottage in the country. He warmed to this theme as if he'd rehearsed it.

"I don't love you anymore, Spence."

It was clear that it anguished Ellie to declared this. They were on the lawn outside the Empress Hotel, where their graduation dinner had taken place. Spence looked up at the imposing brick-clad walls; the quaint turrets with copper domes weathered to the colour of powdered jade. Ivy clung to the exterior like a cozy on a teapot.

Stupid temple to nostalgia.

He saw that a little coterie of her girlfriends had stationed themselves near the stairs that led to the veranda. Vultures, he thought, feeding on this pathetic drama. He turned and looked out over the harbour. To his left, in the twilight, he could see the bronze statue of Queen Victoria primly presiding over the expansive lawn leading to the legislature.

What am I doing in this ridiculous town? This museum strangled in ivy.

And for a moment it occurred to him that he had been born in the wrong place, at the wrong time, to the wrong parents. But he didn't say that.

"You never loved me," he said, instead.

"That's not true." She was crying now.

"You only ever wanted to domesticate me," he said.

And though he was feeling cruel and wanted to hurt her, he felt there was some truth to this. Some part of him still loved her. His anger was like leather wrapped around a ball of tenderness that he could not express. And at that moment, he still desired her but could not explain why. Even if he were partly right about Ellie's aspirations, was there anything really wrong with the things she wanted? Yet he could not help but feel that he needed to smash everything that they had shared for the last two years.

I just want to fuck something. Fuck something until the whole stupid world of people you love and who are supposed to love you just disappears. Just fuck it all out of existence.

"I need a drink," he said.

Behind him, the old-fashioned street lamps flickered on, their white globes floating in the gathering darkness. In tears, Ellie ran up the stairs to the veranda where a cluster of girls, scarcely recognizable in their graduation gowns, surrounded her. Just out of earshot, they had witnessed the whole exchange—a little diaphanous bouquet of whispers. They floated with Ellie back through the arched entrance-way and into the gracious splendour of the Empress. A scene from an E.M. Forster novel.

Spence was drunk as he drove a circuitous route out of town, avoiding any roadblocks intended to corral teens returning from graduation celebrations. He might have made it unscathed had he not noticed the well-kept sign: DND CANADIAN FORCES HOUSING BASE. He spun the steering wheel too late to avoid careening into a wide ditch. The pair of headlights on the driver's side—the ones that had not been smashed—starkly illuminated the steep grassy slope. Spence spun the wheels for a minute before deciding he had best shut off the engine to avoid attracting attention.

He was only a couple hundred feet from the entrance to Belmont Park, his home for much of his childhood. For no reason he could explain, he left his car nearly on its side in the ditch and walked over the narrow bridge that led to the base. The sound of his footsteps in the darkness made the familiar streets seem strange, as though he were wandering through one of the vivid dreams he had experienced as a boy. He passed the little duplex where his family had lived and found himself in the garden outside the Catholic church—Our

Lady of the Sea. The lawn was neatly trimmed and two floodlights were recessed into the grass, illuminating a life-size figure of the Virgin Mary.

Spence ambled to the statue, as tired and alone as he had ever felt. He lay his flushed cheek against the Virgin's cool limestone face. Absurdly, he kissed her. He felt a trace of grit on his lips, as he caressed the outline of her stone breasts, scarcely perceptible under the frozen folds of her white dress. Glancing down, he jumped, startled by the curled outline of a crudely moulded snake under her sandal.

He laughed at his own stupidity. He laughed until his body began to shake with violent sobs. He unzipped his trousers, desperate to replace emotion with sensation, as though he could somehow obliterate himself.

At dawn, an MP on patrol found him asleep on the damp grass. He examined Spence's ID. "Is Chief Petty Officer Spencer your father?"

Spence nodded and looked at his feet.

"Get in," the MP said, pointing with his chin at the jeep. "I know your dad. I'll drive you home."

Spence hoisted himself into the passenger seat, turning to look at the windows of the little rectory. As he did, some unseen hands drew the curtains open. They swayed briefly and settled. He was trying to remember something but his aching head could not seem to focus. The jeep turned directly into the glare of the rising sun and Spence closed his eyes.

Thierry reminds me I haven't showered for more than a week. The situation must be dire if Thierry is giving me advice on hygiene.

"You not goin' to impress Khaleesi next door, Mudder o' Dragons, smellin' like dat, *mon chum*."

I am cajoled into the shower. Once there, I find I cannot leave. Opening the window, the cool air rushes in. Many apartment buildings in Montréal have this peculiar feature, one I never encountered in Vancouver. In the absence of an exterior window, bathrooms on successive floors exhaust through an interior window into a kind of shared chimney leading to the sky. Though not an intentional attribute, the chimney behaves like an amplifier, transmitting the bathroom conversations of one's neighbours. I can hear whispering in the dense fog produced by the cold air and strain to make out the words. I think about the woman next door. Why was she sitting there in Nick's Subaru? And who was the bald guy? I've seen him somewhere. Then the sound of Thierry's voice, shouting through the bathroom door.

"Hey, *mon chum*! Nature call! If you gonna be in dere all day I gonna do my business on de floor like before!"

I open the door. The porcelain of the sink and toilet bowl glisten with condensation. Thierry sighs. He opens the door of the cabinet under the sink a crack and climbs as far as the handle. As he kicks off, the door swings toward the toilet and he dismounts onto the toilet seat.

"Dat move is 'ard enough. You dun gotta turn de joint into a skatin' rink." He does his business, tears off a square of tissue, fashions a makeshift parachute and floats to the floor. The tiles are wet. He slips and lands on his ass.

"*Tabarnac!*" A pause. "*J'veux dire marde!*"

It is not as though Thierry has suddenly become a paragon of virtue. But recently he has modified a few of his more egregious

vices. He tidies. He uses the toilet. His *sacres* are a little less pro-
fane. The last couple of days he has offered some French lessons in
exchange for instruction in reading.

With my palm I clear the fog from the bathroom mirror. There
are dark circles under my eyes. My lips are cracked. Little tufts of
hair sprout from my ears and a couple of renegade bristles spring
from my eyebrows. More grey. I put a fresh blade in my razor.

"You're a disgrace," I mutter.

"I 'eard dat, *ostie!*"

"Not you!" I shout. And add quietly. "*Petite merde.*"

You're the only thing keeping me together.

JEUDI

There are no groceries. Thierry can literally live on crumbs but last
night even he was complaining.

"I know man dun live by bread alone, brudder, but you gotta eat
something."

I have been sitting on the edge of the bed for half an hour. One
sock on, the other dangling from my hand. *L'épicerie* is less than a
block away. You can do this.

Another hour passes.

Finally, I'm dressed and I stuff my coat pockets with reusable
shopping bags. Apparently, I still give a shit. In *l'épicerie* I stand
motionless for a long while. Everything's labelled in French and I
feel as though I have forgotten all the French I've learned. At length
it dawns on me that bread and cheese look the same in any language.
I find I am very hungry. So, naturally, I buy enough groceries for a
family of six. Lugging four overstuffed bags home, I get through the
main entrance easily enough. The doors are propped open because
a delivery truck is unloading a mattress. I am so laden down that
I must press the elevator button with my forehead. Outside my

apartment door I struggle to find my keys. I'm unwilling to set the bags down because I feel certain the contents will spill out.

"*Est-ce que je peux vous aider?* "

She is there behind me. She shuts the door to her apartment and when she smiles, I hear a great roar like a sea. It is blood rushing to my face and ears.

"*Oui. Merci. Je ne peux pas trouver mes clés . . .*"

She reaches for the two grocery bags in my right hand.

"*Ouah. Ils sont lourds!*" She laughs.

A fountain in a garden. The streams of Lebanon.

I open my door and she passes back the bags. My hand touches hers. A faint scent of perfume.

The rose of Sharon and the lily of the valleys.

"*Bonne journée.*" She smiles again and moves a silver strand of hair from her face.

Thou hast doves' eyes.

"*Merci,* " I say. Then add, "*Bonne journée à vous.* "

I shut the door and peer through the peephole.

I am such an idiot.

VENDREDI

"I dun like to ask, man, but I dun know who else gonna help."

"I'm here for you, Thierry. You know that."

Early evening. We are sitting on the balcony drinking tea and watching some kids toss around a frisbee in the park across the street. Thierry is on the arm of my chair. He has a tiny snuff spoon which he uses to draw sips from my cup. An elderly man on the first floor has a little collection of antique snuff boxes and spoons. He's deaf and nearly blind. I don't suppose he will miss one tiny snuff spoon.

"*Tiens. Je ne suis pas la seule souris à vivre dans cet immeuble?*"

"I guess I've never really thought about it. So, just how many mice live in our building?"

"Hmm. A bit 'ard to say. You know, dey come an' go."

"Ballpark estimate."

"*Quoi?*"

"*Environ combien?*"

Thierry taps the snuff spoon on the lip of my cup. "*A peu près cinquante ou soixante.*"

"Fifty or sixty? Thierry! That's like an . . ."

"*Une invasion?* An infestation?" He regards me steadily.

"How can I help?"

He nods.

"Mebbe you dun know, but a lotta mice die in de winter. Not jes de cold. But bein' inside an' not enough food. They wanna move outside soon. But right now, dere not enough food out dere. If nobody do nutin' more mice gonna die. Not jes our buildin'. De 'ole neighbourhood."

"What do you need?"

"*Pain.*"

"Bread? *C'est tout?*"

"Mebbe some peanut butter an' jam. De little kids like dat."

Five small loaves of bread. One jar of extra crunchy. One jar of strawberry jam. Enough food for several days. Following Thierry's instructions, I cut the sandwiches into one-inch squares and set them on plates in the middle of the living room floor. Around midnight a crew of maybe a dozen mice arrive. They arrange a sort of bucket brigade from the centre of the room to somewhere under the sofa. The whole operation takes less than half an hour.

"*Merci, mon frère!* De mice 'round 'ere not gonna forget dis. *Je promets.* We dun a good thing together. Like de man say: 'elp de sick, feed de 'ungry."

"How many do you think we fed, Thierry?"

"*Beaucoup. La multitude.*" He winks.

I'd made a promise.

I'd promised Clara I would visit her apartment every Saturday and attend to her plants. I could excuse myself the first time I missed that commitment. That was the day after our *petit cambriolage*. I had been busy reviving Thierry after freeing him from the safe. I could forgive myself that lapse.

The second time was the day I had found all that information on Mallory Parent on Cynthia's Blog. I suppose I didn't feel like passing St. Raymond's, knowing his portrait was hanging there in the entrance vestibule. Truthfully, I don't think I even clearly registered that the day was Saturday and that I had responsibilities. I could forgive myself that, as well.

The third time I was drunk.

That I can't excuse.

I consider calling Clara but I can't seem to figure out the time difference. Lately, my mind seems to be in a bit of a fog. Clara and I have not talked once since she left. That isn't really unusual. Even for those two—nearly three—years that I was still in Vancouver and she was studying in Montréal, we rarely talked on the phone. When we did, it was typically when she was suffering a panic attack and I would sit helplessly on the other end and listen to her hyperventilating. At Christmas, we talked over Skype. I used to write letters to people. I haven't written a real letter in years. Computers. Cell phones. So much potential for communication; so little connection.

Strangely, I think I feel closer to her standing alone in her empty apartment than I might have if I'd telephoned. Why is that? Perhaps we never understand other people, at all. We simply inspect the emblems of their lives—their clothes, the books on their shelves and the pictures on their walls. We drop clues for one another and pray we will be understood. Some days, even language seems like some elaborate deception. Some complex game of vague associations swirling on the air as strangely as those vast flocks of starlings I used to see in Vancouver, swarming in the evening sky like thousands of mysterious, shifting glyphs being shaken in a kaleidoscope.

The plants seem to be okay despite my neglect. Maybe I had been overwatering them. I press a finger into the soil of the pots as I make the rounds. Life is resilient. If the whole city were emptied of people tomorrow, how many years before vegetation reclaimed this island? Likely the plants I am now fussing about would be crawling through the walls, cracking windows, and bursting pipes. We think of nature as somehow benign. Yet, with time, and a bit of light and water, a forest could rage through this city like a slow fire. Am I nurturing plants on this visit, or am I really dousing flames?

I am not usually quite this philosophical. Since quitting my French classes, all my mind seems to do is wander. I stand in the bathroom for a few moments and look at my reflection in the mirror. How did I get this old? For no reason at all, I flush the toilet. I hadn't even used it. Back in the living room, I stand in front of Clara's bookshelf perusing the titles. I notice she has borrowed my copy of Thomas Merton's *The Seven Story Mountain*. The book that, perhaps, had heralded a brief revival of a more compassionate Catholicism, for Americans, at least. Today, that hope feels like a cruel joke. American bishops have hitched their wagon to Trump's malignant star. I don't even want to think about it.

Desmond gave me the book. I recall he had mentioned all three of us were Bob Dylan fans. And Merton was a poet, too. Quite a good poet. I take the book off the shelf and a photograph falls out. Cyrene. I haven't thought of her in years. Sometime after Serenity died, when I first began teaching, I'd had a brief, passionate affair with Cyrene. I was convinced I was in love. Perhaps I was. Or perhaps I had simply been staving off grief. Maybe both. I don't know anymore. Truthfully, she was too young for me. A lot too young. Not much older than some of my senior students. I suppose I should be ashamed to admit that, but I'm not. Clara had hated her. Maybe just jealousy. Maybe she understood something I did not.

I suppose I had been flattered that someone young and beautiful could find me attractive. Our affair was brief and, wisely, she left. I couldn't blame her. But after that, I guess something changed in me. I recall being heartbroken for about a year. After that, I never fell in love again. Not once in more than twenty years. It is as though the part of me that understood how to fall in love has forgotten how.

LATER . . .

"We all know what part dat is, *mon chum*."

Back home, Thierry is checking out the photo. He grins and sips some ginger ale through a paper straw. Out of concern for me he no longer drinks booze in the apartment. He still smokes plenty of reefer. I've decided to stop. Okay. I've decided to cut back.

"You're hilarious, man. You should be on *Just for Laughs*," I say.

"She is way too 'ot for an old guy like you."

"You know, I wasn't always this old."

Sometimes, I wish my life were more like his. Food, sex, sleep. Rinse. Repeat. But hadn't sex been just another kind of drug for me? Something to get lost in? It strikes me that Cyrene was nearly the same age as Serenity when I first met her. Does that mean something? Had I been trying to start over with a clean slate? I can't organize my thoughts sufficiently to even consider the question. At least I am eating again. Sleep comes in fits and starts. Sex?

I think of the woman who has moved in next door. What did I even know about her, the woman with silver-white hair? She likes jazz and she sings a little off-key. She's generous—she did tip the movers—and considerate. Didn't she help me with the groceries?

"*Écoute*," says Thierry. "*Je vais aller l'espionner.*"

"What?"

"You got a crush. *C'est évident.* I just gonna check out de merchandise."

"Don't you dare."

"You wanna meet dis woman or no? I tink some pussy will do you a lotta good."

He disappears into my bedroom. I see he has left the better part of a joint on the table. I take it out onto the balcony and blaze up. Nearly eight o'clock and it is still light.

Unbelievable.

In the driveway leading to the parking garage is a white 1963 Vauxhall Viva. No one inside. The engine off. My father had owned that exact car. Bought it used in 1970. Same colour. Same year. I had learned to drive in that car. Surely the ugliest car ever produced by GM, who bought out British Vauxhall sometime after the war. You see them everywhere in English movies from the sixties. And in Canada, they were one of the first compact models, beside the Volkswagen Beetle, that made any headway in the market. A stupid, squarish little two-door with no side mirrors. About as sexy as a box of stick matches. Or a coffin, I think. It is the car my father died in. How Ian, Babs and I all fit in the cramped backseat I can't imagine. Then it occurs to me. I'd had sex in the back seat of that car. Well, not exactly sex but whatever passes for sex for a boy of sixteen with about zero experience.

I run inside to tell Thierry. I guess I just want him to witness this little phantom from my youth. It takes me a moment to recall that he left to go spy on the woman next door.

Je retourne au balcon. C'est disparu. It's gone.

Mom

Being sixteen and possessed of a driver's licence meant that Lyle could be recruited to drive Babs to and from Brownies, pick her up from the skating rink or perform any number of chauffeur duties for his ten-year-old sister. On this Friday evening though, his mother had a different request. He was instructed to pick up his father from the Chiefs' and Petty Officers' Mess. Lyle knew this meant his father was too drunk to drive. He could see it in her eyes and by her tightly compressed lips that he had best not argue.

Lyle had never been to the mess. The Duty Officer at the entrance to the base gave him directions. He could hear the muted sound of recorded country music as he stood in the parking area. Considering the two entrances—Men, or Ladies and Escorts—Lyle walked a little farther to get to the men's entrance. The interior was dimly lit and cigarette smoke hung in the air. The washroom was near the entrance so that the smell of urine blended with that of spilled beer.

"Chief Petty Officer Spencer?" he inquired of a waiter passing nearby. The man gestured indifferently with his chin to the opposite side of the room. All the round table tops were wrapped in green terrycloth. No one wore their caps but everyone was in naval uniform except the staff, so at first Lyle could not distinguish his father from the other sailors. Someone pointed at Lyle and his father, who had had his back to the door, turned and gestured for Lyle to join him. He was sitting with a man Lyle did not recognize. A woman, also in uniform, sat on the man's lap. He whispered something in her ear and she slid off his knees to slouch in a nearby chair, pouting. It was nearly ten o'clock and the mess was not busy. But Lyle felt self-conscious as he crossed the room. He was the only guest in civilian dress and was clearly too young to be there.

"Sit, sit," his father said. His father introduced him to the others. Distracted by the strangeness of his surroundings, Lyle immediately forgot their names.

His father was in an expansive mood, and Lyle knew, roughly, how to gauge the degrees of his father's drunkenness—the more he drank, the more carefully he tried to conceal the effects. Lyle was relieved that his father was still in the friendly stage.

"He's cute," the woman said. She took a drag of her cigarette and blew the smoke in his direction. The man whose lap she had vacated laughed. He was a little younger than Lyle's father and sported a full beard of thick black hair, a sign, Lyle knew, that he had recently been to sea, On a voyage, the captain granted sailors permission to grow a beard.

His father slid a glass his way.

"We'll have one more round and then we'll go," he said.

"Mom said—"

"Your mother . . . " he laughed. "Never mind what your mother said. I said we'll have one more beer." He signalled the waiter who gave Lyle the once over and shrugged.

Lyle had some experience with drinking. His earliest ventures had involved consuming too much too fast, and there had been some vomiting. And some blackouts. He was more cautious now and decided he would observe his father and carefully match his intake.

The woman whose name he could not recall got up to use the washroom. She gently brushed his cheek with the back of her hand as she left. She winked and Lyle noticed the clumps in her mascara and the little line of black dots that the excess had traced onto her eyelids.

"You putting the moves on my woman?"

He glanced at his father, confused. Matthews was the other man's name. Lyle saw it printed on a plastic name tag attached to the pocket of his uniform jacket hanging over the back of his chair.

"No, sir," he said.

"Don't call me sir," he replied. "I'm as good a man as you." He laughed, then stood up saying he needed more smokes. He went to the bar to make change for the cigarette machine.

"You only call lieutenants and above 'sir,'" his father explained. "Anyway, he's pulling your leg. She's trying to get him into bed. Not going to happen. He's not interested. You watch."

Lyle was taken aback by his father's frankness. A part of him sensed that his father was taking pride in initiating him into the manly arts of drinking and discerning the motives of women. It had never occurred to him that a woman might play the role of instigator in a seduction. And when she returned, he watched with interest as Matthews calmly ignored her increasingly unsubtle appeals.

One beer turned into several. When Lyle got up to use the washroom he was startled when his father unexpectedly appeared by his side at the urinals. It was another unsettling milestone in what he imagined must be some sort of rite of passage. When they returned to the table, Lyle boldly took the cigarette that Matthews offered him. His fathered frowned but said nothing. The woman leaned in and lit a match for him. Provocatively, it seemed to Lyle, she blew it out in such a way that he could feel her breath on his face.

The next time she got up, his father abruptly announced that they were leaving. Matthews asked if he could catch a ride. Lyle walked a little unsteadily and both the men laughed when he announced that he couldn't remember where he'd parked the car. He wasn't certain what was so funny but he laughed too.

Matthews half sat and half lay in the back seat. His father stretched and put his arm around his son's shoulders. Lyle was concentrating on the speedometer, keeping it at a steady thirty-five miles per hour. He didn't want to attract the attention of a police cruiser. He felt reassured by his father's arm on his shoulders, a rare moment of affection.

"You guys queer?" Matthews shouted from the back seat.

Lyle's father removed his arm.

They dropped Matthews at a shabby-looking apartment building. After he had gone, his father explained that Matthews had recently separated from his wife. Lyle understood that to be some sort of explanation for something. The girl. The disreputable building. They drove the rest of the way home in silence.

Lyle entered the house through the basement. He went directly to his room and lay on the lower bunk, his brother's old bed. Ian had moved out a month ago after a bitter argument with their father and was living with his girlfriend's family now. Lyle's father went in through the front door. He heard his mother's voice. She was obviously not happy about the late hour. At first, his father tried cajoling her, but before long he could hear them both shouting. A door slammed. Then it was quiet.

Lyle's bedroom was more or less under the bathroom. After a few minutes he heard footsteps. The sound of his father peeing. The toilet flushing. After all the beer he had consumed, Lyle needed to pee as well. He briefly considered just going in the backyard. He waited as long as possible, hoping both his parents had retired for the evening. Then he cautiously mounted the stairs. At the top he was confronted by his mother.

"You had one job. Bring home your drunken father from the mess. Not sit drinking with him and his worthless buddies for another two hours and getting half drunk yourself."

Maybe it was the effects of the alcohol. Maybe it was the sense that somehow, after spending an evening drinking beer, smoking, and being halfway propositioned by a grown woman—maybe Lyle felt like he wasn't a boy anymore. He was a man.

"For fuck sakes, Mother! Next time you fucking pick him up then!"

Immediately he wished he hadn't spoken. Too late. The door to his parent's bedroom swung open abruptly and his father emerged with a suddenness he had never before witnessed. He felt two quick punches. A left, which glanced off his cheek. Then an uppercut that caught him squarely on the jaw. There was a flash of light that seemed to come from behind his eyes, like an electric charge, then he felt himself falling.

It must have been only a few moments later that he realized his father was now half carrying and half dragging him to the front door. At first, he did not understand that he had lost consciousness for a few seconds. He reasoned that he had been injured and now he conjured the scene of his father's regret. He was just carrying him to the car. They must be going to the hospital.

"Get out!" he heard his father shout. "Get out!"

His mother held her husband around the waist. She was screaming something through her tears. Lyle's head cleared a little. Enough so that he became aware that his father was ejecting him from his home.

"No," he said thickly. "No. I'm only wearing socks."

It was starting to rain. If he was to be thrown out, he wanted his shoes.

"I live here," he said. "This is my home, too."

Lyle saw his father's eyes go empty.

"You're just like your mother," he said, apropos of nothing it seemed to Lyle.

He released his hold. Lyle leaned over the porch railing and vomited. His head was swimming. And then he peed himself. He felt the warmth and saw the dark stain spreading down the front of his pants. The wetness quickly grew cold. The shame and misery were too much. He began to sob.

"No!" he shouted as his mother reached to comfort him. "Don't touch me. I don't want to be touched."

"So how were Mass?"

"I didn't go."

"You wanna talk?"

"I don't think so." I'm looking over my bicycle. I haven't gone for a ride in nearly two weeks. The frame could use a good cleaning. The chain is a disgrace and the sprockets of the cassette are covered in grime. Likely the tires need air. Somehow, I have come to resemble my own bicycle, the way people seem to resemble their pets.

"Dey say it jes like ridin' a bike, brudder."

"What is?"

"Sex."

I look over at him. He has a raisin in one hand that he probably found on the floor. He takes a bite and holds my gaze as he chews.

"Mebbe it been a long time since you 'ad sex wid a woman. But once you is on *c'est comme faire du vélo*. You dun forget 'ow to ride."

I look away. I test the pressure of the front tire with my thumb. Definitely needs air.

"*Elle est veuve comme toi.*"

"She's not that old. Neither am I."

"*Pas vieux. Veuve.* I dun know 'ow you say dat in English."

"You mean widow?"

"No. Dat what you look out for to check if it rainin'."

"That's window, Thierry."

"Yeah. Made from glass, *ostie*. She ain't made from glass. I seen 'er in de buff. She still got nice ones."

"What the hell, Thierry!"

"What? You see me in de buff all de time."

"Whatever. You were next door. You saw her. She's a widow. *Une veuve.* Her husband's deceased."

"*Oui. Décédé. J'ai vu une photo de lui à l'hôpital. Cancer à coup sûr. Y'est Frère André quand on a besoin de lui?*"

195

"*Il n'y a jamais de miracle quand tu en as besoin.*"

"You dun need a miracle. You jes need to learn more French. 'cause she talk English worse den you butcher French."

"*Vraiment?* I really butcher it?"

"Jack de Ripper, man. Dere oughta be a law."

"Okay. Teach me."

"You teach me to read, like we said."

"Like we said. But no more spying on her. Especially naked."

"Naked is nutin', *mon chum*. You dun wanna know some o' de things I seen."

He's right. I don't.

LUNDI

While I was on my bender, Thierry appears to have dedicated himself to some sort of ad hoc self-improvement program. He is still a dope-smoking, over-sexed, thieving, foul-mouthed rodent. It's not that he's mellowed. More that he has cultivated a range of new interests. He's begun to sketch a little. He struggles to read but persists. His personal hygiene habits have improved. Strangely, he's become rather fastidious about the housework. In general, he's a bit more cosmopolitan.

His strangest preoccupation, though, is his newfound interest in Frère André. He still professes to be an atheist. He still harbours a palpable animosity toward religion in general and the Catholic Church in particular. But he has discovered an affinity with Frère André.

"*Son père est mort quand il était petit.* Jes like me. *Aussi,* 'e were born on a farm, like me."

Evening. I still haven't gotten out of bed.

"How did you learn this stuff, Thierry?"

"Dat lil book, you buy? At *l'Oratoire?* It 'as some pictures. *Aussi—* YouTube, man."

"Hmm. Born on a farm. How did you get to Montréal?" Thierry is sitting on the bed near my feet.

"I were a teenager an' one day *maman* were really mad at me 'cause she found my stash. I know she mad 'cause she shoutin' THEODORE!"

"Theodore?"

"Yeah. Dat my real name. But everyone call me Thierry. Except *maman* when she is mad. Den is THEODORE!"

"Okay, Theodore." I smile.

"Hey, you smile."

A pause.

"Anyway. I end up in de poultry truck on accident 'cause I were tryin' to hide. Dey slam de big doors shut an' dere I am for hours in de refrigerator truck wid all dem butcher chickens. Like a fuckin' 'orror movie."

"My God."

"When we stop in Drummondville, I'm about to get off but jes den Jean-Guy get on. 'e say 'e is goin' to Montréal. I say, *Comment tu sais que ce camion va à Montréal?* 'e say: *Fais-moi confiance.*"

"Stowaways," I say.

"Throw away? Nobody throw us away. We jes gotta get outta dem hick town, man, an' into de big city. Dat were de beginnin' of a beautiful friendship, man."

"I didn't mean . . . never mind."

"*Puis.* Me an' Jean-Guy end up in *Collège Villa-Maria* jes up de street. Guess where Frère André end up in Montréal?"

"*Collège Notre-Dame?*"

"Bingo! *Maria? Notre-Dame? Coïncidence?* I dun tink so!"

"Well . . ."

Really half of Montréal's place names make reference to Mary.

"*Aussi*, guess what day Frère André die? *Le six janvier! Le même jour que mon père!*"

"Sixth of January? Epiphany. Same day my wife died."

"*Frère André? Mon père? Ta femme?*" He slaps his forehead and falls straight back onto the mattress as if in a faint.

"Dats too weird, man! Spooky! I got goosebumps!" He scrambles to his feet.

"So, you gonna get outta bed or what?"

"No. I think I'll just go to sleep."

The thing with miracles and coincidences? You only notice those rare times when they occur. You never notice the rest of the time. When nothing special is happening. When nothing seems to mean anything anymore.

MARDI

Someone is pounding on the door. I check the time. Past noon. More pounding. My sweat pants are on the bedroom floor. I pull them on. I put my glasses on. Through the peephole I see Nick, carrying a box of black heavy-duty garbage bags. This is it. This is how my dismembered body gets carried out. I realize I'm not wearing a shirt. Just as well. No sense ruining a good shirt if I am going to be sawed into pieces anyway. I open the door.

"Spence." Nick is smiling. "Everything all right?"

He knows. But he wants proof.

"Fine," I say.

He's got no evidence. Thierry muddied the waters by falsely implicating the guy next door. My share went to booze and a crummy hotel room. Untraceable.

"Look," he says. "It's spring. A lot of tenants will be doing some spring cleaning. Usually, we get swamped with extra trash. I'm asking tenants to put their excess in these heavy-duty bags. Keep things organized. You know what I mean? Things can get out of hand."

He offers me a bag. *Things can get out of hand.* A veiled threat?

"Okay. Thanks."

He nods and looks past me into the apartment. "How's your French coming along?"

"*Bien. Lentement. J'essaie.*"

"That's good." He shifts the box of garbage bags so it rests on his hip. "*Bonne journée.*"

"*Bonne journée.*"

I close the door and lean against it. I know what this is. He's signalling to me that he's willing to accept the return of my half. No questions asked. Just put the money in this special bag or he'll put pieces of my body in the bag instead. Spring cleaning. That's gangster code. I haven't got $2,950 and I no longer care.

I mention Nick's visit to Thierry later that evening. He is unconcerned.

"Nick dun got nutin' on us. *T'inquiète pas. Je suis un pro.*"

Thierry has the little pamphlet I got for him from St. Joseph's Oratory. He is sprawled on the sofa struggling to read. His lips are moving. I doubt he knows that, historically, an oratory was a simple chapel, often a sort of roadside rest-stop for weary travellers. A place to pause and reflect. Sometimes there wasn't even an altar for the celebration of Mass.

Frère André's original St. Joseph's Oratory was a fifteen- by eighteen-foot wooden chapel. Spruce for the structure. Pine for the altar. Nestled in a cluster of birches, it was assembled in about a week. Seating capacity, ten souls. With the doors flung open, perhaps another hundred could stand outside for Mass. Except for the steeple, which rose twenty-five feet, it might have been mistaken for a large garden shed. I explain this to Thierry.

"Dats a lot smaller den de one I seen in de movie." Thierry is referring to *Le Frère André, un film de Jean-Claude Labrecque.* He'd watched it on YouTube.

"They expanded it a few years later because it proved too small," I say. "They built that little upstairs section that you see in the movie. It looks a bit different now but—"

"It still standin'? Why you dun say so? Dat I gotta see!"

I can't tell if he is genuinely excited or if he is just trying to create an excuse to get me out of the house.

"*Demain. Peut-être.*" I say.

MERCREDI

Strictly speaking, the fire and the shattered angel were not Thierry's fault.

Inside and out, Frère André's little chapel dedicated to St. Joseph is clad in pressed tin siding. That is not quite as aesthetically dire as it sounds. The pressed tin is embossed and painted. White exterior and a kind of flat emerald green inside.

The chapel was damaged by fire in 1951. I suspect the tin cladding was applied during restorations as a fire preventative measure. As a further precaution, two fire extinguishers are mounted near the entrance.

Here's a peculiar thing about the Oratory, in general. There is almost no visible security. Back in March, a priest celebrating morning Mass was attacked by a knife wielding assailant. Fortunately, the priest's wounds were not serious. Encouraged to increase security, church officials declined. Isolated incident, they said. They didn't want visitors to feel unwelcome. I have been to the basilica several times. No visible security. No metal detectors. No searches. Before tourist season, go early enough on a weekday and you essentially have the whole place to yourself.

The original chapel is across the parking lot from the large basilica. As you enter, there are a half dozen shabby chairs scattered in front of the old-fashioned communion rail. The altar is pre-Vatican II style. Up against the wall so that the celebrant would have his back to the congregants. A statue of St. Joseph holding the child Jesus occupies the place of honour. In front of him is a small cross festooned with bare light bulbs like a cinema marquee. Above Joseph, a halo of lightbulbs. One of the bulbs is burnt out. There is a childlike charm to this tawdry display of piety. Joseph is flanked by two ceramic angels. Further to one side, a statue of the Sacred Heart of Jesus. To the other, one of Mary, Queen of Heaven. All in all, it is the devotional equivalent of a fifties' diner with an empty tabernacle where the jukebox might be.

For Thierry, it is heaven.

"Dis a lot like de church back 'ome when I were a kid—*avec maman.*"

It is early morning. We have the place to ourselves. Thierry runs around freely. He is pretty excited.

"What the hell, Thierry. I thought you hated the Church."

"I do. *Mais, je l'aime ben, le Frère André. Je me sens nostalgique.* What dem things say?"

"Sound out the words, Thierry."

He is referring to the dozens of engraved marble plaques mounted on the walls, all expressing gratitude to St. Joseph for healings. Neatly folded and tucked into the space behind every plaque within reach of the communion rail are hundreds of small pieces of paper. Prayer intentions, petitions, *notes de remerciements.* Stuck there like gum under a table in some greasy spoon.

"*Re..con..nais..sance à Saint Jo . . . seph. Re . . . mer..cie . . . ments. Gra . . . ti . . . tude.*" Thierry climbs the altar for a closer view. It is then that a nun enters. She is in a traditional habit: black tunic, black veil, white coif and wimple, white scapular, silver cross. Thierry freezes. He is poised on the altar next to the ceramic angel. Proportionately, he might be mistaken for a heavenly dog seated at the angel's feet. I am in a chair near the railing.

Sister places some coins in the box near the rack of votive candles. The tall sort in coloured glass. Tall as a sleeve of beer. She picks one up and sets it alight, closing her eyes as she prays. When she opens them, she sees Thierry. She screams.

Instinctively, she launches the candle at Thierry. It hits the ceramic angel, which shatters, and the flame from the candle ignites the neatly folded notes behind the marble plaques. Thierry tries to blow out the spreading blaze, which only feeds the flames. Sister panics and runs from the chapel. I expect her to cry *Au feu! Au feu!* Instead, I hear her screaming, "*Une souris! Une souris!*" Through the window I see her white scapular billowing behind as she runs.

I grab a fire extinguisher from near the door. In my haste to remove the pin, I cut my hand. Whoosh! With one blast the flames are dead. Thierry stands still under the Sacred Heart of Jesus. The fire extinguisher has thoroughly dusted him. He is as white as an albino lab mouse. Through the haze of smoke and chemical propellant, his black eyes shine.

"*Tabarnac! Je déteste les bonnes soeurs.*" He blinks and adds, "You is bleedin'."

Blood from my hand is dripping onto the wooden floor.

"I think we should go now."

"*D'accord.*" To my surprise, Thierry joins me in making a hasty sign of the cross. "For Frère André," he says.

JEUDI

Today's headline in *Le Devoir: Un individu non identifié met la feu à la chapelle du Frère André.*

And below, in a smaller font: *Des inconnus sont salués comme des héros pour avoir éteint l'incendie.*

"*Tiens! Nous sommes des héros, mon chum!* De unknown heroes!"

Agonizingly slowly, Thierry begins to read the whole article aloud. I listen while fussing a little with my bandaged hand. A half page column. It is going to take him an hour. I decide to do some laundry—I have no clean underwear.

La salle de lavage est au sous-sol. La place pour le recyclage est dans le garage du stationnement. I have lugged a bag of recycling down as well. I unlock the door to the parking garage, drag the bag to the central concrete column and heave it into one of the bins arranged there.

It is then I realize I'm not alone. *Je ne bouge pas.*

A car engine roars to life. The noise rumbles off the walls of the garage. It is a red 1965 Plymouth Fury. As a boy, I had this model in my Dinky Toy collection. For a moment, I flash on an image of myself "playing cars" on the floor of my bedroom. It is a strangely vivid memory. As though something flings me into my past and then slingshots me back to my present. The sensation leaves me dizzy.

The driver revs the engine then accelerates straight toward me. I throw myself among the plastic bins and cower there. The Fury circles me twice, tires spewing smoke and throwing a spray of grit my way. It exits through the tunnel. I hear the clunk-clunk as the automatic door rolls open. Another menacing revving of the engine. The scream of tires. He's gone. The door rolls shut with a bang. Then silence again. The dripping from the pipes. Fluorescents flickering. A cloud of exhaust disperses and I crawl out.

Je suis presque certain que le conducteur était le propriétaire.

I leave my laundry in the basket on top of a washing machine. Thierry needs to hear this. It could be both our lives are in danger.

"You sure dat was Nick?" he asks.

"Yes . . . no . . . maybe . . . I don't know. It all happened so fast."

"Nick dun drive no '65 Plymouth Fury. I only ever seen 'im in dat ten-year-old Subaru."

"But, I thought, well . . . I just assumed he likes to collect old cars. The underground garage is full of them. Maybe a dozen or more. All under covers. You've seen them."

"Sure, I seen dem. Dey is not Nick's. Nick dun 'ave dat kinda money. 'e got property, for sure, but 'e dun 'ave no good cash flow. I 'eard 'im talkin' on de phone."

"What? In his office? Again? You're not . . . you know you almost died during our last job."

"Relax. I ain't plannin' no job. I jes gotta know what goin' on. *L'instinct de survie.* 'ow you say dat *en anglais*?"

"Pretty much the same. Survival instinct."

"Man, you guys totally steal our language, you know dat? You should get yer own language. Anyway. Dos car ain't Nick's. *En fait*, some of dem change all de time. Some never 'ere more den a few week. Mebbe a month."

"Really?"

"*Vraiment.* You jes dun notice 'cause dey under dos covers all de time. Also, you not always awake when de cars comin' an' goin'. Something weird goin' on down dere, for sure."

"Why have you never mentioned this before?"

"You never ask about dis before. Anyway, I dun keep alive dis long stickin' my nose in udder people business."

LATER . . .

"Dis bedder be good 'cause I break a date for dis."

"Really? What's her name?"

"Never mind about name, brudder. Let's jes get dis over wid."

"Thanks for doing this, Thierry. I couldn't do this alone."

"Anything to get you out o' de 'ouse, *mon chum*. Even if it only de garage."

3:00 am. We are in the underground parking garage. The same musty dampness and thick almond scent of leaking oil. Droplets from the overhead pipes plopping into puddles. Thierry is on my shoulder. He tugs my ear.

"Wait."

A pause.

"What is it?" I whisper.

"Shh." He is still. "A radio. Like one o' dem walkie-talkie."

"I can't hear it."

" 'cause you dun 'ear ultrasonic man." He scrambles to the floor. "Never mind. Jes static anyway. It stop."

We tiptoe a little farther.

"Wow. So much piss down 'ere."

"I don't smell it."

"You is standin' on it."

"What?"

"It glow in dis ultraviolet light. You dun know I got super powers, *hein?*"

"Okay. Let's see what we have here." I lift the tarpaulin off the hood of one of the hidden vehicles. My hands are shaking.

"Holy shit! It's a fucking Phantom V. It's a Rolls Royce Phantom V!"

"How you know dat?" Thierry has scampered down and is leaning on the hood ornament.

"Well, for one, the Silver Lady."

He turns and examines the hood ornament.

"Ooo. Sexy."

I don't dare tell him the winged figure is also called the Spirit of Ecstasy.

"The grill is unmistakable. Trust me. John Lennon had one of these. Elton John. The Queen, for God's sake."

"You mean Elton John de queen or Elton John an' like 'er Majesty de Queen?"

"Either. Both. Trust me. I had the Dinky Toy."

"De what?"

"The Dinky Toy. A die-cast metal facsimile. You know, a toy car, for kids. *N'importe quoi.* This is worth a fortune."

"*Dinky? C'est un nom étrange pour un jouet d'enfant.*"

"Don't start, Thierry."

"*Désolé.*"

Discovering the Rolls Royce has flung me back to 1967. The Summer of Love—I was only ten, so I suppose I missed the love part. But I remember seeing photos of John Lennon's Phantom V painted electric yellow and adorned like a Roma caravan. *Sgt.*

Pepper's Lonely Hearts Club Band—like a circus-come-to-town but filtered through a jumbled garden of half-remembered dreams. The album cover with faces unknown to me then, but strangely familiar. The only one I recognized with certainty was Tarzan from the movies, Johnny Weissmuller. The drumhead in the centre of the LP like a mandala in the window of a church.

My hands are still shaking as I lift a corner of the next tarpaulin to reveal a Pontiac Parisienne. It is the cream-coloured Parisienne I glimpsed from the balcony two months ago. Back in March. I run my fingers along the chrome trim that extends from the fender to halfway down the driver's door.

"I'm certain this is a 1963. I had one of these back in '75. It was the first car I ever owned."

"No Dinky Toy?"

"Yeah. I think, maybe, I had that, too, when I was little. I can't remember exactly. This is not a luxury car but, man, mint condition."

I press my face against the driver's side window. I half expect to see the eight-track tape deck and the speakers I'd had installed in the door panels. Blasting Bob Dylan's *Before the Flood* while cruising into town.

We carry on snooping for about half an hour. An emerald-green VW Karmann Ghia Coupe. It is the '67 I saw the day Thierry spent sulking about our misunderstanding over the box of mousetraps. For a moment I am overwhelmed with memories. Ian and me at the auto show with our father. Me on my bicycle delivering *TV Guide* magazine. Our duplex in Belmont Park, housing for the families of men serving at the naval base, CFB Esquimalt.

A powder blue Fiat 600. 1960 Ford Fairlane. It must have been a month ago that I saw that guy with the shaved head and sunglasses pull into the parking garage driving this Fairlane. Without even checking, I am certain that the Valiant I saw months ago is under the tarpaulin next to it. A dizzying moment as I flash back to high school. Passing the auto shop on my way to rehearsals and seeing Phil Cucovich's '66 Valiant up on the hoist.

Cherry red Aston Martin. Incredible. VW Beetle convertible. A half a dozen more immaculate sixties vintage autos. Some luxury. Some sporty. Some sedans. Many of them I recognize from my Dinky Toy collection or from my brother's or some friend's.

Then, there it is. The white 1963 Vauxhall Viva I'd seen a couple weeks ago. I remember being pretty stoned so I wasn't completely sure whether I'd seen it or if it were just a trick of my imagination. This is the car that my dad died in.

"Get down!" Thierry hisses in my ear.

The interior door into the garage slowly opens. I replace the tarpaulin over the Viva, then Thierry and I slide under the car and out of sight. I am feeling strangely disoriented. I can recall, as a boy, being on the BC Ferries, sometimes, in rough weather. That's sort of what I feel, as if I am being tossed about on a sea of memories. And now, lying under my father's car—well, not exactly his—but it feels like my whole childhood is rolling over me.

The beam of a flashlight rakes the floor, accompanied by the sound of footsteps. The brisk, clipped heels of a woman, travelling from car to car. Each time they halt I hear a whoosh, like a parachute opening as each cover is flipped up. Then a pause, as though someone were making notes.

The steps come closer.

Closer.

Finally, the tarpaulin over the Vauxhall is swept away. I hold my breath. I am inches from a slightly scuffed pair of black pumps. With a crisp snap the cover is replaced.

My new neighbour.

Lyle's sister was named Margaret, but everyone called her Babs for reasons that may have had something to do with a long-deceased relative's nickname or it may have evolved from a mispronunciation of "baby." Ian and Lyle were seven and six, respectively, when Babs was born.

Everyone doted on Babs except Lyle's father, who seemed concerned that affection would somehow spoil her. He was of the opinion that children were perpetually on the brink of succumbing to waywardness if they were not properly disciplined. For Lyle and Ian, this involved the administration of "lickings"—sound whippings across their usually bare buttocks with their father's belt. Lyle once had a painfully swollen testicle for nearly a week from his father's heedless aim.

Lyle was thirteen and Babs had just turned seven when the family moved from Belmont Park into a newly built house, no longer renters but proud homeowners. There was a period of about a year where everyone worked to turn the new place into a home. Ian and Lyle laboured hard on weekends and after school to collect all the rocks on the property and raked soil into an even layer over patches of hard, bare earth so a lawn could be seeded. New furniture was delivered. A second car—a used Austin 1100—appeared in the driveway. It was for Lyle's mother who had started a job, her first, as a cashier at Safeway. Lyle's father took on a second evening job with a janitorial company. As the family's social status advanced, so did their debts. And the general levels of stress.

Babs had been spared many of the chores assigned to her brothers and the lickings the brothers still sometimes received, though less frequently now that they were in their teens. But shortly after the soil for the new lawn had been spread, she had made the error of coming into the house through the front door without removing her shoes. When Lyle's mother returned from work and saw this little trail of dirty footprints on her new carpet, she was furious. Babs burst into panicked tears and ran to the bathroom where she gathered a handful of toilet paper and began rubbing the soiled spots on the carpet.

"You're making it worse!" her mother screeched. It was then that Lyle's father came in.

"Who was supposed to be watching Babs?" he said looking at Lyle. "Right."

Lyle winced at the familiar sound of the loosening buckle of his father's belt and prepared himself for a licking. He was surprised when his father grabbed Babs by the hand and dragged her to the centre of the living room.

Bab's screamed.

"No," Lyle shouted. He ran and picked up Babs by the waist, but stumbled and they both fell. Babs scrambled up and opened the door to the entrance closet, disappeared inside and slammed the door shut. Lyle flung himself against it.

"Move," his father ordered. From the depths of the closet Babs muffled voice repeated, "I'm sorry, I'm sorry, I'm sorry." Lyle's mother was shouting now as well.

"You have spoiled that child for too long," Lyle heard his father say.

"It's my fault! It's my fault! I'm supposed to watch her after school." Lyle grabbed his father's belt and felt one of his fingers go numb as his father yanked it away.

"Fine. You want your sister's licking. Fine."

Lyle put his arms over his face and cowered against the wall, trying to shield himself. His father wielded his belt erratically, delivering quick, powerful swings. Most of the blows landed on Lyle's back and arms. His ear stung as one of them clipped him on the side of the head.

"Stop! Stop! He's bleeding." His mother was crying now.

The beating ceased. Lyle could feel one of his cheeks swelling near his eye. The finger that had been caught in his father's belt now ached unbearably. He could see a patch of blood spreading on his shirt near his armpit. Thinking of the new carpet, he quickly walked into the kitchen. He turned on the tap and put his finger under cold water as the front door opened and slammed shut. An engine roared and and tires squealed.

Lyle's mother stood leaning against the refrigerator, crying. Babs appeared, flung her arms around Lyle's waist and clung to him.

"It's okay," he said. "It's okay."

VENDREDI

The mystery woman.

It was nearly morning when I got to bed yesterday. While I slept, Thierry did a little more reconnaissance next door. This time I didn't object. He reported back this evening.

"Nutin'. Everything seem pretty normal. Only thing weird, she got a two-way radio. D'expensive kind. Remember I tawt I 'eard one last night? An' when she checkin' dos car, I were pickin' up a lotta ultrasonic. I tink mebbe it were her radio."

Thierry thinks that Nick may be involved in moving stolen vintage cars. That makes sense. None of the tenants park in the garage. Just Nick. The only time tenants go down there is with garbage or recycling. Private. But private in plain view.

"You think she is in on this?"

"I dunno, man. I tawt first she jes some nice old lady. Now—"

"Old!"

"Okay, okay. Middle-age, *ostie*. Mebbe she de brains o' de operation 'cause, for sure, Nick ain't no genius. Anyway, none o' our business. We gonna keep our nose outta dis. Okay?"

Just when I think, maybe, I am turning a corner, all my sadness comes back full force. The days are warm and pleasant but I don't feel like venturing much farther than the balcony. Why do I have this ridiculous schoolboy crush on a woman I hardly know? My silver-haired widow is a criminal mastermind?

"All right, brudder. Time fer my readin' lesson. *Et le temps pour toi de parler un peu français.*"

Seated on my knee, he reads aloud from *Le Petit Prince*. Listening and repeating, I improve my grammar and pronunciation. Occasionally I must look up a word that neither of us understands.

"*Adieu, dit le renard. Voici mon secret. Il est très simple: on ne voit bien qu'avec le cœur. L'essentiel est invisible pour les yeux.*" He pauses. "Okay. De 'eart dun got eyes. You can't see wid de 'eart."

"It's a metaphor, Thierry. When I say *je vois* it can mean 'I see' or it can mean 'I understand.' He's saying only the heart can understand certain things. They can't be reasoned. They can only be felt."

"Uh huh. Like what?" Thierry reaches over and grabs his fixings off the arm of the sofa. He rolls a joint.

"Well. Have you ever been in love?"

He stops. His tongue is just about to wet the glue on the rolling paper.

"Mebbe." He licks the paper and rolls it pensively.

"Well, love isn't visible. Not even under a microscope. And no matter how you try to explain it, something essential still remains a bit mysterious."

"Okay." He lights the joint, takes a long drag, and passes it to me. He reads: "*Les hommes ont oublié cette vérité, dit le renard. Mais tu ne dois pas l'oublier. Tu deviens responsable pour toujours de ce que tu as app . . . appriv . . . apprivoisé.*"

He struggles a little with the final word.

"Dat mean 'tame,' *n'est-ce pas?*" He laughs. "Dat mean you is *responsable pour moi parce que* you tamed me? Dat what you tink? You tame dis mouse?" There is a bit of a challenge in his voice.

"I don't think he means tame exactly. I think he means something closer to connection. Like friendship. Friends have a responsibility to support each other." I pass back the joint. He flicks a bit of unburnt paper off the ember. "You and I know what friendship is, Thierry."

He takes another long drag and thinks.

"Yeah. Dats when you dun want nutin' from de udder person. You dun use de udder person for nutin'. You jes like each udder an' hang out. An' also give a shit when dat person goin' tru a bad time."

We sit quietly for a few moments.

Nailed it, Thierry.

"*Parlant d'amour, j'ai rencontré quelqu'un.*"

"You've met someone? Is it, you know, serious?"

"*Peut-être*. I tawt mebbe I introduce you two."

"I'd like that, Thierry." Then after a moment. "I'm happy for you."

SAMEDI

His name is Benoît. ·

He is sleek and black and very handsome. He speaks only French with what, Thierry tells me, is a Haitian accent. I don't understand a word. There is an awkward moment when we meet. Then Thierry says:

"*Un prêtre, un rabbin et une souris gay entrent dans un bar. Le barman lève la tête et dit: Est-ce que c'est une blague?*"

It takes me a moment.

A priest, a rabbi and a gay mouse walk into a bar. The bartender looks up and says: Is this a joke?

I smile. Thierry smiles. We laugh. Benoît smiles.

"I thought, um, I thought . . ."

"You tawt I were straight?"

"Well, you know all that macho talk about women."

"*L'instinct de survie, mon chum*. Also, mebbe I tawk macho but I never tawk about women *exactement*."

"But that night, I saw that girl. With the pearl earring?"

"*Pis*? You can tell de boy mouse from de girl mouse now?"

"Not exactly."

"You jes see what you wanna see, brudder."

"And the church mouse girls across the street at St. Augustine's?"

"No girls dere, man. Jes, you know, a place for guys to meet up."

"And Jean-Guy?"

A pause.

"*Oui*."

He takes a moment to translate for Benoît.

"Dat one o' de reason I dun like de church, man. I dun like dem hypocrite. Lotsa *prêtres* is queer like me. Dey jes dun admit it. I dun tink you can talk 'bout love on Sunday an' den pretend you somebody you not de rest o' de week."

I'm not going to argue with that.

"Dat why I leave de farm, too. I dun get trap in no *frigo* truck. *Ma mère ne pouvait pas accepter que j'étais gay.* I rather die in dat truck den see dat look on 'er face. I like dat lil Frère André and all, but dat Catholic stuff jes not my style. Hey! Benoît's *grand-père* were a vodou priest! 'ow cool is dat?

Benoît talks for a little and I understand nothing. Thierry translates, explaining that they met at Le Musée des beaux-arts. I think now I understand Thierry's recent enthusiasm for a more cosmopolitan way of life. The sketching, the reading and the hygiene. He has been trying to impress Benoît.

After dinner, Thierry and Benoît grow more serious. It seems that after the new fluorescents were installed in the basement, the signs that mice were present had been discovered. Thierry and Benoît look at me solemnly. They had witnessed a meeting in Nick's office; present at the meeting were Nick, my silver-haired neighbour and someone named Rocco.

" 'e's a bald guy. Wid black eyebrows."

"I think I've seen him. Sounds like the guy who delivered a car. A Fairlane. More than a month ago."

They tell me that Rocco insisted Nick lay traps and poison in the garage. The cars were too valuable, he said. He didn't want mice anywhere near them, chewing the upholstery and scratching the paint. Now three mice are dead from poison.

"Jes kids," says Thierry. "Some kids explorin' an' 'aving some fun. Dey dun know nutin' about poison. De udder thing is dis. We learn dat dey is feelin' de heat. Something makin' 'im nervous an' dat bald guy, Rocco, wanna move all de cars outta de garage on *lundi*. 'round midnight. Nick an' Khaleesi say dey dun like dis idea but de bald guy insist. *Il veut emmener les autos à un autre emplacement.*"

Thierry has a plan.

Naturellement.

TROISIÈME DIMANCHE DE PÂQUES

Thierry has never been on a bicycle before. He took a nap in the wee hours last night so he could wake this morning and attend the early 8:30 Mass with me. The day is warm and sunny.

"*C'est pas mal moins chiant que de marcher!*"

Straddling a clamp bolted to the head tube, he grips the little white front reflector like a steering wheel. He is wearing a pink helmet and pink sunglasses which he claims he's just borrowing from the little girl down the hall who has Bicycle Barbie in her collection.

"Dat kid got too many toy, anyway. She not gonna miss dis stuff."

The final touch to his cycling garb is a long, white silk scarf. Caught by the wind, it flows well past the tips of his flattened whiskers. The ends flutter just under my chin.

"*Fais attention*, Thierry! Affectations can be dangerous."

"*Quoi?*"

Our voices are drowned in the wind. Perhaps some other time I will describe for him Isadora Duncan's death by silk scarf strangulation and Gertrude Stein's morbid humour.

"*Rien.*"

Thierry stays in my pocket until the scripture readings conclude. Then he wanders the church freely. During the Sanctus I catch sight of him lapping up some holy water at a small font by the side door. By the *Agnus Dei*, I can see him spread-eagled and fast asleep under the little shrine to St. Joseph.

The priest: The peace of the Lord be with you always.

The people: And with your spirit.

The priest: Let us offer each other the sign of peace.

I nod to the two women in the pew behind me. I shake hands with a few other people across the aisle. I have been attending Mass here for nearly a year and I know no one's name. Except Carl, the greeter. In church I sit near the sparse choir of elderly women and directly behind the organist. He's middle-aged. Still handsome. I think, maybe he is from somewhere in Central America. His wife and sons usually sit nearby. No one ever sits next to me. Probably because there is no cushioned hassock for kneeling in this pew due to the position of the organ. I prefer this spot because I can stretch out my legs. And I am actually more comfortable kneeling on the ground.

At this point in the Mass, the organist's two teenage sons come over and each, in turn, give him a hug. His third son, the youngest boy, is about nine or ten. He kisses his father on the cheek. His father kisses his youngest on his forehead. I have no recollection of ever hugging my father. Ever. Certainly, he never kissed me, nor I him.

I begin to cry. It's absurd. I am a grown man. But seeing a little boy kiss his father's cheek is just too beautiful to bear. I make no sound. Just a flood of tears. And I can't stop them.

Cycling home, I cry.

In the elevator, I cry.

At the table, I cry.

Before the mirror, I cry.

Thierry is fast asleep the whole time. He'd opened his eyes briefly when I settled him in my pocket. Now I put him gently on the sofa and position my handkerchief over him. Still crying, I lean over and give him a kiss.

In 1967, Lyle Spencer was an enterprising ten year old. He had taken over a *TV Guide* route from another boy, delivering the magazine to over forty households in Belmont Park. Over the course of a year, he'd expanded the route to more than sixty. Lyle rode his bicycle to pick up the magazines from the depot in the Colwood Plaza after school on Tuesdays. Deliveries were on Wednesday and, sometimes, Thursday evenings.

Subscriptions were sixty cents a month. Of that, Lyle kept a dime. Hitherto, his weekly allowance had been seventy-five cents a week. With the *TV Guide* route, Lyle tripled his monthly income. He even received the occasional tip. Sometimes, particularly around Christmas, a customer might hand over three quarters and cheerfully remark, "Keep the change."

Father Mallory Parent always gave Lyle a crisp dollar bill.

Lyle had delivered *TV Guide* to the rectory for a month before actually meeting the priest. Our Lady of the Sea was not far from his house and was the final delivery on his route. For those first three weeks, he had approached the church a little warily. On the rectory lawn was a statue of the Virgin Mary. The sidewalk formed a little roundabout where she stood and Lyle would usually ride his bicycle in circles around her a couple of times before leaning it against the wall of the church. Spence's family never spoke about religion, though he had briefly attended Sunday School before he began kindergarten. And for a few years, each Easter and Christmas, everyone in his family donned their best attire and trooped to the Anglican church. The service was what was then known as low Anglican and Lyle vaguely understood, from his upbringing, and from his lessons in Sunday School, that he was, nominally, a Protestant.

He knew that those of his friends who were Catholic went to catechism every Tuesday after school until their confirmations but he never inquired too closely about that process. On Sunday mornings, he had seen women emerge from Our Lady of the Sea, their heads draped with white lace veils. He had once caught a glimpse of the interior with its stained-glass windows and garishly painted statues swathed in a haze of incense. So different from the austere interior of the Anglican church—oak pews, a few amber panes added to the windows, and a severe, unadorned cross.

And so, it was with some surprise that upon meeting Parent on collection day, he found himself confronted with an unprepossessing, middle-aged man wearing a baggy cardigan sweater over an ordinary black shirt with a too tight clerical collar. The scent of camphor lingered about him. Lyle later learned that that particular odour was from the snuff Parent took from time to time, placing a pinch from a little tin near the base of his thumb and inhaling it extravagantly. Typically, a powerful sneeze ensued and Parent would pull a handkerchief from his trousers and apply it vigorously to his nose.

"Hello, young man," he said. He had a French accent. "Please come inside."

That first time, Lyle stayed for only ten minutes, chatting about his *TV Guide* route, about Cub Scouts and baseball and school. They stood side by side and examined the exotic fish in the priest's large aquarium. Lyle left with a crisp one-dollar bill that Parent had tucked into his shirt pocket. The priest had asked him to knock on the door each time he made his delivery and Lyle willingly complied. When Lyle asked his name, he told him to simply call him Father.

"Everyone calls the priest Father. It's the custom, Lyle. It is respectful but . . . affectionate?"

Lyle nodded.

That second visit, Parent asked if Lyle was thirsty. "A little," he said. The priest brought two tall glasses with ice and a bottle of Coca Cola. He portioned the soda and handed one to Spence. They clinked glasses and Parent said, "*Santé.*"

"What does that mean?" Lyle asked.

"To your health. To your very good health."

"*Santé*," Lyle repeated and they clinked glasses again.

The television was on but the priest had turned down the sound when Lyle rang the doorbell. Now he walked over to the TV and turned the sound up. They watched a bit of *Gilligan's Island* together until Gilligan was transformed into the White Goddess, Gillianna. Then Parent rose abruptly from the sofa and turned the TV off.

"That's not very funny," he said.

Mallory Parent was patient. Those first few weeks he would invite Lyle into the living room of the rectory under some pretext of hospitality. Are you hungry? I have some lovely pastries. There is a new fish in the aquarium. I have a little gift for you—something I thought might interest you. Would you like to see the church?

Lyle received an invitation to attend Mass one Sunday. The priest suggested that he invite his parents, as well. Lyle had spoken to them, a little, about Father Parent. About how nice he was. To Spence's surprise, his mother and father accepted the invitation and, afterwards, he introduced them to Parent.

"This is Father . . . Father . . . "

"Father Mallory," he said. Everyone shook hands. Lyle's mother remarked that she had enjoyed the music. His father called him "Padre." He mentioned the name of a priest who had served aboard the HMCS *Qu'Appelle* with him some years earlier and did Parent know him? They had been at seminary together. What a coincidence.

The next Sunday, at his parents' invitation, the priest came over for dinner. Roast beef and Yorkshire pudding served on the good china and with the silverware that they'd received as a wedding gift. Lyle's father wore a tie. Parent said the blessing.

On the strength of these introductions, Lyle's parents put their confidence in Father Mallory. He was a priest, after all. Lyle's parents were agnostic, but some years ago they agreed to "let the children find their own way." Our Lady of the Sea was just down the street from their house. They were neighbours.

After dinner, Lyle's dad and Father Parent retired to the living room. Lyle and Ian washed and dried the dishes while their mother tidied. Babs played in her room. Parent sat in the armchair that was always reserved for his father. Lyle had never seen anyone else sit there except his grandfather. Over the course of the evening, Father Parent did not once speak to Lyle directly. In fact, he so thoroughly ignored him that Lyle wondered if he'd said or done something to offend him.

When he left, the priest shook hands with everyone, including Lyle. It was raining and Lyle stood on the porch and watched as Parent walked down the driveway to his car. For some reason it seemed strange to him that a priest would drive a car. Parent gave a little toot of the horn as he backed out and Lyle waved goodbye.

The wrestling did not alarm Lyle. He had told Parent about a fight he had witnessed at school. Parent affirmed that boys should have some knowledge of self-defence. He offered to share a few wrestling moves. Once a week, under the tutelage of the priest, Lyle was incrementally introduced to the subtleties of the manly art of wrestling.

At first, Parent showed Lyle some useful wrestling holds. The priest's size made it difficult for Lyle to perform these effectively. Yet, Parent would not allow him to be discouraged. Often Lyle would, for some several minutes, find himself with his arms wrapped around the priest's legs, or waist, or neck. Always Parent would exert just enough force to keep Lyle engaged, but not enough for either of them to break off from their sustained embrace.

After some weeks, Parent suggested a contest, offering to wrestle Lyle using only one arm. On these occasions, he would contrive a victory for Lyle. But he insisted it must be complete victory. In order for Lyle to win, he must completely immobilize the priest. This required him to lie flat on top of his opponent, exerting all his force to keep the priest subdued.

"I can still talk," Parent kept repeating. "How can you stop me from talking?"

Lyle understood. He compressed his lips and placed them on the priest's mouth. He felt the rough sandpaper of his whiskers.

In due course, Parent invoked the traditions of the ancient Greeks. Naturally, it would be inappropriate to be completely naked. Perhaps, Lyle should just remove his shirt. In time, they wrestled in their underwear. Occasionally, Parent would get an erection but Lyle had no clear understanding of what this might portend. He had some rudimentary knowledge about sex from a book his mother had given him to read: *A Doctor Talks to 10- to 12-Year-Olds*. He had been required to read it over the course of several evenings, seated alone at the kitchen table while his mother did the dishes. She had assured him that she would answer any of his questions.

"Mom, what are testicles?"

"Those are what you probably call your balls," she answered with a frankness that embarrassed him. Her back was to Lyle. He could make out her reflection in the window over the sink. He would ask no more questions. In any event, the book taught him nothing about sex, only the rudiments of the reproductive organs. So, when the tip of Parent's penis would poke over the elastic of his underwear, Lyle would politely pretend not to see. He would be confused—a little anxious, perhaps. But never outright alarmed. There was so much that was mysterious about adults that they would not explain.

When you're older. You're too young. One day you'll understand.

Parent's machinations were cautious. Each progression vaguely plausible. As when Lyle dutifully donned his rubber boots and went outside to tramp in the snow. Parent had challenged him to punch his belly in order to demonstrate the strength of his abdominal muscles. He even invited Lyle to stand, balanced on his belly, as he kept the boy steady by holding him by the buttocks. Then he sent him out into the frozen garden. Lyle traced a short route in the snow around the statue of the Virgin, as he had often done with his bicycle. He returned with snow still clinging to his boots. Parent lay on his back and loosened his trousers. He lifted the elastic of his underwear. Lyle stood on his belly and slipped his boots onto the priest's groin, the cold rubber on either side of Parent's now erect penis. This ritual they repeated several times that afternoon. This feat of strength. This test of manhood.

It was December 29, 1967. Feast of the Holy Family.

Spring came early. By the Victoria Day weekend, in May, the weather was warm, almost summery. Parent had proposed a camping trip. He and three boys would head out to Elk Lake on Sunday after Mass and be back by Monday evening. The other two boys, James and John, were twins. They were Catholic boys and their father knew Lyle's father because they sometimes drank beer together at the Chiefs' and Petty Officers' Mess. At the last moment, John came down with a fever and had to stay home. It was just Parent, Lyle and James.

The lake was not far. Less than an hour's drive. Their camping spot was near a rickety dock. A row boat with peeling white paint was secured there and the priest promised the boys that they could row out onto the lake in the morning. Together they set up the canvas tent they would share that night. James and Lyle played soccer for a while with a group of kids who were visiting from up the island. Later, they roasted wieners and marshmallows. The priest taught them a few words to a song in French.

It was well past nine o'clock before it was completely dark. He sent them into the tent with instructions to get into their pyjamas. A little later he came in himself. Lyle could smell liquor and he supposed the priest must have had a drink. The tent was nearly tall enough for a man to stand upright. Parent undressed in the dark and settled into his sleeping bag.

When he woke, Lyle could hear raindrops on the tent. Something had roused him from a deep sleep. He heard Father Parent whisper.

"Lyle. It is so cold. Come warm me up a little."

The tent did not seem quite so dark now. Lyle could just make out Parent's form next to him. He was holding his sleeping bag open and beckoning Lyle. He patted a spot next to him. Still half asleep, Lyle obediently slid next to the priest and, at once, fell back to sleep. Some time later he woke again. He could feel Parent's fingers fondling his penis. Alarmed, he pushed his hand away. He felt the priest shift position until he was poised over him. He guided Lyle's hand to his own erect penis. Closing his fingers around Lyle's, he moved the boy's hand in slow, rhythmic strokes. Lyle tried to pull his hand away but the priest was stronger.

After a couple of minutes, Parent stopped. Lyle crossed both his hands over his chest and held them there tightly. The priest repositioned himself, his erection brushing against Lyle's still flaccid penis. *This must be a dream.* Lyle remembered a trick he used to escape his dreams. His lucid dreams. He just needed to be alone for a moment. A place where he could close his eyes and bury his head in his arms. When he awoke, he would be safe in his own bed.

Then, Parent's mouth was around Lyle's penis. He could feel the stubble of his beard, the intense sensation of his tongue moving, the strange suction of his mouth drawing on his penis as if it were a paper straw. A moment later he was startled as the priest roughly lifted his testicles and licked his anus. Lyle cried out, half in pain, half in baffled surprise and embarrassment. Fully awake now, he pummelled Parent on his head and cheeks—wherever his fists could reach. The priest sat up. He slapped Lyle soundly on the cheek. Lyle could feel hot tears on his face. Nearby, James rolled over in his sleeping bag. Parent glanced in that direction. He pushed Lyle aside.

"Go. Go back to bed."

He scrambled into his own sleeping bag and zipped it to his neck. It was then that James rolled over again. For a moment their eyes met. Then James turned his back on Lyle. He heard a few soft grunts from Parent. He waited until he heard the priest's slow, rhythmic breathing before he dared to close his eyes and sleep.

The next morning, after breakfast, Parent took the boys out in the rowboat as promised. He rowed a little way from shore and abruptly stopped. All morning the priest had been moody and impatient. For a panicked moment, Lyle wondered if he was going to toss them both overboard and let them drown. The boat rocked perilously as Parent instructed the boys to change positions with him. He told them they would row back to shore. They struggled ineptly and Parent scolded them for being the sons of sailors and knowing nothing of boats. He continued to complain after they had docked and were walking back to camp.

Annoyed, Lyle muttered under his breath, "*Sacrebleu.*"

The priest turned and slapped him hard across the cheek. Lyle stood seething with fear and embarrassment and a suppressed rage that he could scarcely acknowledge.

"Never say that again!" Parent's finger was in Lyle's face.

Lyle did not even know the meaning of the phrase. He had heard it uttered in a Bugs Bunny cartoon. He thought it an innocuous French expression.

Lyle continued to deliver *TV Guide* to the rectory, slipping it through the mail slot and hurrying away. He no longer collected the subscription price. In any event, he figured he was more than breaking even after months of accepting Parent's tips. In July, the rectory door opened as Lyle approached. A young man stood there. He was wearing a black short-sleeved shirt with a clerical collar. He greeted Lyle kindly and explained that Father Parent had been transferred back to Montréal. He did not require a *TV Guide* as he rarely watched television.

"Are you owed anything?" he asked and reached into his pocket for change.

"No," Lyle said.

"All right, then. Bless you and have a nice evening."

The best laid schemes o' Mice an' Men
Gang aft agley,
An' lea'e us nought but grief an' pain.

I'm squatting on a plastic milk carton inside an empty recycling bin. I have brought one full water bottle. And one empty. Both contingencies covered. I have been here for a little more than an hour, keeping watch through the tiny peepholes that Thierry and Benoît have gnawed through the plastic. At Thierry's suggestion, I've glued sheets of newspaper to my umbrella. When open, it gives the impression that my bin is full. Over the walkie-talkies, which Thierry has stolen from my neighbour, he refers to me by my code name.

"Rainman, Rainman, come in. Over." Thierry checks in every half hour.

"Everything's quiet, Thierry. Over."

"*Qui?*"

"Everything's quiet, Baobab Boy. Over."

He has chosen that handle from *Le Petit Prince*. It amuses him because it sounds a bit like Be-a-Bad-Boy. Apparently, my umbrella inspired the name Rainman. Thierry claims he has never seen the movie with Dustin Hoffman. I dread the moment when I must use the other absurd codes Thierry has devised.

"Roger dat, Rainman. Baobab Boy out."

Thierry and Benoît have chosen this evening to exact revenge for the death of the three hapless mice who were poisoned here. My job is simple. Report to Thierry when the drivers arrive. Keep track of their activities. Advise Thierry when the engines start. Give a final warning when the first car goes up the tunnel exit toward the street.

The recently installed fluorescents produce an irritating hum. Surprisingly, some of these new ones already flicker off and on.

Thierry says the humming may prevent him from hearing the car engines starting. That's one of the reasons I am here. I am not entirely sure what Thierry and Benoît have in mind or what will happen the moment they exact their revenge. I've been told not to leave the recycling bin under any circumstances.

"Except if dere is a fire. Den get out."

"Fire? There could be fire?"

"*C'est possible mais peu probable.*"

If this bin is to be my funeral pyre, I am keenly aware that it is constructed entirely of plastic.

"Rainman, Rainman. Come in. Over."

"Nothing to report. No . . . wait."

I hear the low whirring hum and the clack-clack of the garage door opening. The squeal of tires. A van emerges from the tunnel, followed by a second van. Doors slide open and men leap out. They are nearly all attired in blue coveralls. Several have caps pulled low over their eyes. They wear gloves.

"Baobab Boy, Baobab Boy! *Les renards sont dans le poulailler. Je répète. Les renards sont dans le poulailler.* Over."

"Roger dat, Rainman. Over."

Another of Thierry's absurd codes: the foxes are in the henhouse. I am relieved that my neighbour is not among this mob. The men set to work removing the dust covers from the vehicles. The vans are still running their engines.

"Baobab Boy. Come in. Over." I hiss into the walkie-talkie then hold it to my ear. The volume is set low.

"Go ahead Rainman. Over."

"*Les renards* arrived in two vans. The vans are leaving now. *Les renards sont toujours dans le poulailler.* I repeat. The foxes are still in the henhouse. Over."

"Roger dat, Rainman. Over."

The door leading into the building swings open and Rocco enters, followed by Nick. The men in coveralls gather round as the vans depart. Rocco has a clipboard. He gives each man a sheet of paper. Nick hands out keys. Maybe the drivers are only just now learning which car, which route, and their destination. That would make sense. A good precaution if you think there's a snitch.

"Baobab Boy, Baobab Boy. Pinky and Dinky are in the henhouse."

"Roger dat."

The hum of the fluorescents intensifies. One of the tubes flickers and goes out. My eye is drawn to the three rows of old-fashioned electricity meters, because I can see Benoît standing on one of the topmost. From my vantage he appears to be holding aloft two long sticks of smouldering incense. Is it my imagination or is he wearing the ornate feather necklace of a Vodou priest? He seems to be praying. The dials on the meters begin to spin wildly. This is absurd.

Most of the men are seated in their cars. Engines come alive and spew clouds of exhaust. The roar of a dozen engines drowns out the humming from the lights. I shout over the din.

"Baobab Boy, Baobab Boy! *Les renards ont commencé—*"

I have no opportunity to give the final code. Overhead the fluorescent tubes begin to explode, one after another in quick succession. After each burst a shower of brittle white glass descends. The garage is plunged, briefly, into darkness. Moments later, I am blinded by a flood of headlights. The drivers are disoriented. Horns blare and tires screech. As my eyes adjust to the shifting light, I see Rocco run to the mouth of the exit tunnel, shouting and waving his arms. Headlights illuminate the far wall and I catch a glimpse of Benoît scaling the metal casing of a conduit as he ascends to the ceiling. Below him the electricity meters are glowing red. I have no idea what sort of sabotage he has wrought, but they explode and glass is blasted across the garage. Nick turns and pulls his jacket over his head. Rocco shields his face with his arms. Several shards pierce the recycling bin and poke through the plastic inches from my face.

Above the blare of the horns, sirens wail. Flashing blue and red lights dance on the walls. Dozens of uniformed police swarm the garage, guns are drawn. A single shot is fired, maybe by accident. At the sound of a ricochet, everyone ducks. All around, engines are switched off and voices echo in rapid French. The beams from flashlights crisscross everywhere and drivers emerge from the cars with their hands held high in the air.

There is a deafening screech from my walkie-talkie and the lid to my hiding place is flung open. My camouflage—my newspaper umbrella—is torn away. The glare of a flashlight. I try to stand and raise my arms but my legs are numb from sitting cramped for so long. I lose my balance as I try to hoist myself up and the bin topples over. I land painfully—half in and half out. I look up through the white light. Her face floats above me: the silver-haired widow.

She is leaning over me. I reach toward her and am embarrassed when my hand accidently brushes against her breast. At that moment, the cacophony ceases and everything in the parking garage goes utterly silent.

A profound silence, like nothing I have ever experienced.

It is as though the very atmosphere has surrendered and the garage has been transformed into a vacuum. The total absence of sound is even more disconcerting than were the sirens and explosions. Now everything is darkness except for the flashlight that shines directly in my eyes.

"Please," I say. Like a goldfish in a bowl, my mouth moves but I have no voice. I place my hand over the lens and fumble with it for a moment as it falls into my grasp. Still no sound. My other senses seem less reliable without my ears confirming what I can see and feel. It is like switching off the sound from a television, except the whole world is now that television. I turn the light upward but my beautiful white-haired neighbour has vanished.

No one is going to believe me. I know that. I'm not sure *I* believe it. There is a white, life-size statue standing where my neighbour should be. At first, it looks as though she has, somehow, been frozen. As though a blast of arctic air has transformed her.

I must be dreaming.

The concrete floor is covered in snow. Or is it simply covered in those delicate shards of glass that fell when the fluorescents exploded? How can that be? I set the flashlight on the ground and stand up. The snow is nearly a foot deep. I am in rubber boots. Where did they come from? I walk around the statue of my neighbour. Except it is no longer her. It is that statue of the Virgin Mary that stood on the lawn outside the rectory of Our Lady of the Sea. She has Tadla's face. I am walking around her in my rubber boots. In the snow. But I might as well be walking on clouds. I can feel the crunch of the snow but everything is still. It is the kind of complete silence that makes you wonder if your own heart is still pumping blood. Even that nearly imperceptible pulse is absent. Where I have put the flashlight down, I now see a pair of lights recessed into the lawn. Their heat has melted the snow and they illuminate the statue from below. I turn toward the windows of the rectory. The curtain parts. He is standing there waving.

Father Mallory Parent.

This must be a dream.

The statue of the Virgin begins to soundlessly disintegrate. Briefly, it looks like the statue in the little courtyard at Queen of All Saints. The peeling paint, the missing fingers, the crumbling nose. Absurdly, I am reminded of *Ben Hur*, the caves with the lepers. The scene where Charlton Heston embraces his mother and her leprosy is healed. I remember seeing the movie on TV. I panic.

I can't be here.

Inexplicably, I am back in the parking garage. At my feet is the umbrella I used to conceal myself in the recycling bin. The pages of newspaper come unfastened and begin spinning madly like in a movie from the forties before a headline appears on the screen. Then they become propellors—the old-fashioned wooden sort on biplanes. Did I will that transformation? Oliver and Wendell. I mouth the names but no sound emerges. Besides, that is wrong. What am I thinking of? *TV Guide*? *Green Acres*? Orville and Wilbur? Arnold Ziffel? The wind from the propellors displaces the snow around my feet and it starts to rise. I am not cold. I should at least hear the wind whistling by my ears but there is nothing. I can feel it, but there is no sound at all. Snowflakes hang in space—swirling around me like thousands of tiny, crystalline ornaments dangling from a Christmas tree. Rudolph the Red-Nosed Reindeer. I look around for the flashlight but it is gone. I can see but I cannot determine any source of light.

Picking up the umbrella, I feel myself begin to float upward. I am briefly panicked as I rise through the ceiling in the garage. Passing through my own apartment on the third floor, my bed is visible below me. I want to lie down on it but I continue to clutch the umbrella. Mary Poppins. Propellors and snowflakes whirl around me. All in silence. Below, I try to recognize my neighbourhood in NDG. I must fly to Clara's apartment, I think. I need to water the plants.

But I am not in Montréal, now. I am in the house where I lived as a boy in Belmont Park. My father is raining blows down on me with his belt. It's my fault. I didn't water the plants. I didn't do any of my chores. I should have been minding Babs. The belt strikes me on the cheek and one eye becomes swollen shut as though I had been stung by a wasp. Where is my umbrella? Maybe I can use it as a shield.

My mother is sitting on a chair at the kitchen table. It is one of those Formica-topped tables that everyone had back in the sixties. Stainless steel trim and legs. She is crying but making no sound. My father stops and hands me the belt. I'm not sure what I am supposed to do with it. He sits down next to my mother and, he too, begins to cry soundlessly. I feel sorry for them both. They're so young, I think. They must have been children, once. What must they have suffered?

Without warning, I am transported to my crib. Not transported, really. I am just there and, now, I am crying too. I'm a baby. But old enough to stand up. My gums are aching and I gnaw on the headboard of the crib. It produces no sound. Little yellow ducklings marred by jagged lines where my baby teeth have scraped the paint. Somehow, I can still see my parents, though they are downstairs in the kitchen, still crying soundlessly. None of this is making any sense but it feels very good to cry. I feel as though I want to cry forever, it feels so wonderful.

Now I am certain I am in a dream. Or, perhaps, I am inside a memory of a dream that I had as a child. Perhaps all those dreams are assembled somewhere in my mind like books on a dusty shelf. Perhaps I am simply repeating a dream, the way you read a book and it is only when you are halfway through that you realize you've read it before. Is that how we recall our own lives? Stories we half remember? Yellowing paper and faded ink. Crumbling volumes stuffed with the secrets we keep from ourselves.

A horse is a horse, of course, of course.
Why have I got the theme song from *Mister Ed* stuck in my mind? It is as though I am turning the channels on an old black and white TV. I lose my balance and noiselessly fall backward onto the mattress of my crib. What is that smell? Urine? Johnson's Baby Powder? How can I sense odour but not sound? There are plastic sheets under the cotton ones. I can feel them crinkling when I move but still no sound. I'm a newborn baby. A wooden clothespin is fastened to my umbilical cord. That can't be possible. Why a clothespin? I abruptly stop crying as I reach down to touch it. Fascinated, I bring my tiny, plump fingers to my face. I can smell the sea. Clara.

Now I am flung upwards. Up through the ceiling of the bedroom. Up and up and up until I am floating among the stars. They surround me. As thick as a fog. Like the foam that gathers at the surface of steamed milk, but everything glitters as brightly and as varied as crystals of sand under a child's microscope. It is all incredibly beautiful. If only I could dissolve and become a part of it all. But I know I cannot stay here.

I must deliver my *TV Guides.*

I set my bicycle against the wall of the church. Our Lady of the Sea. Crushed shells on the ground in the tidy space that divides the foundation from the sidewalk. I ring the doorbell to the rectory. The door opens. I am expecting Mallory Parent but it is a boy wearing only a pair of white underpants. He is maybe ten. It takes me a moment to recognize myself.

What is he looking at?

I realize he is staring at my eye. The one swollen shut by my father's belt. I want to say something but I cannot find my voice. Everything is wholly silent. So, I reach out and hand him a *TV Guide.* There is a picture of Bob Denver on the cover. The actor who played Gilligan on *Gilligan's Island.* He shuts the door.

I have the odd sensation that I am outside of my own body. I am simultaneously on the porch and inside the rectory. I turn and see the statue of the Virgin on the lawn. No. That's wrong. Her hands are supposed to be open, her arms parted, as if she is about to enfold the world. I am certain that is how I remember her. She looks like the actress on *I Dream of Jeannie.* She is holding a little figure of the child, Jesus. He is maybe two years old. His arms are outstretched the way children reach out when you have been holding them for a while and now you are passing them back to their mother.

I see myself passing Clara to Serenity, when she was that age. How she would lean out of my grasp as though she were absolutely convinced that she could just float from me into her mother's arms. As if gravity held no sway over her. Life held no dangers. I start to cry again. Again, I make no sound. Maybe I am crying for Serenity. Or for Clara. Both? Perhaps I am crying for Jesus because he too, is just a little kid. I suppose Joseph wanted to protect him, too. Except he didn't. Maybe he couldn't. He just disappears from the story. No one knows why.

Abraham begat Isaac; and Isaac begat Jacob; and Jacob begat Judas and his brethren.

All those fathers busy begetting but where are all the men when Christ is suffering on the cross? Only the three Marys remain. Three faithful women. Disciples—absent by the dozen. All those distant fathers. The Church full of men hiding from themselves. Hiding from women. Hiding from Christ. Hiding their sordid crimes. Daring to call themselves fathers.

It would be better for them to have a large millstone hung around their neck and to be drowned in the depths of the sea.

I hear something, at last. It is far away. Like geese approaching with a hoarse fanfare. I cannot open my eyes. It is as though someone has placed a pair of coins over them. Sealed like tombs. "This is a dream," I say. My voice, I think, is coming back to me. The rectory and the church dissolve. The statue of the Virgin and Child wavers. I lie down in the snow and bury my face in my arms, the way I did when I was a boy and needed to escape a dream. I can recognise the sound now. It is a siren.

TUESDAY

Elle s'appelle Manon. The woman next door with the silver hair. Her name is Manon. She is sitting on my bed in what must be the Emergency Ward.

"*J'étais tellement inquiete pour toi.*"

"*Je suis désolé,*" I murmur. "*Merci pour votre . . .*" I search for the word. "*. . . votre . . . gentillesse?*"

"*De rien. Je suis tellement heureuse que tu ailles bien.*"

She is addressing me in the familiar form.

"*Tu parles très bien français.*" She smiles.

That's not true. But it's an encouraging fib. We chat for a while. Me in broken French and Franglais. Her occasionally in hesitant English with an accent that makes each word sound as if it had been born anew at that exact moment.

I am suddenly sleepy, hypnotized by the vision of her legs, one crossed over the other, and by one shapely calf moving rhythmically. The long heel of her slightly scuffed black shoe rising and falling on the horizon of my bed like the slender bill of a bird feeding in a spring marsh.

A nurse comes by with one small paper cup full of water and another with a pill nestled in the bottom. I am too tired to resist. I suppose I slept for a while because it is noon when I next open my eyes and Manon is gone. Was she really here? Or did I imagine her?

I remember.

Manon was standing between the open rear doors to the ambulance speaking rapidly in French to the paramedics. I recognized the words *tomber* and *tête*. I must have passed in and out of consciousness several times before I finally arrived in Emergency. Before we parted, it seemed to me that Manon was about to climb into the ambulance. But Nick put a hand on her shoulder and shook his head no.

Strange.

Another doctor comes by. Not the one who examined me when I was admitted. He is a little man with unusually thick lenses in his glasses. Through them, his eyes appear to be too large for his face. I don't feel like talking, so I provide laconic responses to his questions and am pleased when he seems to lose interest. I sleep for a while. It is late afternoon when I wake and I decide I will walk home. A police officer has been stationed a few feet from my bed.

"*Je suis désolée, monsieur, mais vous ne pouvez pas partir.*"

The cop is younger than Clara. She appears to be about the age of one of my senior students back at Queen of All Saints. I realize she is a police cadet. Am I in the custody of this child? She sits in the chair next to my bed and scrolls through her phone for the rest of the afternoon.

WEDNESDAY

I spent all of yesterday in Emergency. I have a splint on my sprained right wrist and a bandage over the abrasions on my cheek. Several young cadets have taken turns sitting near me in shifts. Not one has acknowledged me. Perhaps I have become invisible. This morning a cop arrives. He looks like he spends most of his leisure time in the gym. Maybe because of my injured wrist, I am not handcuffed as I am escorted to a police cruiser and placed in the back. By 9:00 am we are at Hôpital Douglas, *institut universitaire santé mentale*.

The officer leaves and I am escorted to a small room. On the single bed is a white towel and facecloth, a thin brick of soap wrapped in paper, a toothbrush, and a small tube of toothpaste. I put my belt, my keys and my wallet in a blue plastic container and they are taken away. Surprisingly, I am permitted my phone. I turn it off.

THURSDAY

Breakfast is Corn Flakes with skim milk and a banana.

I take a nap.

A nurse rouses me for lunch. An egg salad sandwich, an apple, and two Dad's Cookies in a cellophane wrapper.

Another nap.

Dinner is *pâté chinois* and green Jell-O.

Medication.

I lie awake on my bed, staring at the ceiling.

I hope Thierry's okay.

FRIDAY

Yesterday's *Gazette* is on the table. I stare at the crossword puzzle for an hour. One down. Four letters. Denizen of the sky.

Bird? Dove? Wren? Star? Moon? Mars?

Who can decide such things?

Thierry might know.

More medication.

SATURDAY

I spend much of the morning being interviewed by the resident psychiatrist. So many questions.

Tentative diagnosis: unspecified delusional disorder.

More medication.

I need Thierry.

FIFTH SUNDAY OF EASTER

Yesterday, the psychiatrist had explained that I am involuntarily committed to the hospital but that, with medication, she was confident I could shortly be released as an out-patient. This morning, I take a shower and sit in my room for two hours in a hospital gown while staff launders my clothes. Later, I am allowed to visit the little chapel in another section of the building. I am escorted there by one of the attendants. He is dressed informally in jeans and a black Cat Stevens T-shirt. Beneath the white portrait is the word *meow.* The chapel is small, austere, and designed to suggest a vague atmosphere of non-denominational spirituality—oak pews, a shelf-like fireplace mantel that I suppose is meant to resemble an altar. On it is a single electric candle in a plastic red cup.

"Psst!"

"Thierry!"

He is sitting in the pew beside me.

"*Tabernac!* We been lookin' for you for days. You know you gotta take two different Metro an' a bus to get 'ere? I get lost so many time."

"How did you know I was here?"

"What? You tink mice dun know what goin' on in dis city? Me an' Benoît, we preddy famous for givin' Rocco what 'e got comin'. People talk to us. I 'eard it tru de grapevine, brudder, like de song say."

I stare at him for what seems a long while and neither of us speak.

"What de matter, *mon chum?* You got dat faraway look in yer eye."

"Nothing. I was just thinking . . ."

"Tinkin'? I tawt you is retire, man? You dun 'ave to do no more tinkin'. Not in dis lifetime. Too much tinkin' mebbe what got you in dis nuthouse in de first place."

"Thierry, what are you doing here?"

"I come to spring you, man. Get you outta 'ere. I got a plan—"

My mind is spinning. For a moment I am back in the recycling bin. The explosions. The glass flying. The lights and sirens.

"Thierry, stop! Stop. Just stop for a second."

He removes his pork pie hat, smooths his ears back and replaces it at a jaunty angle. He looks at me calmly.

"I have a hat just like that," I say. I focus on his hat. It calms me.

"Nice. Why you never wear it?"

"I'm on the bike a lot now. But I used to wear it all the time."

"Uh huh."

"It looks better on you."

"What can I say, man?"

The attendant in the Cat Stevens T-shirt opens one of the oak doors to the chapel and tells me I have a visitor. A visitor? I don't know anyone, really, in Montréal. I glance down at Thierry, but he is gone. He has left his pork pie hat. I reach to pick it up, but when I open my hand it's gone as well.

My visitor is a priest. He is wearing a blazer over a black shirt with a clerical collar. I stand a bit awkwardly and am embarrassed when I flinch a little as he extends his hand to shake mine.

"Father."

"Please, just call me Omer." The priest is about my age and has soft, plump hands. He slides into the pew in front of me and turns, extending his arm along the oak top. I sit back down. I watch him fuss with the ribbon that marks his page in the little black book he is carrying. For a moment, I think he is going to read me a Bible passage but then realize it is simply one of those old-fashioned moleskin notebooks.

"Mr. Spencer?" he smiles.

"Just Spence."

"Spence." He makes a note of this in the book. "I was in the Urgent Care Ward down the hall and they told me you were here."

"You were looking for me?" Why would he be looking for me? Absurdly, I think about the fire at Frère André's chapel.

"No, no. I'm just making my rounds. I work for the Diocese of Montréal. I'm a sort of liaison."

"Liaison to what?"

"Correctional institutions, hospitals, mental health facilities, that sort of thing."

"I see." He notes my confusion.

"When you were admitted to Emergency on . . . " he looks

in his black book, "On Tuesday, you may recall answering a few questions?"

"I remember a doctor asking questions. Two doctors." I don't mention the succession of police cadets taking turns supervising me.

"Ah, yes. Well, one of the questions is about religious affiliation. It's optional, actually. That should have been explained to you. In any case . . ." He shrugs and gestures as if to say "so here I am."

"I really can't remember. Apparently, I'm a little..." I point a finger at my head and waggle it as if to remind him we are in a mental hospital.

"Of course. I hope the diagnosis you've received is helping you in your recovery."

"Unspecified delusional disorder."

"Ah," he says. "That means they are uncertain."

We sit in silence for a moment.

"May I ask, are you a practising Catholic?"

I nod a bit hesitantly. I am and I'm not, I think to myself.

"Well then, you must be accustomed to being diagnosed as delusional."

We both smile.

"Are you native to Montréal? A member of a parish?"

"St. Monica's," I say. He makes another note.

I explain that I've recently moved from Vancouver. For some reason I suddenly feel quite chatty. Maybe it's the medication. Maybe it's because I haven't spoken to anyone for a while. Except Thierry. I've spoken to Thierry. I tell him a little about Queen of All Saints. I mention JF and stupidly ask if they've ever met. Why would they have ever met? I prattle on about JF and mention that everyone in the Sauvé family was grateful to Frère André for his father's seemingly miraculous recovery from polio. For some reason, I feel overwhelmed and become a little tearful. Maybe talking about JF has set me off. "Sorry. It's the medication, I think."

Father Omer nods.

"Frère André has been a source of inspiration for many."

"Yes," I say. I am about to mention Thierry and stop myself. Instead, I say: "Someone did a presentation at Queen of All Saints. After he was beatified. Or canonized. Something-ized."

"I suppose you heard about the fire at the chapel by the Oratory?" He watches me closely as he asks this.

I can feel the blood rush to my face. His look turns quizzical.

"Mr. Spencer." He hesitates. "Spence. I can see you are a sincere person. I am guessing you are an honest person, as well. And I'm sorry that I have not been entirely forthright with you. But . . . "

Father Omer opens the little black book again and takes out several newspaper clippings.

"Spence. When you were first admitted to Emergency you were not conscious and you had no identification with you. Staff found these in your pocket."

He carefully unfolds three newspaper clippings. Two of them are in French and one in English. They all pertain to the fire at St. Joseph's Chapel. "Please understand, no one is accusing you of anything."

"You stole my . . . why?" I'm not sure what is happening. I'd saved the clippings for Thierry. For reading practice. How could this priest possibly know I had been at the chapel the day of the fire?

"There was a police cadet assigned to you, Spence. That indicated to me that, likely, you were being detained. It was sheer coincidence that I saw you at all, because I was there for a different matter. I spoke to a woman named . . . " he consults his notebook again... "Manon. She'd arrived sometime after you were admitted. In fact, it was she who initially identified you. Anyway, seeing the clippings, she was very concerned that the police might think you were involved because she felt you were . . . That you hadn't done anything wrong and that you were not well."

"A nutjob," I say.

Father Omer shrugs. "I'm sorry. I don't know why I kept them. I shouldn't have and I apologize. Manon was afraid that the clippings might have cast suspicion on you. She didn't want you to be falsely accused and, given your recent . . ."

He trails off.

"I suppose neither of us was thinking very clearly. Manon seemed very sweet and obviously concerned. I think I just went along for the ride. In retrospect, it all seems rather silly. Anyway, I felt I should return them to you."

"A nun," I say.

"Pardon?"

"A religious sister," I say. "She threw a candle. It wasn't her fault. She was startled. Thierry—"

I stop. Father Omer is looking at me as if I am a lunatic. Perhaps I am.

"I'm sorry, Spence. I have no idea what you are talking about?"

"The chapel," I say.

"The chapel?"

"The fire at the chapel. A nun threw a candle. It set all those little paper prayer intentions ablaze. I used the fire extinguisher. I should have stayed but I guess I panicked. I know I should have gone to the authorities but . . ."

Father Omer looks down at the clippings he is holding and then up at me again. He blinks several times. He starts to speak but stops himself. He sits looking at me for a long while.

"Am I hearing you correctly? You are saying it was you who put out the fire at the chapel?"

"With the fire extinguisher. There were two of them right by the door. I cut my finger taking out the pin." I hold up my hand to show him the thin scar on my finger, still a little red around the edges.

"So, you were bleeding? Your hand I mean?" he asks.

"Just my finger. Yes. Quite a bit, actually."

He sits staring at me, evidently dumbfounded, for a full minute.

"Are you going to tell the police?" I ask, finally.

"What? Yes. I mean no. I mean the police are still looking for the culprit."

"Really?"

"It must be someone troubled," he says.

"It all happened so fast," I say. "Maybe I'm mistaken. About the nun."

I feel certain I saw a nun throw a candle. But it is possible I have not been seeing everything entirely clearly lately.

"Which fire extinguisher?"

"Sorry?"

"Which fire extinguisher did you use?"

"The one on your left as you enter. You know, nearest the candles."

Father Omer nods solemnly.

"Where were the flames? Exactly?"

"Mostly along the wall next to the altar where there is the Sacred Heart of Jesus. One of the angels was shattered. I remember because—" I can see Thierry's moist black eyes blinking through a dusting of chemical suppressant. "I just remember."

"This is a very bizarre coincidence. When I spoke with Manon in Emergency, clearly, she was trying to avoid you being implicated in the arson. I mean, those three clippings and you hiding in a . . . I can't recall what she said."

"A recycling bin." I sigh. "I was in a recycling bin."

Omer can't prevent himself from smiling.

"May I ask why?"

"I don't know anymore. Maybe I thought I could get myself reincarnated."

Omer got permission to escort me on a walk around the hospital grounds, which are very pretty and extend almost to the river. We exchange phone numbers before we part.

MONDAY

I am released today with the caveat that I must attend an appointment, tomorrow, with a psychiatrist at Jewish General Hospital. I have been enrolled in some sort of outpatient program.

My apartment is as I left it but it seems somewhat more chaotic than what I recall.

"Thierry?"

I call several times. No response. I look under my bed. Under the sofa. I drag the stove away from the wall. Dust and two long, greasy smears on the floor. I pull the fridge out. More dust. Under the sink, there is the box of mousetraps. Almost a hundred traps neatly stacked.

TUESDAY

The psychiatrist at Jewish General seems nice enough. Dr. Tremblay. There are some long questionnaires to be filled out. I am given a prescription for antipsychotics. I say nothing but I decide I am taking no more medication. I don't like the way it makes me feel, as though I am a visitor in my own body.

Back at home, I pick up my old companion, *Le Petit Prince*.

J'ai ainsi vécu seul, sans personne avec qui parler véritablement, jusqu'à une panne dans le désert Sahara, il y a six ans. Quelque chose s'était cassé dans mon moteur.

So, I lived all alone, without anyone with whom I could truly talk, until a breakdown in the Sahara Desert, six years ago. Something was wrong with my motor.

Something is certainly wrong with my motor. Clearly, I have had some sort of breakdown. And the only person with whom I've truly talked for a long time is *une petite souris*. A little mouse named Thierry.

Wednesday

I can't find the copy of Camus' *L'Étranger*. The copy Thierry gave me. Stole for me. I spend much of the day fruitlessly searching. Come evening, I start to feel a little calmer and I take a chair out onto the balcony. Nearly 8:00 pm and it is still daylight. A group of men are playing cards at one of the picnic tables across the street in the park.

Then I hear it. The familiar sound of the garage door opening below my balcony. First comes the green Karmann Ghia Coupe. Right behind it, the Rolls Royce Phantom. The men in the park look up from their cards and break into a spontaneous round of applause. The putt-putt of the VW convertible. The top is down and two middle-aged men in matching polo shirts sit in the front. The driver has his arm around his passenger. One by one the cars that Thierry and I checked out in the garage emerge. The blue Fiat 600. The cherry-red Aston Martin. Whoever is driving the Ford Fairlane revs the engine and his tires squeal as he turns onto Boulevard Décarie. Not one vehicle shows any sign of damage.

I race down to the parking garage. It is nearly empty. Carefully folded tarpaulins sit propped against the walls. The odour of exhaust hangs in the air. I look over at the glass utility meters on the far wall. All perfectly intact. On the ceiling all the fluorescent burn brightly except the one directly over the recycling bins. The two metal ends are still fixed in position but it has, evidently, exploded. I spend a few moments trying to find the peep holes that Thierry and Benoît gnawed through the plastic of the bin.

They are gone.

Thursday

"Gibeau Orange Julep," Nick says. I am sitting in his office. Nick is behind the desk.

"Gibeau Orange Julep." I repeat it back to him.

"It's a Montréal landmark, Spence. A tradition."

"And every Wednesday night?"

"A hundred, maybe two hundred vintage cars, hot rods, MGs, Mustangs, you name it. Wednesday night, they all converge on Orange Julep."

"And those cars are parked here?"

"Well, not all of them. But a few. My brother belongs to a kind of informal classic car club. He likes to say he's the president of the club but really, he's full of shit. He just knows a lot of guys who are like him. Guys who love vintage cars. Every Wednesday night, once the weather is good, they all hang out at Orange Julep. It's ten minutes up Décarie. Huge parking lot. Total car nerds. But I make a decent buck storing the cars over the winter."

Nick sits smiling at me. Part of me thinks I should be afraid. But I'm not. I don't quite know what I'm feeling but I have a sudden need to get everything off my chest. So, I just blurt it out.

"It was me."

"What?"

"It was me. Who robbed the safe."

Nick tilts his head and squints a little as though I've gone out of focus.

"I'll pay you back," I add. "I just need some time."

"What safe?"

"The one under your desk."

Nick seems amused. He reaches below his knees, pulls out a blue produce box and sets it on his desk. It has FRAIS AU QUÉBEC printed on the side.

"This safe?"

"What is that?"

"It's a cardboard box, Spence. I use it for recycling."

"No money is missing?"

"Am I an idiot? What? I'm going to keep money in this office?

Don't be crazy." He frowns. "Sorry, Spence. I didn't mean that. I know you've been going through a hard time."

I feel a wave of relief wash over me and I burst into tears. I cry for several minutes, while Nick stands awkwardly with a box of tissues, occasionally giving me a little pat on the shoulder.

"I'm sorry about the guy next door, too," I sob. "That was all my fault. I didn't mean for that to get out of hand."

"Next door to who, Spence?"

"Me," I blubber. "The guy who was living next door to me."

"Spence. Until this month, nobody has been living next door to you. The apartment was being renovated. Sorry about the noise."

Another tenant knocks cautiously on the open door to Nick's office. I excuse myself and, averting my face, hurry to the lobby. There is mailbox 105. The one where Thierry started the fire. His distraction. Someone has pasted an adhesive sticker to the metal door. It is black and vaguely star-shaped. On it, in bold white letters, is printed EXTINCTION REBELLION. That's all. No smoke. No fire.

How long have I been dreaming? I'm not a thief. I've never stolen anything in my life. Some cookies, maybe, when I was a kid. Even something that minor might have earned a round with my father's belt. Maybe I just needed to be a bad boy for once in my cowardly life. Take a risk. Live a little.

I think back. How much of my life has actually been delusion? All those bizarre memories of childhood. Had I invented them? The lucid dreams. Burying myself in the roles I played in the theatre. A decade lost to drunkenness. The strange experience in the cathedral that finally got me sober. Even as a teacher—had I spent a twenty-year career playing make-believe? What of my religious convictions? Just some crazy story. Have I spent so much of my life in my imagination that I no longer know how to parse fiction from reality? Maybe a recycling bin is exactly what I deserve.

I jump at the unfamiliar sound. It takes me a moment to realize it is the intercom. The only other time I've heard that alarming squawk is when Clara and Gabriel came over for Christmas.

"Yes?"

I hear a distorted reply in a vaguely familiar voice.

"Who?"

"Omer."

The priest. Why is he at the entrance? Has he brought the police? Truly, I did nothing wrong. Maybe it wasn't a nun who started the fire. But I had no part in that. I put it out. I can't be mistaken. Can I? Though I suppose, if I am capable of robbery . . .

Even if nothing went missing.

"Come on up."

I watch through the peephole as he approaches. He's alone, no police.

"I'm sorry," I say. "The place is a mess. I can make you some coffee but I don't think I have any cream."

"I can't really stay, Spence. Another time, maybe."

"How did you find me?"

"I tried texting you and I tried calling but you didn't respond. I was a little concerned so I stopped by St. Monica's. Normally they wouldn't share your address, but in the circumstances . . . "

I vaguely recall turning off my cell phone at Douglas Hospital. I haven't used it since. More than a week ago. It's there. On the table.

"Sorry. I turned it off because . . . I don't know why I turned it off."

"Not to worry, Spence. Can we?" He gestures to the table and we both sit.

"Spence, I've been thinking about what you described. Your experience at the chapel. The fire and so on. And I wanted to assure you that I believe your recollection is, substantially, accurate. Someone wearing a black hoodie was seen running from the chapel across the parking lot. Given your, um, illness, is it possible you saw the hoodie and imagined a traditional black religious habit?"

"I suppose."

"And rather than lighting a candle?"

"I really can't say for sure, Fa—Omer."

"Spence, everything else you describe—blood on the fire extinguisher, the location of the blaze—none of those details were in the papers. The chapel, itself, has been closed until yesterday. There is no way you could know those details unless you were there."

Omer reaches into his pocket. "In any event, I've spoken with the archbishop and he is of the same opinion as me. We haven't mention this to the police because we feel you have gone through enough. But I think we'd be remiss if we didn't offer you some token of our gratitude. The chapel is of tremendous importance to the diocese. To the whole city, really."

He hands me a tiny black box. It contains a silver medallion depicting St. Joseph and the Infant Jesus. I've seen them at the souvenir shop at the Oratory. Thierry, I think. Thierry would love this.

"Who's Thierry?"

Did I speak aloud?

"No one," I say. "A friend. Just a friend."

"Friendship is a great blessing."

"Yes," I say. "Thanks. Thank-you."

"God will not give up on you, Spence. You're not alone. And you can call me if you need me. I hope you don't mind but I also spoke to Larry."

"Larry?"

"Father Larry at St. Monica's. He's a good guy. He'll talk your ear off about books and movies, but he's also a good listener."

I stand at the door to my apartment and watch Omer as he departs. He gives me a little wave as he turns the corner toward the elevator. Back inside, I switch on my cell phone. Two voice messages and two texts from Omer. A text from Dr. Tremblay's office reminding me about my next psychiatric appointment. One from Clara: "Love you, Daddy! Be home June 1."

Next Friday. One week. I have a week to pull myself together.

SATURDAY

Lately, I have been reading *Le Petit Prince* quite a lot. I have more passages memorized now. I can readily recognize the verb conjugations. Most of the book I can read aloud with a moderate degree of fluency. Even my dreadful pronunciation has improved, I think.

I have had time to reflect on some of the characters *le petit prince* encounters on various planets: *le roi*, who believes he rules the stars; *le businessman*, who is convinced he owns them; *le géographe*, mapping worlds he has never seen. *L'allumeur*, faithfully genuflecting to traditions that no longer shed light. *Le vaniteux*, doffing his hat to a need that feeds on itself. *Le buveur*, drinking to smother the shame of being a drunkard.

Except ye turn, and become as little children, ye shall no wise enter into the kingdom of heaven.

Trouble with being a little child? It is vulnerability that gives one wisdom. But our world sees vulnerability as weakness, weakness to be exploited. Perhaps, in the cloistered environment of my studio at Queen of All Saints, surrendering my power had been the source of my strength. But in the real world? "Behold, I send you forth as sheep in the midst of wolves; be ye therefore wise as serpents and as innocent as doves."

The psychiatrist, Dr. Tremblay, suggests I feel isolated from the world because of the onset of mental illness. But what if it is actually the world that is crazy? What if I am beginning to go sane? I don't think there's a pill for that.

SUNDAY

I attend Mass in the Basilica of St. Joseph's Oratory, climbing the ninety-nine wooden steps as I did on Good Friday, the day Thierry disappeared. I visit the Votive Chapel where Thierry lit a candle for Jean-Guy, then I walk across the parking lot to the Chapel. All of the neatly folded paper prayer intentions have been plucked from behind the marble plaques, a few of which still have some smoke damage, as does the altar. The fire, at least, was real. Omer is real. I touch the little St. Joseph medallion through my shirt. Manon? Real. Omer spoke with her. The vintage cars? I suppose I was a little confused there. Getting drunk? There are certainly several days I can't remember.

MONDAY

This morning I ride my bike to Cimetière Notre-Dame-des-Neiges. How long since I last rode? Two weeks? Three? The day Thierry rode to Mass with me with his pink Bicycle Barbie helmet and sunglasses? I dismount as I pass under the lichgate at the entrance. Behind me I can glimpse the dome of L'Oratoire Saint-Joseph above a fortress of apartment buildings.

I walk past the working-class section. Row upon row of ordinary headstones, almost uniform in shape and height. It is as though a giant scythe has harvested this section, leaving only stubble. I am startled when a groundhog waddles out from behind a nearby head-stone, nibbling at grass and dandelions.

At the crest of the hill, I pause near a row of family tombs built into a knoll like hobbit homes. I read the inscription on one of them: *Agnus Dei, qui tollis peccata mundi, miserere nobis.* Lamb of God, you take away the sins of the world, have mercy on us.

Thus far the graves and monuments have been both lovely and

grim. But now I come to a newer section that looks like the shredded remains of a Christmas morning in the rain. Faded pink and purple wreathes dangle from headstones. Crumpled bouquets languish in the grass.

Mothers' Day. I forgot Mothers' Day.

TUESDAY

I telephone my mom today and we speak for an hour. She's fine. I'm fine. Babs and Ian and their kids are fine. Everyone is fine.

Afterward, I walk down to St. Raymond's and stand in the vestibule looking at the photo of Father Mallory Parent OSM 1968–69. He is real. That was real. I open the interior doors and perform a little genuflection before walking down to where a candle wavers in the red lamp above the tabernacle. I am about to lower the bench of the front pew when I notice it has one of those old-fashioned—what are they called? Misericords? A little protuberance on the upright edge of the hinged pew bench. A place where a fatigued worshipper might lean and sit partly upright during the portions of the Mass that require one to stand. *Petites miséricordes.* Little mercies.

The bell sounds. Clanks. It must be noon. I recall a portion of *Le Petit Prince* that I have memorized.

Et j'aime la nuit écouter les étoiles. C'est comme cinq cent millions de grelots . . .

And I love listening to the stars at night. It is like five hundred million little bells . . .

Alors les grelots se changent tous en larmes . . .

Then the bells are all changed into tears . . .

WEDNESDAY

Several times today, I have knelt on my bed with my ear to the wall that adjoins Manon's apartment next door. Over the course of the past week, I thought I'd heard some muffled sounds of activity. But no music. No off-key singing. I'd even stood outside her door trying to work up the courage to knock. But what do you say to a woman with whom you've exchanged only a few words in halting French and who discovered you cowering in a recycling bin? Yet hadn't she visited me in Emergency? Didn't Father Omer explain that she had tried to . . . what? Shield me from suspicion about the arson at the chapel? Hadn't Omer said she'd identified me while I still lay unconscious? But did she even know my name? Nothing makes sense.

It is Wednesday evening. I ride my bike up to Gibeau Orange Julep. I have to take a somewhat circuitous route to avoid traffic. The last few blocks I dismount and push my bike along the sidewalk. It is getting dark, and this section of Boulevard Décarie is too dangerous to cycle even in ideal conditions.

It is twilight when the enormous orange ball looms into view. It has all the vulgar charm of one of those gigantic roadside attractions you sometimes encounter along the highway: some huge menacing beaver or a tyrannosaurus rex or a thirty-foot-tall Canadian nickel. It's not exactly in the middle of Montréal but not quite what you'd expect in the outskirts of a metropolis, yet here it is. A colossal hotdog stand, akin to those A&W drive-in restaurants I knew as a kid. But on the scale of an orange asteroid surrounded by concentric rings of parking packed with mint-condition vintage cars.

This is surreal.

Nothing Nick had described could have prepared me for this. It is like a scene out of that movie. *American Graffiti*? All those teenagers swarming Mel's Drive-In with the glare of neon lights piercing the hormone-laden gloom. Except this evening, it is mostly middle-aged men. A midlife crisis on steroids, but who am I to talk?

There is nowhere in the parking area to lock my bike so I must leave it secured to a bench at the bus stop. I am just crossing the street when I hear a voice shouting, "Spence! Spence!"

Rocco. The sheen of his scalp shaved bald. The thick black eyebrows. Thierry had called him Rocco. The guy running the stolen car ring. Except . . .

I suppress an impulse to run.

"You're Spence? Right?" He extends his hand and shakes mine vigorously. He is not what I expected. In my mind Rocco is a laconic, no-nonsense gangster. This guy is smiling broadly and is, incongruously, rather garrulous.

"We met once. That is, I've seen you around a couple of times. In the garage? My brother has told me a bit about you. You were in hospital, yes? How are you doing?"

"Your brother?"

"Nectarios."

I stare at him blankly.

"Nick."

"You're Nick's brother?"

"Uh huh." He still has my hand. He gives it a few more quick shakes and then leads me over to where he is parked. A couple of men are holding what must be orange julep drinks and sipping them through straws. They are admiring a car that I recognize is a 1960 Ford Fairlane. The men raise their orange cups and seem to offer a little toast to Nick's brother and then move on to the next vehicle.

"I'm Andreas. Call me Andy."

Andy?

"You know my wife, I think."

"I don't really know anyone in—"

"Manon?"

The parking lot begins spinning as though all these shining vintage cars have been flung into orbit around an orange ball the size of a small moon.

"You better sit down, Spence. Have you eaten today? Here. Have some of this. I haven't touched it. Really. Try some."

Andreas—Andy—opens the passenger side door and I settle half in and half out of his Fairlane. He hands me a tall orange cup. I take a sip. It tastes a bit like an orange Creamsicle, except sweeter. I drink it about halfway down and hand the cup back.

"Sorry. I think I forgot to eat today."

"You sit," he says. "Take this." He hands me back the cup. "I'll only be a few minutes."

I watch him disappear into the line-up leading to what looks like a service counter that extends about halfway around the base of the Orange Julep ball. Married? Of course she is married. Why did I think she was widowed? Thierry said . . .

I finish Andy's orange drink just as he returns with another slightly smaller version and a cheeseburger with fries.

"Eat, eat." He goes around to the driver's side and settles in behind the wheel. "Mind the upholstery, though. This is my baby."

I begin to feel a little better. Mercifully, Andy does all the talking. I nod and mumble a little between mouthfuls. After a few minutes, it begins to become clear that Andy and Manon had asked Nick to do renovations on the apartment next to mine to prepare it for their youngest son who would be starting at McGill come September.

"Nick gave us a deal, naturally. Manon and I were going to stay the summer until Alex arrived. That's our son. But, you know, she has her boutique back in Louiseville—"

"Boutique?"

"Yeah. Women's fashions. Accessories. Hats. The hats are big sellers. Who knew? She even gets tourists. Anyway, she's already gone home. You know Louiseville? Not far from Trois-Rivières. Me, I'm retired. Semi-retired. I still have a few clients that I help out with payroll and taxes. I'll probably stay a few more weeks. But back and forth, you know. We're taking our son—he's our youngest, did I say that?—to Paris in July. Just for three weeks. Alex. Right, I told you. Alex and you will be neighbours. You'll like Alex. He's a quiet kid. More like his mother, really."

Andy talks for nearly an hour. "You scared Manon half to death when you came out of that bin. Hilarious!" I decline his offer to drive me home. I walk my bike much of the way. I need time to digest both the burger and everything Andy has told me.

I feel a little ashamed that I painted Nick as a villain in my mind. From what I can glean from Andy's rambling remarks, Nick has been, in his own way, acting as my guardian angel. He didn't say it outright—simply remarking that Nick and Manon had noted that I was going through a bad patch—but I got the impression that the two had conferred on the subject of my general wellbeing.

What's that phrase from *Catch-22*? Just because you're paranoid, doesn't mean they aren't after you.

Couldn't the opposite be true? What if everything in the world is actually conspiring to achieve our salvation but we are just too busy being suspicious to take notice?

THURSDAY, ASCENSION DAY

"Hey dere, brudder!"

I am propped up in bed. Thierry is there. In my doorway. Almost exactly as I saw him that evening on Ash Wednesday. I close my eyes and open them again. We both sit in silence for a while.

"Your hat?" I say.

He shrugs.

"I tink I lost it somewhere. I is gettin' forgetful."

"I hear you."

He scrambles onto my bed. I suppose I must have seemed startled.

"You okay?" His ears swivel as he regards me. I feel a little unsettled, as though his ears are, somehow, performing a scan.

"No, Thierry. I don't think I'm okay. I don't think I've been okay for a while."

"You need something? I could—"

"Look, Thierry." I take a moment to choose my words. "I think I have to do this on my own. I appreciate everything you've done. And it's nice of you to offer, but . . . "

He blinks.

"Dats alright. Whatever you gotta do. I'm gonna support dat."

He blinks again.

"We is chums. *D'accord?*"

"*Oui, nous sommes des chums, Thierry. Nous sommes des frères.*"

He nods.

"*Frères,*" he says.

"*Écoute, j'ai quelque chose pour toi. Un petit cadeau,*" I say. I hand Thierry the box that Father Omer gave me. The silver St. Joseph medallion.

"Oh, man! *C'est magnifique!* I love dis!"

"I'm glad, Thierry."

He runs his hand over the image. St. Joseph holds a lily in one hand and the boy, Jesus, cradled in his other arm.

"But I tink you should keep dis."

"*Moi? Pourquoi?*"

"Well, first thing: I love St. Joseph an' all, but dis way too 'eavy for me to wear. *Mais aussi,* I tink you de one could use de extra 'elp."

He hands it back to me.

"*Maintenant, tu as un autre père.*"

Perhaps I do have another father. How many fathers now? My dad and Father Mallory Parent—two fathers who, in their own fashion, made and marred me. Father Desmond, I suppose. Good old Normand, too. Certainly JF. And now, St. Joseph, the father who might lift up the boy I once was and carry that child in his arms.

"*Je suis désolé, Thierry.*"

"You is sorry? You dun got nutin' to be sorry for."

"Maybe. Still, I'm sorry, anyway."

"*Tu es fou, mon chum.*"

"*Dis-moi que tu me pardonnes.*"

"*Quoi?*"

"Tell me you forgive me."

"*Il n'y rien à pardonner.*"

"Just say it. *S'il te plait.*"

"Okay. *Je te pardonne. Content?*"

"*Merci.*"

"*De rien.*"

"Ain't you finish dat book, yet?" He points to my paperback *Le Petit Prince* next to my pillow.

"You know. Still studying."

Thierry stays a while longer. We finish reading *Le Petit Prince together.*

. . . soyez gentils! Ne me laissez pas tellement triste: écrivez-moi vite qu'il est revenu . . .

"I read my first book, *ostie! C'est un miracle!*"

And then he is gone.

Spence met Clara and Gabriel at Station Lionel-Groulx as they disembarked the 747 bus. When Clara caught sight of her father, she abandoned her luggage on the sidewalk and ran to him, almost knocking him down. Gabriel stood sentinel over her belongings and offered Spence a smile and a quick wave. Abruptly, Clara ran back to her fiancé and kissed him on the lips. They exchanged a few words in French which surprised Spence since, hitherto, Clara rarely spoke it.

After a handshake and a few pleasantries with his future father-in-law, Gabriel took the escalator down to the platform heading east to Station Mont-Royal. Spence and Clara were going west to Station Vendôme. She leaned over the barrier to watch Gabriel descending and they blew each other kisses. Spence was a little embarrassed by this display but it occurred to him that the pair had not spent a night apart for nearly three months. When they got to Clara's place, she threw herself on the bed and declared she could sleep for a week.

"Oh, wait! I have something for you. I bought this in Notre-Dame. At the gift shop."

She dug through her carry-on bag. Spence sat on the edge of the plump little sofa.

"Here."

It was a slender black box. The sort that you used to get when you bought an expensive pen. On the lid, embossed in silver, was a cluster of stars around the letter M. Inside was a silver medallion on a chain.

"It's not real silver, of course. I think it's coated maybe. The real silver ones were way too expensive. Do you like it?"

"Love it," said Spence.

"Do you know what it is?"

"Yes, I think so. It's a *médaille miraculeuse*." He traced the image of the Virgin Mother with his little finger. "It's a very famous design. Inspired by a Marian apparition, I recall."

"Yes. I have a pamphlet explaining all the symbolism. Somewhere. I'll find it later. Or you can Google it." Clara was sitting on her bed. She jumped up and hurried to the room she used as a studio. "The plants look great, Dad. Good job."

Spence looked down at the image of Mary nestled in his palm. He remembered the statue of the Virgin that stood in the courtyard outside the window of JF's office. The Marian shrine in the garden hidden behind St. Francis of Assisi near where he lived with Serenity when Clara was a baby. Another in front of Our Lady of the Sea in Belmont Park.

"I was going to give you this before I left," Clara called from the hallway, "but the paint wasn't quite dry. It was supposed to be for your birthday but, you know."

She came back to the living room cradling the portrait that Spence had discovered in the linen closet some weeks ago. The portrait of himself as a boy. It occurred to Spence that Clara was nearly his own mother's age when he was the boy depicted in this painting. Had Serenity lived, she, too, would have been about Clara's age when her daughter was the age of this boy. It was confusing to think about. How people who die young are frozen in time. How a man such as himself could grow old and still be that boy in the painting.

In the bright light of the living room, the portrait was more vivid than when he had first encountered it. The boy's eyes more vulnerable. His eyes. Before, he had thought the eyes looked wary. Now they seemed to be hiding something. The boy's lips were full, almost feminine. The sort of beauty that seems always to imperil children. Clara had exaggerated the dark circles under the eyes. Resignation? Weariness? How do artists do that? Make the eyes follow you? Capture the illusion of thought? The moment before someone speaks? It was unsettling.

"Do you like it, Dad?"

Spence had no words. He was gripped by panic. Swept up by memories he could no longer suppress. He felt himself shaking. This was not what he had planned. He had resolved to keep the past few weeks a secret. To quietly slip away once a week for a few sessions of—what? Therapy, he supposed. The long winter was over and summer was almost upon them. A few decent bike rides and some healthy meals and he would be fine. Spence had been sitting on the very edge of the sofa and now he slipped onto the floor and lay on his side.

Please stop hurting me. Please stop hurting me.

"Dad?" Clara knelt down beside him. "Who are you talking to?"

Had he said that aloud? Even as he lay whimpering this over and over, there was a part of Spence that berated himself for his weakness. The boy in the painting had survived after all. Maybe even thrived. What was the big deal? He was a grown man. A father. Maybe, soon, he would be a grandfather. He hated himself for being weak in front of his daughter, ruining her homecoming.

"I'm not going to hurt you, Dad. I wouldn't hurt you." Clara lay down on the floor beside her father. "Breathe. Breathe. Deep breaths, Dad. I think you are having a panic attack."

"I'm sorry. I'm sorry." Spence whispered.

"It's okay, Dad. You don't have to be sorry."

"I'm so sorry your mother died. I'm sorry I couldn't keep her alive."

"That wasn't your fault, Dad. That was nobody's fault."

"I couldn't look after you, Clara. I wasn't a good father. I just kept fucking up."

"It's all right, Dad. It's all right. You always loved me. You did your best. See, you're here now, aren't you? You're looking after me now, aren't you?"

"No," Spence wailed. "You're looking after *me*."

They both began to laugh. They laughed and cried and laid together on the floor, until the flood of feelings that had been released in Spence finally subsided.

Spence sat up and looked around dazed, feeling strangely elated.

"Are you hungry, sweetie?" he said, finally.

"I'm starved." Clara sat up too and rested her head on his shoulder.

"Me too. Should we order a pizza?"

They spent much of the evening sitting on the floor with their backs against the sofa, as if it were safer there. Clara talked about Paris. When she mentioned the fire at Notre-Dame, he told her about the fire at Frère André's chapel, leaving out the part about the nun. And Thierry.

"Look," he said, taking the St. Joseph medallion from around his neck. "This is my official reward. Well, I guess not official, but Father—his name will come to me in a second—and the archbishop gave—not the archbishop personally but—it's complicated."

"Very cool, Dad."

"Here," he said. "You should have this."

"The chain is way too long," Clara laughed.

"We'll switch. The chain on the *médaille miraculeuse* is a bit short for me."

He switched the chains and fastened the St. Joseph around his daughter's neck. "I prefer to have Mary with me, anyway. All those Hail Marys when I was getting sober. I kind of got attached to her."

"I'm going to check this out in the mirror," Clara stood and walked to the bathroom.

"You want this last piece of pizza?" Spence called.

"Do you want it?"

"Not if you want it."

"You sure?"

Spence nodded as she came back into the room.

"Would St. Joseph let his child go hungry? I don't think so."

"You know St. Joseph dies when Jesus is just a kid, right? I mean, that's the tradition. Dying is easy."

"Comedy's hard," Spence quipped.

"Keeping going, Dad. That's hard. Not giving up. Learning. Growing."

Spence nudged the pizza box toward her, and Clara took the last slice.

"Want a bite?"

He shook his head. "I'm just going to close my eyes for a minute. Okay? Wake me if I fall asleep."

And he did.

MONDAY, THE FIRST DAY AFTER PENTECOST

"And then what happened?"

I look out the window and down onto the flat gravel roof of the adjacent building. Dr. Tremblay's office is on the seventh floor. A pair of gulls are on the roof squabbling over some tidbit.

"Like I said. I saw the mouse several times. It would sit in the doorway of my bedroom and look at me. So, I did what I've done in the past. I set traps. Four of them."

"And?"

One of the gulls flies off with something in its mouth. The other follows. It is early June and the window is open though there is no breeze. I can hear the shrill lament of the second gull in pursuit.

"Just before daybreak the trap was sprung. I was still in bed. The sound woke me. I could hear squeaking and the sound of the trap being dragged. So I knew it hadn't been a clean kill."

"And what did you do?"

The gulls fly behind the dome of a church and out of sight. I look at Dr. Tremblay. She has removed her glasses and is polishing them with a little cloth. Her hair is just beginning to acquire a few streaks of grey, but she looks almost young without her glasses.

"I didn't want it to suffer. I found the mouse. One rear leg was caught in the trap. It was clearly terrified of me and tried its best to escape. It dragged the trap under the sofa."

She repositions her glasses and looks at me over the rims. Her expression is neutral. Even kind. There is no judgment.

"I filled the kitchen sink with cold water. I moved the sofa and picked up the trap with a pair of tongs because I didn't want to be bitten. Then I drowned the mouse in the sink."

She nods.

"It was upsetting to watch. I held him under and he struggled for his life. I could see the panic. At one point he tried to swim in the direction of the plug, as though to let the water drain. But, how could a mouse possibly know about plugs? And then it was over."

I look out the window again.

"I was upset. I felt like . . . I felt like a monster. I mean, I know a cat or an owl or a snake or such wouldn't have flinched. I know mice are considered pests."

"But?"

I look back and ours eyes meet.

"I felt like I had killed something that had been a guest. Not like a friend or anything. But someone who dropped in from time to time. It was upsetting."

"What did you do with the remains?"

"I buried him. In the park across the street. I wrapped him in paper towel and I dug a little hole with a trowel that I use for camping. But I didn't want him to be alone. So stupid. I have this little Christmas Nativity scene. The little figurines? I've had it since my daughter was a baby. It was March but I still hadn't put it away. So, I buried him with the little ceramic St. Joseph."

A pause.

"Probably the squirrels dug him up, anyway. I just . . . it's so stupid. "

I look out the window again. The second gull is back. Or maybe it's a different one. Does it matter? I suppose it might matter in a world where every hair on one's head is numbered. It seems to be searching for some morsel.

"Hey."

I turn and look at her again.

"It wasn't stupid to bury the mouse with a little St. Joseph figurine. I think that was a compassionate thing to do."

She hands me the box of tissues. She knows I'm going to cry because I always cry when she says something kind about me. Apparently, I haven't learned how to accept being loved, or so she says. Something about shame and feeling unworthy.

"Do you think it's possible that you became depressed after your retirement? That moving to a new city where you have no friends, your money worries, struggling with an unfamiliar language, confronting memories of this priest—is it possible all this was overwhelming?"

I blow my nose. Out the window the gull has given up on whatever it was searching for. It takes flight again.

"I think you magnified your very natural feelings of remorse over trapping and drowning this mouse. I think this may have been a factor in triggering a psychotic episode. It may help explain the delusions and the paranoia."

"But some of it was real. The fire in the chapel was real. The stolen cars were real. I mean, they weren't stolen, but they *were* real. Maybe I wasn't seeing things clearly but I was still connected to reality."

"Some people who experience even very anguishing mental illness can be high functioning, very perceptive and, by all appearances, perfectly sane."

"I sincerely doubt that I have ever appeared perfectly sane to anyone."

"Okay, consider this. Have you ever been dreaming? And half asleep you hear, say, the radio or television? Or street sounds or a conversation in the other room? And later you realize you had been incorporating those sounds into your dream?"

"Yeah. For sure. I've done that."

"Something similar can happen during a psychotic episode. Psychosis can manifest in many different ways and we don't fully understand them all. In your case, you needed a friend. So, you brought this vulnerable little mouse back to life in your—"

"My delusions? My imagination?"

"In this metaphor, let's say. In your waking dreams. You integrated the real world—"

"Whatever that is—"

"—into your dreams. And vice versa."

I hand her back the box of tissues.

"You named him Thierry? Yes?"

"*Son nom était Thierry. Oui.*"

She smiles.

"You understand, don't you, that Thierry is an aspect of yourself? And, in many ways, this delusion, or dream, or call it what you will—"

"Thierry."

"Yes. Thierry helped nurture you. And you, him. In befriending him you were befriending yourself. And he was helping you reach the little boy in you who had been hurt."

She hands me the tissues again.

"It's so ridiculous. I'm a grown man. I'm older than you are. I've helped educate a generation of schoolchildren. I shouldn't be such a fucking mess."

"Do you think, perhaps, that is a factor? From what you have told me, you made a lot of positive changes in your life. But struggling with your wife's addiction, your challenges as a single father. It sounds to me that you were a positive influence as a teacher, but maybe a bit of a workaholic? When did you leave time to just work on you?"

I sob for several minutes. When will the crying stop? I'm ashamed because my suffering seems so insignificant compared to the Simard boys, to Clara, to so many of my students. So much suffering. Millions of people suffering. It is as though I haven't earned my sorrow.

"So, my guardian angel is a gay, lapsed Catholic, bilingual mouse?" I say, finally.

She laughs.

"Thierry is who you need him to be."

"And now he's gone," I say.

"*Du sacrifice vient le renouveau,*" she says.

I stand up and walk to the window. I can just make out the gull in the distance. A faint brush stroke of white. Then after a moment, only sky.

As I leave the hospital, I am happy to see Clara is waiting for me on a bench in the little garden outside.

"How did it go?" she asks.

"Okay, I guess. This is a nice surprise. How did it go for you?"

Clara had an appointment this morning at the Catholic Centre. She and Gabriel have decided to have a church wedding, and she had to make arrangements for certain interviews and to register for the marriage preparation course.

"Great! Dad, do you remember a priest named Omer?"

"I think the priest who gave me that was named Omer."

I point to the little silver St. Joseph medallion that she is wearing around her neck.

"Exactly!" She is excited. "He was at the Catholic Centre dropping off some books at the library and I literally bumped into him. Anyway, he asked me about it. The medallion. And I told him how you got it and how you gave it to me. And he says, 'Coincidence!' You know, because he was the one who gave it to *you*."

"Woah. Slow down. "

"And then he asks what I'm doing there and I say signing up for marriage prep. And he says if I need a priest, he'd be happy to do the job. And guess what?"

"What?"

"He says that he is friends with the archbishop and that he is pretty sure, under the circumstances, you saving the day and all . . . He's pretty sure he can get special permission to have the wedding at the little chapel. Frère André's little chapel next to the Oratory. And you can walk me down the aisle."

"There's no aisle, sweetie." I laugh. It feels good to laugh. "You've seen it, right? It's tiny."

"I know. I don't care. We're going to have a really small wedding anyway. It'll be perfect."

Her eyes are shining. She's going to be all right, I think. *Ça va bien aller.* Everything's going to be all right.

"The chapel's not far from here. We can walk over and check it out, if you like," I say.

She slips her arm through mine and we set off. This is just the sort of coincidence that Thierry would have called a miracle. A Frère André–St. Joseph sort of miracle. For a moment, I wonder if Thierry is still practising his reading. Does he have a copy of *Le Petit Prince*?

Then, I remember.

But what does it matter? Believing the impossible isn't really all that crazy. We do it all the time. Or at least, as we say in the theatre, willingly suspend our disbelief. Isn't that a kind of crazy? So many of the things that seem truest in my life are just stories. Fictions, yes. But who has read *Hamlet* and doesn't feel they know Hamlet better than they know many of their own friends? If not Hamlet, then, maybe Holden Caulfield or Scrooge or Elizabeth Bennett? What we call *real* can be a slippery business.

Seeing is believing? What if it is really the other way round? What if, sometimes, believing is seeing? What if the essential really *isn't* always invisible to the eye? My hand is in my pocket. I feel a coin. It is a little silver dime. 1957. Coincidentally, the year I was born.

Adieu, mon petit prince.
Merci, brudder. Merci.

FIN

Acknowledgments

My heartfelt thanks to my old friend, Michael Ireland, who read an earlier draft of the novel and who generously offered encouragement and expert editorial advice.

Thank you, Yann Lapalme, for reviewing my French in the early stages. *Mes remerciements à* Louise Roy for thoroughly reviewing my French in the final manuscript. Any errors in French spelling and usage that survive are entirely my own.

I am endlessly grateful to my editor, Kilmeny Jane Denny, whose insights and encouragement have made me a better writer and who has guided me to a better book than I could ever have managed without her kind ministrations.

Thanks as well to Lynn Duncan who provided a fresh editorial perspective in the final stages.